# SACRIFICE OF THE GUARDIANS

Sacrifice of the Guardians
by Darius C. Modi

Paperback Edition
First Published in 2023 in India by

Inkfeathers Publishing
Vivek Vihar, New Delhi 110 095
www.inkfeathers.com

ISBN 9788119483839

# SACRIFICE OF THE GUARDIANS

DARIUS C. MODI

Inkfeathers Publishing
www.inkfeathers.com

*To my wacky friends.*

*(kidding, you guys are the best)*

# PREFACE

Books have always been the script for their respective movies. The movies may not be the exact replica of the books, but if the books were best-sellers, the movies would generally be blockbusters. There are many famous movie series that had their origins in books.

Growing up reading fantasy books and watching the movies, I felt that this was one genre where I could establish myself. With virtually no limits in this genre, writers can create their ideal world and immerse the readers into pages of whatever tickled their fancy. I am no different. I prefer non-linear storylines, preferably with plot-twists and a sense of mystery. People say that the book cannot deliver the same feeling as the movie, but the books give you something that the movies do not. The fresh smell of the pages of a new book, the papercuts people sometimes get when turning the pages, the crisp print on the pages; these are things no movie can ever give you. I am not putting down any movies, but I do prefer books to movies. Books allow you to read lines and simultaneously imagine the scenes that are being played out, subject to immediate change in your mind only. You can decide what soundtrack to play in your head while reading the lines.

I can only hope that this book does justice to its predecessor. This particular one was maybe 4 years coming, but I do feel it would be worth the wait.

# CHAPTER 1

Ake fell down the side of the waterfall silently. His hands held the struggling form of his Wolf, Hadver. The bleeding from Hadver's side had slowed down a bit, but Ake was not going to take a chance with his Wolf. He hit the bottom of the waterfall sooner than he had expected. He could see the lights of the city far ahead. He was glad that the bottom of the waterfall was shallow. The water came only up to his ankles.

He still had a league of forest to get through before he got to the city. He could feel Hadver's pain, and it almost made him cry. But he steeled himself and ran on. It was not easy picking up a two-hundred-pound animal and running at the same time, but Ake refused to leave his loyal companion to die. He struggled to keep Hadver awake, but did not stop. He had covered half the distance from the waterfall to the city when he felt Hadver unmerge. He set Hadver down on the ground and sat next to him. What he did not realise was that he was being stalked. He heard a soft growl and spun around. Behind him was a creature slightly bigger than the one Hadver had fought on top of the waterfall. He crouched, ready to wrestle the animal. But the animal was not interested with him. It passed him and licked Hadver's wound. The big canine heaved a sigh as if it was ready to take its last breath. And the Wolf did not move a muscle again. The boy looked at the retreating form of the other creature and then back at Hadver. The wound on Hadver's side had sealed itself, but it was evidently too late for the Wolf. He had lost too much blood.

As Ake watched, Hadver's form began to dissolve into green vapour, until all that was left was an Emerald the size of Ake's palm. Ake picked it up and studied it. It had the silhouette of a wolf's face on it. The Emerald gave off a brilliant green light and the light pulsed, as if it had a mind of its own.

Ake slipped the gem into his pocket and trudged on towards the city. He felt hollow. His one true companion was gone. He reached the city gates, but did not bother calling out for the guards to open it.

Suddenly, the gates opened, noiselessly. He slipped inside the gates and had barely taken ten steps, when he felt a sword at his throat. A man spoke, "Do not even think about moving. Who are you and how did you get in here?"

"My name is Ake. I am from Logder. The gates were open when I came in."

The sword came away from his throat and was sheathed. A torch was lit, and Ake could see the man who was ready to kill him. He was about fifty years old, with battle scars on his face and neck.

"Come with me." He said. Ake did not even resist. He walked behind the man and was blinded by a gold flash. The next thing he knew, he was standing in a throne room like the one in Talis. In front of him stood a man about his height. A sword was strapped to his side, as if he expected a fight. He had arms that made Clint's look like toothpicks. He sent Ake's captor away and motioned for Ake to follow him. He led Ake through a maze of corridors and stopped when they came to a fork in their path. The man then spoke, "Tell me your story. Only then I will send you on your path."

Ake first bowed and said, "Lord Xast." Then he told Lord Xast his life's story. At the end, Lord Xast said, "Very well, you may stay here."

"But how do you know I have not lied?"

"I can discern lies quite easily. I hear none from you. I will show you how your Emerald works tomorrow. Rest now."

Lord Xast guided Ake down the left corridor to a room where Ake crashed out on the bed.

# CHAPTER 2

Gonth straightened himself as the doctor made him drink some sweet liquid. He could feel it fixing his backbone where Emmanuel had smacked him. They were the last people fighting the battle the Trainers had made them do. Even though they were from Tauris, they had to fight each other for one to come out on top. Trest was attacked by all three Leonids, and was the first one to be taken out. He looked around the room, which contained everyone except Clint and Emmanuel. Clint was going to get a new trident since Vincent had broken his original one.

As soon as he could, Gonth got out of the room and headed back to his bedroom to sleep for some time. His dreams were anything but pleasant.

He stood on a cliff overlooking a forest. Suddenly, the whole forest burst into flames. Even at a height and in a dream, Gonth could feel the heat. Suddenly, a wave of ice covered the fire.

He heard a female voice next to him, "Shame, isn't it?"

He turned and saw a woman who was white as snow. She wore a crown that sparkled like an icicle. Her features were sharp, and her nails were long, at least three inches.

Gonth bowed. "Lady Ara."

"Just Ara will do. As I was saying, if you cannot stop Yedgal's rise, there will be a war. Each District will pool its resources into fighting the other five. All I can do to keep this from happening is separate the Districts."

Gonth was confused, and it showed on his face.

Ara looked at him and said, "I am the Goddess of ice. I keep the Dividing Mountains in place to prevent a war. Sadly, your enemy has decided to use that to his advantage."

She looked at him, as if expecting something. Then the truth struck Gonth.

"His base is somewhere in the mountains, right?"

"Yes. I do not know where it is, though. That is where your friend Dan is being kept. You must rescue him fast."

Gonth snapped awake and got out of his bed. He knew that if he told any of his comrades about this dream, they would not believe it. But the Trainers might believe him. He got out of the room and searched for his own Trainer, Latyu. He told Latyu of his dream and asked if it was significant or not. Latyu said, "I believe you. If this turns out to be true, we will have to get you prepared fast. I will take this up with the others and Lord Veryu. Don't tell anyone of this dream."

Gonth nodded and turned around to head to his room. Just then, a thought struck him. He asked Latyu, "What does Yedgal want with Dan?"

Latyu stared at him for ten heartbeats before answering.

"Think of yourselves and Yedgal as two sides of the same coin. If Yedgal is to come to power, you are born to your respective Tribes. But, he needs your powers, six in total, to come to life. If you are not born, he will not come to power. If he does not come to power, you are not born. Since the Wolf Tribe is no more, there should not be a rebirth of Yedgal again, once you defeat him this time."

"But Elesa, Ake and Garon are from the Wolf Tribe. If they start their respective families, surely the Wolf Tribe will be started again."

"Not necessarily. You see, if they marry any normal human being, the gene of the Wolf Tribe is lost forever."

"So this is the last time Yedgal has to be defeated. But what will happen to the Tribes after that?"

"They will live on. Children will be born to them. But they will not have the same destiny as you. They will live on to be advisors to the King of Lasgalan and the Lord of their District."

Gonth was satisfied with his answer and went to the armoury, where he picked up a sword and shield. The sword was much heavier than what he was used to, though it was the same shape and size as his. He went to the training ground and started hacking at one of the straw dummies. He could not get much power swinging the sword the width he was used to, so he swung it from behind his back, using the momentum to hack the dummy. He found a small button near his thumb on the hilt. He kept the sword on the ground, with the blade facing away from him, and pressed the button.

A second blade jutted out from the hilt. Only Gonth's quick reflexes saved him. He jumped to the side and looked at the sword. It was deadly and he liked deadly weapons. He picked up the sword. It felt better balanced. He took his normal swing at the dummy. This time, the dummy was cleanly cut in half at its waist. Clapping sounds came from behind him. He turned and saw Clint holding a cylindrical piece of metal in his hand.

Clint said, "Looks like you got a new weapon too. Looks nice, but not as nice as mine."

"Show me yours. Then we can have a duel to see whose is better."

"You are going to regret challenging me."

Clint slashed his metal piece outwards, like a sword. The piece extended from both ends until he held a spear seven feet tall, with sharp points at both ends of it. Clint turned it upside down and turned the smaller point down towards the ground. He did not appear to do anything to the spear, but the larger point opened quickly and silently, becoming four more points.

Gonth admired Clint's weapon. He had seen these weapons before, but those were just experimental weapons. He had never seen or heard of someone use a quindent. He whistled appreciatively and said, "Did you ask them to make it for you, or did they make it on their own?"

"I asked them. Now, let us battle."

Gonth gripped his new sword tightly and ran at Clint. Clint levelled the quindent and waited for Gonth to come at him. The first clash of the two involved the quindent slamming into Gonth's shield, denting it. Clint had the advantage of his extra reach, which kept Gonth out of sticking distance. Gonth cursed under his breath and pressed the button again. The second blade went back inside and Clint's quindent seemed to get shorter. That was all that Gonth needed. He pressed the sword point under Clint's chin and said, "I win."

"Not so. Look below."

Gonth glanced below and realised that the quindent had not gotten shorter; Clint had just pulled it back to create the illusion. If this had been a real fight, Gonth would have been dead long before he could put the sword under Clint's chin. He glanced behind Clint and noticed the six Ring-bearers watching them. He pulled his sword back and said, "What happened?"

Adrian, his District's Ring-bearer, spoke up in a thick voice, "The Trainers and Lord Veryu want to see you two in the throne room."

Clint and Gonth exchanged uneasy looks, but went in. They found all their Trainers looking at them expectantly. Lord Veryu was looking very seriously at Gonth, though Clint did not know why. They stopped and waited for someone to say something.

Latyu spoke first.

"Gonth, we have discussed your dream and come to a conclusion that it was not just a random dream, but one that Lady Ara herself wanted you to have. This means that she favours you, which is a good thing."

"What is the bad part of it?" Gonth had learnt a long time ago that when there was good part to something, there was always a bad part to it as well.

"Well, it stands that you will have to lead all of your friends against Yedgal. However, you have to choose somebody to be your co-leader. Who that is, you have to decide now."

Gonth did not hesitate. "I choose Clint."

Clint, who obviously did not expect his name to be said, spoke, "Why me? You barely know me. You could have chosen anyone from your District."

"You are from the army. You would be useful to help give courage to our friends. Also, if they do not listen to me, they will definitely listen to you."

Clint nodded. He asked Sens, "What do you want us to do?"

Sens replied, "Go back to the field with all the Guardians. Since Dan and Ake are not here, we will have you train the others in all types of combat. Armed, unarmed and using the Rings."

"But neither of us know how to use the Rings."

"You will manage. Have a little faith in yourselves."

"Alright, but they will become hardened fighters, if you want me to train them."

"Fine."

Ten minutes later, twenty teenagers were facing Clint and Gonth. Clint said, "I want full attention and discipline paid to the both of us. We are assigned to train you in all types of combat. First we start with unarmed combat. I want you to pick pairs. But no merging. Understood?"

Soon the decided pairs were fighting it out on the ground, their Guardians watching them. The winners were to face Clint and Gonth. The first person to win was Vincent. He faced Clint and said, "This should be easy."

"Do not take this lightly my friend. I can still knock you out."

They circled each other and charged. At the last second, Clint jumped aside, and Vincent felt a kick in his back. He collapsed on the ground, but got up again. He took a step and stumbled. He got up again.

"Give up Vincent. You will fall before you reach me." Clint's voice seemed to come from far away.

"Never!" Vincent bellowed and got a second wind. He managed to catch Clint off-guard and, grabbing his waist, pushed Clint back. But his extra weight did not help. Clint stopped him dead in his tracks. He picked Vincent up from his own waist and tossed him like a rag doll. Vincent tried to get up again, but instead only managed to sit up.

The next person was Robert. He rubbed his hands together and picked up some dirt to coat his hands. He faced off against Gonth. That match was short and not so sweet for Gonth, who got beaten up badly.

# CHAPTER 3

Ake got up from his sleep and looked out of the window. It was raining lightly outside, but Ake had a thunderstorm raging inside him. Reaching into his pocket, he pulled out the Emerald, the only reminder of Hadver. Lord Xast had promised to show him how to use it, but Ake did not feel like getting out of the bed. He just wanted to cry himself to sleep. Nevertheless, he got out of his bed and had a bath. He walked out of the room to be faced by a guard who guided him to the throne room.

Lord Xast was waiting for him. After dismissing the guard, he took Ake to an open-air stadium. It was small, but big enough for a small platoon of soldiers to defend. Lord Xast turned to Ake and said, "Before we start, I am sorry for your loss. And please, just call me Xast. None of this Lord nonsense."

Ake nodded. He asked, "How do I use the Emerald?"

"You need to think of something that brings strong emotions within you. Any emotion. Then, put the gem in the arm-guard of the hand that you normally use. After that, the gem will power you up to a level which you may not be able to imagine, at first. Do that. I will explain further after that."

Ake held the gem in his left hand and thought of the day he saw Faldor casually take out Hadver. The emotion he felt at that time was rage. He kept the gem over the outline of the wolf on his arm-guard. The Emerald sank in, and Ake felt Hadver back in his mind.

"Now, try to conjure a weapon."

An axe appeared in Ake's hand. It was as green as the Emerald and felt just right in his hands.

He turned to Xast and said, "Now what?"

"The gem connects you to your Guardian. You are now permanently merged with him. Have courage and see that his sacrifice was not in vain. I will train you myself in using the Emerald. The emotion you felt when you passed the Emerald into the arm-guard is the best one to produce a weapon. Now let us duel."

Xast pulled out a double-edged sword from his scabbard. He swung it at Ake's stomach. Ake let his reflexes take over. He imagined a shield and a green shield appeared out of both his arm-guards. The sword struck the shields and glanced off them. Xast smiled and swung again, the sword at Ake's neck level. The shields disappeared and Ake held a broadsword in his hands. He pushed the sword down and forced Xast to release his grip on the sword.

Xast smiled and picked up his sword. For the next hour, they duelled. Ake learned how to produce different weapons to fight. Xast taught him hand to hand combat in a different style than what Faldor had taught him. Soon, Ake was wrestling with the palace guards, putting them to the ground and himself getting put to the ground sometimes. He put all his will into the fighting. He stopped wrestling and tried something new.

With Xast watching him closely, Ake produced an axe in both his hands. Then, he willed them to expand in size. The axes obeyed, but with a little too much enthusiasm. They enlarged till they were three times Ake's height. He did not know what was happening and tried to get them to stop, but they did not. He felt the flat of a broadsword hit him under the ribs and the axes vanished. Ake collapsed onto the ground. Xast's face loomed over him, and he said, "If you lose your concentration in battle, even for a moment, the results will be worse than getting hit with the flat of a sword. Do you understand?"

"Yes, sir." Ake accepted Xast's hand and got up. Xast made him wash up, and then took him to a room filled with chemicals. Ake looked around the room and saw that there were only five windows in the room. There were different coloured liquids in corked glass vials. Some Leonids were pouring them into opaque canteens, which were handed to others, who wrote something on each of them.

Xast led him to the back of the room, where a lot of canteens and vials were kept. They were all in packs of twenty-four, which Ake found very disturbing and coincidental to the number of people in his group, including himself, back in Talis. There were eleven such packs. He was about to open a vial which contained orange crystals, when Xast grabbed his hand, preventing him from doing so.

"Do not open that vial. It is caustic, a solid that explodes on contact with air."

"I see. So why are you giving me these?" Ake gestured to the eleven packs.

Xast snickered. "You catch on fast. You will be taking these back to Talis. Your Trainers will explain everything to you. And before I forget, you will have to teach your friends how to use their gems when the time is right."

"How can you say that with such certainty?"

"I am not only the best potion maker in Lasgalan in this time, but I can see the future as well. The other Guardians will die soon when your friends decide to storm Yedgal's fortress."

"You know where it is?"

"No. But your Trainers have an approximate location. Ask them when you get back."

"Then I am leaving now."

"Right. Then hold two packs. My men will come with you."

Ake again got blinded by a gold flash, but shut his eyes this time. When he opened them, he was back in the training ground in Talis.

His friends looked at him, as if he had dropped out of thin air, which he felt was an accurate description as to how he had appeared. In front of him was Clint, who had James in a headlock. Just then, the Trainers came out and saw the new development. They did not seem surprised that Ake was lugging packs of potions. They took all the packs and set them on the ground. Ake hugged Hasha and told her of what he had been doing. When he told the whole group about what Xast had said, Gonth said, "I had a dream about Ara. She said that Yedgal's base was in the mountains."

"So we know we are going to lose our Guardians in the mountains. Personally, I feel that we Ravens are going to be the safest in the air, so you guys have to be careful." Chris' voice came from the back of the group, now sitting down.

Ake nodded. He turned to Reidan and asked, "How about you show us how to use these potions?"

"Right you are."

# CHAPTER 4

Dan got up in his cell and stretched himself. His senses were now on high alert. He was expecting to be killed while he slept, or while his back was turned to the gate of the cell. Someone had slipped a plate of food into his cell while he was sleeping. He wolfed it down and slipped it out of the cell. He walked to the back of the cell, where he was trying to get a way out. He could not get his arrowhead between the stones, so he decided to try and strike up a conversation with the guards. He managed to get one guard talking, but he could not glean much information from him. He saw that he was in a sort of circular room, and seeing the size of cells in the room and the size of the room itself, guessed that there were eighteen, one for each of the Chosen Ones. He saw Raze coming to him, and readied his arrowhead. Raze came to his cell and smiled at him.

"Good morning."

"Morning. You told Xristos about your folly? I bet he was fuming mad at you."

"Yes, I told him. He was not mad. Like I said, any six will do, dead or alive."

"You want me to die first or would rather have me alive?" Dan growled.

"If we can get five more, all well and good. You were caught with a lot of difficulty. Listro had his chance and failed. I will not."

Dan moved fast and tried to plunge the arrowhead into Raze's abdomen, but Raze stepped out of reach. The guards moved and pointed their spears at Dan's hand, forcing him to rein in his hand.

Raze laughed and said, “Really? You thought we did not know that you had weapons on you? You really are daft.”

“Do not test me Raze. When I get out of here, the first thing on my list will be to take a guard’s spear and put your head on it.”

“Ha. First get out of the cell and find me. Then, if you can, defeat me in combat and kill me. But for now, I advise you to stay put.”

# CHAPTER 5

The twenty-three youngsters settled themselves down in the training ground, while their Trainers prepared to teach them about what Xast had given them. Anne sat in the front row, along with Victoria, Chris, and Jacob.

Her Trainer, Lucia, barked instructions to the others, which they carried out. It became evident that she was the one who knew the most about the potions and the chemicals.

She turned to them and said, "Well, as Ake has said, these packs were given by Lord Xast. He is the best potion maker in Lasgalan in this time. We will show you how, when and where to use them. First up is a potion all of you are familiar with."

She held up a vial containing green liquid. She poured a bit of it onto the grass. There was a small explosion and a crater, about a metre across. Green smoke curled off the edges of the crater.

"Normally, this potion will not leave a mark on the ground where it is dropped. It depends on the amount of iron in it. This is the only potion which is derived from a metal. The starting material is iron oxide. Then, on addition of other liquids, you get this. It is called a flat-bomb. The correct flat-bomb can reduce any standing structure to ashes, but not earth itself. The next one we have is sapphire potion. As the name suggests, it is derived from the Sapphire Rose from Logder. Speaking of which, please forget whatever you were told about legendary items of each of their Districts. They are very easy to find. That is all a farce. We have got Lord Logdan's armour, and bow and quiver. We also have Lord Leonin's mace. Now, I do not need to tell you much about this potion. Just know that it can cure any disease, ailment or injury, no matter how grievous. Its juice can, and has, brought back people from the dead."

"Wait a minute," James called out. "The potion you have may be the same colour as mine, but mine is smoking inside the vial." Sure enough, Anne could see blue vapours coming off the surface of his potion.

"Keep it out of direct sunlight. Too much exposure will make it lose its potency."

"Thanks."

"The next five potions are derived from the blood of your Districts' Legend Animals. The first one is called stampede. It comes from the Unicorn. The person who drinks this becomes a Pegasus, the very embodiment of the Tribe. The Pegasus is, in its prime, an animal which hates to be constrained. It is a loose cannon, which is why we do not wish to give you this potion. But since Lord Xast has sent it, we will give it to you." Lucia held up a vial that contained a red coloured liquid. She kept it next to the other two which she had just introduced to them.

"The next one is my personal favourite. It is called poisoner. It is derived from the blood of an Acid Hound. The drinker becomes one himself or herself. They are invulnerable and wherever their teeth or claws touch on a person or animal, that part burns out. The only animal this potion is not really effective against is a Dragon. Dragons heal as fast as they are wounded. The only body part that does not heal are their eyes. Once gouged or touched, the eyes burn out."

Lucia could see that the youth were giving her their undivided attention. She decided to keep it that way.

"The next one has a very catchy name. It is derived from the blood of a Crow. It is called wings of death. The drinker becomes an eagle. The only ability the eagle has is that it is invisible. It is a black liquid that tastes the best out of all five blood-derived potions. Next is blocker. It is derived from Liger blood and can stop any wound from bleeding. Liger saliva is better, but we use the blood. It is just as efficient." Anne heard a grunt and turning around, saw Ake with his eyes burning with hate. Anne figured that his Wolf was killed by one. Turning back to Lucia, Anne saw her hold a vial full of yellow liquid that was the Liger blood.

"The next one is a highly volatile liquid. It is taken from Xale blood. It is purple in colour and has a dual purpose. Due to its volatile nature, it can be used as a weapon. But it can be used as a smoke-screen if you ever want to get a quick escape out of a tight corner."

"What is its range?" Jacob asked.

"One drop of this stuff can form a crater ten feet wide and deep. Throwing an entire vial of this will not form a crater, since the glass will absorb most of the heat. All you will get is a lot of smoke."

"Right, so how are we supposed to get out of the crater?"

"You will have to run fast. There is no delay for the explosion. It gives off fumes and gases that will incapacitate you within two minutes. But the effect wears off as fast once you are removed from that area. It is, aptly called, smoke bomb. The next three are solid chemicals that are very volatile and difficult to keep together."

"Then why are you giving them to two dozen inexperienced teenagers?" Clint asked.

"You will not fail us, this much we know. That is why. First up, we have caustic. This orange solid is used as a bomb and explodes on contact with air. We keep water in the vials to cover it. When you need it to be used, open the cap of the vial and throw it at whatever you want. It will explode within five seconds. You get this chemical by sieving the water of Fang River. Small particles of this are found and put into water-filled vials. It is an art to get these particles without losing a body part, particularly the hands. Next up, we have epsom.

This is a lilac-coloured solid that can be used as a blinder on your enemies. Particles of this are found in the Logd River. It is collected by the same method as caustic. It burns with a dazzling white light. The last solid we have is the dark red carmine. It is found in the Jet River and can bring a person back from shock. All you have to do is mix a small pinch of this in water and pour it down the person's mouth. They will recover. However, though most of these chemicals are digestible, the Ring bearers cannot have carmine and sweenet."

"What is sweenet?" Adriana asked.

Gonth answered, "It is a drink that they gave us after our fight. I do not what they did for you, but it repaired my partially broken back. It is a very sweet liquid."

"Yes. That is sweenet." Lucia said.

Before she could say anything else, a visibly troubled Talon ran up to her and said, "We have a caravan stuck in the river. We need a lot of help."

Lucia smiled and said, "All of you, get your Guardians and good luck."

Soon, merged figures were crashing through the forest, heading east for the Fang River. They cleared the last of the trees and saw the caravan. It was an absolute wreck. Twenty wagons, each with five people, were in the water. The wagons had come off the bridge, which was now broken in two. The people were not in any danger of drowning, but the actual danger were the rocks around them. They knew that all of them could not get down without making the wagons go down as well.

Garon leapt over the side before they could come to a conclusion about what to do. He landed on the closest wagon and stretched his hand out. A woman passed her baby to him, and Chris swooped down to collect the infant. Then, Garon took the woman's hands and passed her over to James, who had also joined in to help. Soon, five wagons were clear, but Garon could not continue. He jumped back to the bank and instantly unmerged. The Centaurs took over. They nimbly jumped from rock to rock and positioned themselves in a chain like formation. Clint, James, and Chris did the same. But they could not reach the top of the waterfall, where the caravan had fallen from. Ake and Elesa joined in as well, and the trio of Ravens moved higher up, almost making it to the top. There was still ten feet of rock face to go, so Jacob took up position as the last person.

The Centaurs picked up people one by one and jumped to the next person. The Wolves then took them up to the Ravens. The Ravens picked them up and passed them from one to the other, until they reached Jacob, who let the people hold onto his mane, while he leapt from handhold to handhold till he reached the top. Anne could see that the Ravens were tiring, but to their credit, they kept going until the last person was safe and sound. Then, all nine of them started to climb back up. As soon as they made it to the top, they helped the travellers back to the capital, where they were given rooms in three pubs. As they trooped back into the palace, they were met by guards, who levelled their weapons and charged them.

Anne figured that this was some kind of test, so she charged ahead of everyone else and threw herself at the nearest guard, trying to get behind him, but the guard kept facing her, making her task a bit difficult. They were outnumbered two to one, but that did not stop the Wolves. They had already incapacitated their guards and were helping the Ravens with their adversaries. The battle was short and soon the guards were placed in one pile. Luca came out and glanced at the pile. He turned to them and asked, "Do you know who you just fought? These are Lord Veryu's personal guards. To knock them out takes a certain degree of strength. Though you have been under us for a short time, you have shown fighting skill that would have come from being with us for a longer time. We can only assume that you have been trained for a long time. We can start you on your missions now."

"What missions?" Anne asked.

"Yedgal did not just have people in his army. He also had monsters. You already know about two of them, the Battois and the Constries."

Ake intervened. "What monsters are these?"

Anne filled him in and noticed that Ake's eyes regained some of the fire that he had earlier, before disappearing with James.

Luca continued once Anne had finished. "There is only one type of air monster that Yedgal kept. They are called Jides. They are vicious and will eat anything, dead or alive. Their only weakness is fire. They can fly of speeds of up to thirty leagues an hour. Their teeth are capable of biting through the hardest rock and are sharper than swords. The water monsters are the most ferocious ones you will ever meet. They are called Yoknies. They live in the rivers and are the natural enemies of the Battois. However, Yedgal managed to get them to put their enmity aside and fight for him. The Yoknies can survive any pressure underwater and can make anything that touches its skin, adhere to it. Their eyes can see up to half a league underwater and navigate in dark depths using ultrasonic sounds. They have four large fins that can help them speed up and catch up to fast boats. They are not to be engaged unless one has the advantage of numbers. They respond violently to anything that they believe is a threat to them. The last monsters you have to know about are the non-earthly monsters. These are the Underworld Hounds. They are not to be confused with Acid Hounds of Logder, which are the only animals which can bring them down. They are controlled by Esdah, who lends them to a person he believes to be Lasgalan's saviour."

"Hold it there." Gonth said. "Are you saying that Yedgal was favoured by Esdah? That makes no sense. We should not be preventing Yedgal's rise then."

"I knew that you would ask this question. But the answer is yes and no. Yes, because only Esdah's favoured one can control the Hounds. No, because you should not be allowing Yedgal's rise. Even though he was favoured by Esdah, the God of the Underworld cannot keep him alive forever. If he dies, he dies. When Yedgal died the last time, the monsters went back to their old lives and rivalries. But I think that they can sense that he is coming back. Your first mission is to get on the mountains and start snuffing out the Battois population. They are the least dangerous monsters you will encounter. You will be separated into groups and sent away by this evening. If your group has to split up, go in groups of two at the very minimum. We will first send you to the west, towards the mountains enclosed by Backlash River. You will be able to understand why this is necessary. Now, you will be carrying some epsom and sweenet with yourselves. We will be preparing more of these potions and chemicals while you are away. Ake, you are going to get some poisoner since you do not have your Guardian with you. The rest of you will be rested properly. You need to prepare your body for a lot of merging. We will come to get you after you have finished with the Battois. Class dismissed."

# CHAPTER 6

Anne woke up, well rested and eager to get on with whatever their Trainers had in store for them. She strapped on her armour and proceeded on outside to the corridor. She saw that most of her comrades ready with their respective weapons. The most impressive were Chris' mace and Clint's quindent. The two owners had their Ravens on their shoulders. The two Ravens were nipping affectionately at their ears. Anne walked over to Clint and asked, "May I pet him?"

Clint regarded her with a curious and amused twinkle in his eyes. He smiled and said, "Fine. But do not touch his beak, whatever you do."

Anne stroked his Raven's head, which the bird seemed to enjoy a lot. The Raven hopped onto her shoulder and rubbed against her neck. Clint watched this, but did not say anything. He stared at her for a few seconds before saying, "I have never seen Cyrus take to someone so fast and so nicely. You two might get on great."

"Is that supposed to be your version of a complement?"

"Sort of. I guess that being away from people for a long time, with only hardened warriors for company has made my social skills a bit rusty."

"Then why did you not ask for a posting within the city?"

"I like challenges, especially one that seems almost impossible. Some days I regret my decision to join the army, some days I do not."

"You like challenges. How come you do not crack under the

pressure of being away from your family for so long?"

"One learns to deal with it over time. Besides, I prefer being with someone I do not know that well as my own family, to build up a relationship based on trust." He stared straight at her, as if asking her to read between the lines.

Anne took a few seconds to understand what he meant. When she did, she laughed.

"Really? This is your idea of asking me to be in a relationship with you?"

Clint raised his hands in surrender. "I did not say anything like that. As I said, my social skills are a bit rusty."

"Of course, they are. But why me of all people? Surely you would want someone of your own age." She gestured to Adriana, Vesper, and Victoria.

"Maybe. But I can connect with you better. You remind me very much of my mother. It is like her soul has entered you. I know that it sounds weird, but would you mind being part of my group for this exercise?"

"Why not? Let us see if you connect any better with me."

"Thanks."

Just then, Sens came towards them from another room on the corridor. He asked them to gather round him in a circle and hold hands. He then transported them to a clearing in a valley nestled between two small mountains. Judging by the faces of some of their friends, Anne guessed that the trip was not very smooth for them. Sens then spoke, "You will be divided into five groups of four each. The other three will be in one group. Since we want to assess how well you do in smaller groups, I will be taking your groups and placing them in different areas. Good luck."

Another gold flash and he was gone with nineteen of them. Anne looked at her group, which consisted of Clint, Trest, Edward and herself. The only ones who had an advantage in battle were Edward and Trest. Clint too had an advantage, having managed to smuggle his Raven onto this exercise. He merged, and took to the skies. After doing a few loops in the air, he landed next to them and said, "There are some blue flames about five hundred metres into the forest. I suggest we be on our guard from now on."

"Wait." Anne was not sure why she said that. She could feel something wrong. She did not know what it was though. Then Clint's eyes locked onto something behind her. He ploughed into her, throwing both of them to the ground as a large Dragon came in for landing in front of them. The only one who was not surprised was Edward. He patted the Dragon's snout.

"Ontemp. Been a while my friend."

Ontemp made a rumbling sound in his throat and shot flames into the sky. From behind his wing, David, a Claw Lion jumped and landed next to Anne. She hugged David and merged. So did the other two. Trest's Dragon, Dersyu, had also landed. From the forest, a number of loud bellows sounded, like a herd of Bulls.

"Clint, see what is going on." Edward said.

"No need. We got a full herd of Battois approaching us."

As Clint said that the first few Battois broke through the tree line and roared. There were about ten of them, though Anne could hear more crashing through the trees behind. Clint said, "I am going to distract them from the sky. Anne, Trest, flank them and attack. Edward, you are the only one who can stand against them. Blind them from the front with your flames. We should be able to contain them."

Edward nodded. He burst into flames and shot some at the Battois, just to get their attention. He succeeded. They turned to him while the other three got to their respective positions. The Battois snorted blue flames at Edward, who countered with his own flames. Meanwhile, Trest and Anne got to work, killing the Battois together like a well-oiled machine. Clint swooped down and kicked Battois on the head and hit them with his wings, killing them in the process.

They regrouped and waited for the next charge. The crashing continued towards them. The next wave of Battois consisted of about thirty of them. Then, more flooded into the valley from behind them. They had walked straight into an ambush.

Clint levelled his quindent, though Anne knew that he could only pierce a maximum of two Battois at a time. Trest pressed a button on the hilt of her scalpel and a second blade protruded out of the hilt in the other direction. Trest's scalpel itself was two feet long and crafted like a sword. The second blade added another two feet of cutting edge. Edward burst into flames again and sent a blast of fire towards the nearest Battos, as an indication to back off. Both the Talons had scales on their skin, but Anne was not sure they would survive a wave of flames aimed at them. Anne herself could pack a good punch. Because of her lighter frame, Anne could dodge the fire faster than the others. But one mistimed blast and she could die within seconds. It seemed that they were not getting anywhere.

Then, Edward came up with a brilliant idea.

"Guys, take out a vial of epsom. We can use it to escape."

Anne pulled out a vial with the lilac coloured solid. She tossed some towards the smaller group of Battois. Edward waited for the right moment and shouted, "Look away!" He sent a flame at the solid, which burst into white flames that left the four of them seeing flashes of light for a few seconds. They charged the group and overpowered them, which was easy, since none of them had eyes left to see what was happening. The larger group charged down their slope towards them. But it was too late. The four of them ran into the trees and disappeared in its darkness. The bodies of forty Battois littered the clearing.

Edward ignited his fingers. They blazed like a miniature campfire. It was already getting dark and the last rays of the sun could be seen above the tree tops. Behind them, the Battois crashed through the trees. They ran into another clearing where Edward suggested that they split up. The other three did not readily agree to this, so Clint came up with an alternative. They would leave Edward as bait in the clearing, while Clint flew up and waited for a chance to strike. The girls would go back around the Battois and flank them, cutting off their escape. That plan went down better with them. Their sole aim was to hit and run. If they stretched the Battois lines thin, the monsters would get the message crystal clear. They took up their respective positions and waited.

The first few Battois broke the tree line and charged at Edward. To his credit, he stood his ground and flung fireballs at them. A few got incinerated, but soon Edward was going to be overwhelmed. Clint flew down and started helping Edward. But a punch to his back got him on the ground.

Through his hazy vision, Clint could see Edward go under three Battois, with more piling on top of him. Clint tried to stand up, using his spear as a support. The girls came and helped him into the trees, with Anne proving a cover for them as some Battois charged them. But most of them were piled up on Edward.

Clint could see what the Battois could not. From within, an orange light was glowing, becoming brighter by the second. Then, the Battois peeled off, as if some force was pushing them. At that instant, Edward released his full power.

# CHAPTER 7

Trest had never seen Edward ablaze before. At least, not as brightly as he was at that moment. His body was covered in flames, his eyes were miniature balls of fire. He threw fire at the retreating Battois, which burned them to a crisp. When there were none left he turned towards them, a flaming sword in each hand. Clint decided that if he was anyway going to die, it was going to be defending the two girls behind him. He expanded his spear into a quindent, ready to take Edward on. As Edward advanced towards them, Clint levelled his weapon.

Edward was just three metres away, when Clint flapped his wings. He used them to shut down Edward's flames, but did not seem to do the trick. Cyrus' energy was getting spent, but Clint had trained him to push his limits. If Clint could get Edward to get on the defensive, he might succeed in getting the flames shut down. He said, "Sorry about this, Edward."

And then, Clint started attacking Edward with a ferocity that Trest had never seen before. He was getting dangerously close to the flames, which had somewhat contracted around Edward to form a shield. Edward's eyes were still glowing. Trest was sure that was not a good sign. As Anne and she watched, the orange colour in his eyes expanded, covering his whites. His pupils thinned out and spread out across the length of his eyes.

Trest nearly cried. She heard about this happening to Garon from Karen herself. Only a strong shock or hit would get Edward back to normal. But there was no way they could get through the fire wall surrounding Edward. Clint muttered under his breath, "Not this again."

Unknown to them, Clint had one ace up his sleeve.

As they watched, Clint dropped his weapon and hugged his sides like he was having fits. Then he straightened up and turned towards the girls, who backed up into a tree. Clint had red eyes, in the same way as Edward. He smiled, which was very unnerving. He turned back to Edward, who was looking very confused on seeing the new person. He turned his flames faster and charged Clint. Clint did not move. As Edward's fire shell hit him, Clint caught it as easily as if he was catching a ball. With the shell in his grasp, he flapped his wings harder than he ever had, extinguishing the fire easily, and caught Edward in his arms. He punched Edward in the ribs, which probably got him out of his beast mode. Anne ran to Edward and forced some sweenet into his mouth. She glanced up at Clint, who looked as if he expected something from her.

She remembered what Karen had said about giving a strong hit to the person in this state. She swept out her leg, knocking Clint off-balance. As he fell, she punched him in the stomach, though not too strongly. He hit a tree and then the ground. Trest went to him and poured sweenet down his throat as well. It was good that the two boys had not unmerged, because then it would have been troublesome to transport a Dragon as well.

The boys got up after a few minutes. After hearing the story of their duel from the girls, they grinned and Edward told Clint, "Thanks for saving me."

"No problem. Though please do not do it often."

"Sure."

Trest asked, "Are you guys good enough to walk back to clearing?"

"Yes." Both of them said.

They got to their feet and headed to the clearing. When they reached, they saw that there were no Battois bodies. Instead, there was one huge Battos waiting for them. It looked like it could take on all of them with no problem. The only problem was, both Edward and Clint were out. It was taking every bit of their concentration to stay merged, as Trest could see. It seemed like it would be Anne and herself against the giant.

The Battos pawed the earth and charged at them. Anne threw herself to one side while the other three leapt to the other side. The Battos turned to Anne and charged at her. Anne jumped up, but timed it wrong. The Battos grabbed her ankle and yanked it downwards and slammed her into the ground hard. She could see Trest trying to get the Battos' attention by throwing small rocks at it.

When she succeeded, the Battos charged her, and she ran to the side towards Anne. She took out some of her remaining sweenet and made Anne swallow it. Since her back was turned to the Battos, she could not see it charging towards them. As the monster charged towards them, Anne threw Trest to one side and punched the Battos hard. It was propelled backwards through the air and, by sheer luck, onto Clint's quindent. She glanced at him and saw a brief smirk on his face. Just then, a silver flash occurred at the edge of the clearing, and they saw Sens walk out of it. He looked around at the four of them and said, "Well done. Now let us get you back."

He made them hold hands and teleported them back to the palace. He then made all of them unmerge and took the Guardians back to their room. After coming back, he made the girls go back to their rooms while he took the boys to the field outside. As the girls went back to their rooms, Anne caught hold of James and asked him to eavesdrop on Sens and what he had to say to Clint and Edward.

James looked sceptically at Anne, but agreed to do it. He turned invisible and headed for the field. He was not sure that his shadow would show from the fire in the torches, but he still took a chance and stood in front of one torch. Sens and Luca were coming into the field with Garon. Garon looked like he had it rough with his group.

Nevertheless, he still smiled at the other five. Looking around at the other five, James could see that they were the ones who had been taken away for some time the day that Dan had been kidnapped and Ake and he had run all the way to Leonis. There was Karen, Edward, Clint, Vincent, Garon and Robert.

Luca had them sit in a line and started off, "Today was a day I do not think you will be forgetting very fast."

Robert laughed and said, "Like we have much of a choice, considering our brain power."

The others burst out laughing. Luca said, "Yes, well, the good thing is that no one got hurt."

Clint and Edward both said, "Excuse me?"

Sens smiled and said, "We know what happened to you guys. In fact, you guys all unleashed raw power in this exercise. Lord Veryu was particularly impressed by Clint and Garon. You guys managed to go beyond pure savagery that is your Guardian's base instinct. Both of you could control your Guardian. That is very good, but you should also know that it has its side effects. For instance, you can get tired much faster than the others. It is more than just merging. You guys become absolute beasts. Nothing is impossible for you six. There is very little margin for error where you are concerned. That is why we are going to put you through more rigorous training than the others. We will make you precision fighters. If you are captured, it will be very, very bad for Lasgalan. No power can stand up to you in your primal beast mode. But having so much power comes with a cost. Do you want to know what it is?"

Karen sarcastically asked, "We actually have a choice?"

"Yes. Now tell me, do you want to know?"

The six of them huddled together and discussed the issue.

When they decided, Robert nodded to Luca.

"Fine. The one drawback is that you have no conscience in your primal forms. You will kill anything in your path to get to your destination. If we tell you to kill your family now, you will not. Even merged, you will not. But in your primal form, you will not hesitate to kill them. You feel no remorse, no hatred, just rage. You cannot speak complete sentences, but your actions will literally speak louder than what you will be able to speak. You are the strongest there is in Lasgalan now. Even the combined power of the District Rings cannot hold back even one of you. Now think about how much you could accomplish as a team."

"Are you saying we will not fight each other to stay at the top of our game?" Vincent asked.

James knew what he was talking about. He had been there when Vincent went all out on the Battois. James had never seen someone kill like him. All he was doing at that time was trying to get Hasha and Chris to safety. He had them both in his talons, and was trying to put some distance between Vincent and himself. He had just about cleared the tree-tops when something grazed his wing. He remembered Vincent saying that he was accurate up to half a league with projectiles. He had been hit by a branch and that had sent him nearly out of control. He hit them the ground, using his body to shield Hasha and Chris from the worst of the impact. Upon getting up, he saw that Hasha was using her Ring to produce weapons to hit Vincent. He was dodging and smacking them away like they were nothing to him. Finally, Chris got behind him and hit him in his side. That got him back to his senses, though he did not faint.

He had surveyed the destruction around him and asked for some sweenet for his ribs. Sens had come to collect them and then taken Vincent to the field, where he sat right now.

Sens replied, "No Vincent. Though your Guardian has a lust for staying on top as an undisputed beast, you will not have the same urge. Also, if you wanted to be at the top, your other friends are there to hold you back. As you all saw today, it only takes a strong knock to bring you back."

"So we have another weakness to add to our list. But one thing does seem odd."

"What?"

"How come Chris' mace did not shatter when he hit my ribs?"

"It is a metal mace. Because your skeleton is also coated in a metal, iron, the mace did not shatter. But due to the power behind the swing Chris hit you with, your bones cracked a bit."

"Right, so any metal coated weapon will not shatter on impact with my bones."

"No. Spears and javelins can shatter due to the intense pressure your bones exert on them. But enough of all this. From tomorrow, you will be trained under the two of us. It will be a high protein and fat diet, coupled with high level training. Remember, one wrong move on the battlefield and you die. Do not repeat this conversation to anybody, even the others. Understood?"

The six of them nodded. James sensed that the talk was over and ran back to his room. He caught Anne's eye and mouthed, "Tell you tomorrow."

He slipped into his room and the torches extinguished themselves. He heard the six of them pass his room, but did not try to get out of bed. The torches would light up again and his Trainers would smell something fishy. So he closed his eyes and fell off to sleep.

# CHAPTER 8

Vincent got out of bed just before dawn. The excitement of the previous day had got him out like a light. Though he was asleep for just about six hours, not his usual sleep time, he felt even well refreshed than normal. He glanced around his room to see everyone sleeping. Now that Sens and Luca had insisted that the six of them sleep separately, he had five roommates. He was not the eldest out of them. That was Edward and Clint. The youngest was Karen, who he felt protective of. Garon was the same age as her, but he could hold his own, as Vincent had seen.

He stretched his lean frame and walked out onto the corridor. There were just three other rooms, one each for the remaining girls, boys, and Ring-bearers. He was one of the shortest in their group, shorter than fourteen-year-old Karen and Ake. He glanced around and saw that there were no guards around. That did not seem right. He went back into the room and grabbed his javelin. Most of the time, people mistook his javelin for a spear. But it was a javelin. Vincent was sure of that.

He got out of the room and glanced into the three rooms. Normally, he would not have looked into a girl's room without the occupant's permission. But he did not have to.

The Ring-bearers and girls came out from their rooms, walking towards him like sleepwalkers. The boys came out of their room on the other side. They had trapped Vincent from both sides. Vincent resorted to the first rule of combat he had been taught. "Assume you are the target and lead your pursuers away from anyone else."

He did just that. Using his javelin as a pole, he vaulted on top of the boys' heads and landed behind them. He needed to keep them focused on himself, so he backed up slowly. He needed his Guardian, Nilesh, who could give him an edge in a fight. He got to the door to the throne room and turned and ran. He ran straight for the Guardians' room and got inside. He headed for Nilesh, and silently willed the Lion to merge with him. It happened, and Vincent headed out to face his adversaries. Leading the group were the Ring-bearers. Vincent remembered that not even the combined power of all six Rings could bring him down, so he readied his javelin. As the group got closer, he vaulted over them again, and ran for his room. He positioned himself in front of the door, ready for charge after charge. They came slowly. As they got closer, Thomas used his Ring to pull Vincent onto the floor. Vincent tried to get up, but it felt as if the air had become solid on top of him. He could see the six Ring-bearers point their Rings at him, ready to hit him with the full force of the Rings. Just then, he saw a flame behind the group.

Edward caused a good distraction by getting all of them focused on him. Meanwhile, Karen and Garon got Vincent to his feet. The six of them formed a small circle and let their friends form a ring around them. Vincent waited for them to close in a bit closer and then said, "Edward, blaze now."

Edward burst into red-hot flames. He directed them in front of himself, keeping the other five cool. Clint expanded his quindent and pointed it ahead, keeping the part of the group ahead of him at bay. Robert crouched, ready to go hand-to-hand with anyone. Garon's eyes flicked from person to person, as if he was already deciding how to knock off different people. Karen pointed her scythe at those in front of her, as if willing them to back off. Vincent too levelled his javelin and waited for the charge.

The first person who tried to get through them was James. He turned invisible and the others came in closer. However, Vincent could smell him. He lashed out in front of Clint and gripped something in the air. His hands closed around something solid, and James shimmered back into existence. Vincent threw him into the crowd, knocking some of them off their feet. But the bulk of the group closed in on them. Robert charged out of the group and threw himself at some others, keeping them occupied.

Suddenly, the air rippled around Vincent. He turned around to see Latyu standing a few feet behind him, holding a small red casket in his palm. Save the six in a circle, the others got sucked into it. Latyu shut it once the last person was inside.

He smiled and said, "This was a test, the first of many that we wanted to put you through. We wanted to see how you would take down your friends if they were forced to fight you. We could see the way that you were going about it, you were going to win. Your friends are actually sleeping right now."

Sure enough, the others were soundly sleeping away. Vincent raised an eyebrow at Latyu. "Impressive. Just out of curiosity, how much would you give us on ten, for the way we handled the situation?"

"About a nine, I would say. Now come on, breakfast for you guys is ready."

The six of them marched down to the dining hall. Vincent still had Nilesh merged with him, so Latyu made him unmerge and took Nilesh back to the Guardians' room.

The six of them got into the dining room and saw that a feast awaited them. Vincent went straight for the lean venison and helped himself to a lot of it. The others went for the beef and pork. Vincent knew the reason. The fat of the beef and pork would give them extra energy boost whenever needed. Since Vincent had no fat on the meat, he would have to be wise as to how he would be spending his energy. He chowed down his meat and went back to his room to bathe and change.

Once they were ready, they were taken down to the field and saw Reidan and Sens waiting for them. As they approached, Sens said, "We called you here so that you can reach your full potential. Here, we have no problem with you going all out with your powers."

Clint interrupted him. "You do remember what happened last time, Reidan?"

"Of course, I do. But Garon has proved himself capable of controlling his Guardian. So have you, even in a situation of facing someone in his own primal form."

Clint shrugged his shoulders. He glanced at Edward, who was nervously fidgeting with his fingers. Among the six of them, Edward was the most powerful, which also made him the perfect ally but also the worst enemy they would face if he decided to turn against them.

They were made to stand in pairs. Karen faced Garon again. Vincent's opponent was Clint. Edward was against Robert.

"Alright," Sens said. "No weapons in this round, only powers. Vincent, this places you, Karen and Garon at a slight disadvantage. But, if you remember something we had told you back at the old base, all of you are equally powered. Begin."

Karen realised what Sens was talking about. So, when Garon got ready to charge her, she willed her heart to slow down, and saw Garon running towards her very slowly. She got out of his line of sight and charged him from the side. She grabbed Garon's stomach and was about to flip him over, when she felt a sharp pain in her back. She sped up her heart to normal and saw that somehow, Garon had managed to go upright, turn, and hit her. As she let go off him, he let her slide down gently and asked for some sweenet to give her. As she swallowed the sweet liquid, he chuckled good-heartedly and said, "Good idea of slowing down your heart, but you should not have done it with me so close to you."

"You mean you did it too?"

"I did not need to. All I had to do was anticipate what you were going to do. When you went in for the grab, I twisted and got you. You were looking too closely for the shot. You need to observe your surroundings better."

"Got it. You ready for another round?"

"Ready and raring."

The two of them squared off again. This time, Garon went on the defensive. He raised his palms defensively and kept his hands open, as if he wanted to grab Karen as she charged. As she ran at him, she thought that she saw a faint green aura around him. Dismissing it as a trick of the light, Karen went for his stomach with her left hand and his head with her right hand. Then, he did the unexpected.

He grabbed her left hand with his right hand and her right hand with his left. He then twisted himself and came up holding Karen in lock. He had both her arms stretched across her chest, stopping her movement. She swung her legs and tried to get him off-balance. But his legs were not moved. She tried to head-butt him, but he just moved his head out of range. He had got her pinned fast and was in no hurry to let her go. She said, "Alright, I concede."

Garon released her hands and looked at Vincent and Clint. Clint had an advantage with his height, but not in weight. Both of them were trying to go for each other's throat, to get the upper hand in the fight. Vincent was more defensive, protecting his throat without going for a shot at Clint. Clint was exactly the opposite. He was more focused on going through Vincent's defence than protecting his throat. Vincent was getting pushed back by Clint's fast and random attacks. Then, he started going on the offensive. Clint was surprised by this, but got over his shock fast. He started analysing Vincent's attack pattern. As soon as he saw an opening in the attack, he went for his favourite move, the kill move, as he called it. This particular move required the use of his quindent, which he did not have at the moment. He started to back up to a tree with a low-hanging branch. As soon as he was in range, he jumped and grabbed the branch with both hands. He swung himself in a circle around the branch, kicking Vincent on the way up. As he swung down, he released his hands and slammed both fists into Vincent's ribs after flipping twice through the air. But the most shocking part for Clint, was that Vincent had managed to catch and stop both of Clint's fists together with the same hands. Clint glanced at Vincent's hands, crossed over his chest, which were glowing a faint shade of yellow. Clint blinked twice to check if he was seeing things. When the colour did not fade, Clint realised that he was going to use more power. He started to kick, thinking that Vincent would not be able would not be able to defend himself. But to Clint's further surprise and Vincent's credit, the latter used one leg to block the kicks. Clint flipped himself over Vincent and brought Vincent down on the ground with a lot of force. Though Vincent did not appear to have broken bones, Clint forced some sweenet into his throat. Vincent accepted. The last match that was still going on was Robert against Edward.

This was a supposedly one-sided match, since Edward could easily keep Robert at bay with his flames, but Robert was holding his own pretty well. He kept punching Edward hard and fast, preventing him from concentrating and getting a flaming defence up. Robert's punches were fast, but he was not aiming for any particular part of Edward. Out of nowhere, Edward grabbed both his wrists and stared hard into Robert's eyes.

"You know one other use of my flames? They help me siphon power from someone else."

Edward burst into flames again and let the flames wrap around Robert. Robert screamed as he could feel his strength and stamina leave him. Just then, Edward stiffened as if he had been hit by lightning. His flames shut off, and he let go of Robert.

Robert let him fall, and then stepped away from him. He glanced at Sens and Reidan. But they just stood quiet. Robert heard a sound like cracking leaves. He turned and saw Edward trying to get up. He said, "Edward, don't. You do not have the strength."

In reply, Edward stood up and burst into red flames. He snarled and said, "You think?"

Garon shouted to Sens, "Our Guardians, now!"

Sens rushed off to get the five Guardians, while the five of them made a small circle around Edward. Vincent adopted a traditional fighting stance from Leonis. His right hand went behind his back, his body at an angle to the right and his left forearm raised as if he was holding a shield on it.

Garon went completely opposite. He faced Edward head on, both his hands up and palms open, ready to grab Edward if he came too close.

Robert did almost the same thing. Instead of opening his palms, he made a fist in each hand and opened them, keeping his fingers folded, exposing only his palm.

Karen simply made two fists and stood at an angle to Edward, as if she was ready to pound Edward into the ground.

Clint crossed his open palms across his chest, with his fingers straight out, like he was ready to go and chop up Edward with his bare hands.

Sens did not come out, their Guardians did. They took one look at Edward and ran to the people they were supposed to protect. They instantly merged, and Vincent heard Reidan saying, "Come on, let it work."

Vincent glanced at Garon and saw that he was having trouble with his Guardian. His face looked like he was ready to get sick. Reidan shouted, "Let your Guardians take over."

Vincent saw that this was the only way they were going to take out Edward, so he let Nilesh take over his mind. Looking around, he could see that the others had done the same. He saw that each of them had a distinctive aura around themselves that was trying to form a solid figure. Around Garon, a green aura broke and formed the figure of a Wolf mid-jump. Around Karen, her purple aura formed a Bull mid-charge. Clint had a red aura that formed a Raven in flight. Robert's blue aura showed a Horse in a position of rearing up. Vincent could only imagine that his aura had formed the shape of a roaring Lion. There was no holding back now.

Vincent and Garon lunged at Edward from the sides, while Karen rushed him from the front. Robert and Clint got him from the back. With Vincent and Garon holding his arms and forcing him to his knees, Karen started to punch him across his front. Clint delivered a sharp blow to his head and Robert pounded his fists into Edward's shoulders. They kept at it until Edward's flames shut off. Then they put a lot of sweenet into his mouth and got some water into his mouth as well.

With Edward taken away to the doctors, the five of them sat down, exhausted from their workout. They all had received hard hits from Reidan in order to subdue their Guardians. They had not yet unmerged, though. Garon huffed like he had just run up and down a mountain. But he looked better than he sounded. Vincent turned to Reidan and said, "When we let our Guardians take over, I thought I saw..."

"A Raven, Bull, Wolf, and Horse. Am I right?"

"Yes. Is this a condition that we are born with, that makes us more precious than the others?"

"Partly. Until you and your Guardian are strongly united, this does not happen. The animals showing is just a sign of your power. The more your power, the larger your animal appears. This is also a way to scare your enemies before you actually attack them. The only way you can unite with this level of power, is if you are born as embodiment of your Tribe's animal. Clint was the first one to unlock his power. All it takes is a strong emotional trigger to set it off. But once you lose your

Guardians, the gems you get from them will power you up like Ake. You were not there, but he dispatched the largest Battos with one swing of a sword that he produced with his gem."

Vincent spoke up, "Can you please stop saying that we will lose our Guardians? It feels an extra weight on our shoulders."

"Sorry. But this is a sad truth you have to accept. If Lord Xast has said it will happen, it will certainly happen."

Clint said, "Then we do not take our Guardians when we storm the fortress of Yedgal. Simple as that."

"No. You will need your Guardians for that. Since we do not know exactly where in the mountains it is, we will split you up into groups and send you into the six Districts at the same time. From there on, you will be on your own. But to ensure that we do not play into Yedgal's forces' hands, we will not allow more than one of you and one of the Ring-bearers to go together. There will be one of you each per group and two others of your choosing. But we must make sure that we stretch out their forces so that there is a chance you do not all get captured."

Karen raised her hand, "Why not send the groups in one go together?"

"We cannot risk five more of you getting captured, especially not any of you six. The Ring-bearers are of no value to Yedgal. All he needs to be resurrected are the souls of any six of you. Also, if you find the fortress of Yedgal, you must not engage under any circumstances with anyone or anything around it. Just fall back to the closest District and try to get back to us. Then, with our full might, and hopefully, the entire force of Lasgalan, we can storm the fortress."

Karen once again asked, "Why are you not discussing this with the others?"

"Because we will not accept it, and insist that we go District-wise." Jacob's voice came from behind her.

They whirled around and saw the Leonid standing at the door of the palace. His knuckledusters were placed his fingers and he glared at Reidan and said, "That is the reason, is it not?"

Reidan sighed and said, "Sadly, yes. Unlike the twelve of you, these six know the cost of sacrifice. This is something they are born with, an instinct implanted into their brains. They know when to let go. You guys have a common flaw. You will always be loyal to people, even if they are in the gravest of wrongs. You will fight to the death for them. These six do not have that flaw in them. That is what makes them special. Now, you can try and stop us from doing what we wanted to do, or you can do just the opposite. The choice is yours."

Karen could see Jacob's neck muscles tightening as if he was going to fight the two Trainers, or if he was going to try and use his power of being intimidating and force the Trainers into submission. But he just smiled and said, "Have it your way."

Karen watched him as he went back through the door. She turned and asked Reidan, "Why only us? Surely even they can overcome their sacrificial instinct."

"No. Even if we try to train them to do so, they will falter at the most crucial moment. Besides, we are not done with you yet. We will make you face Constries soon. Since there are only six of you, we will send you as one group. Just know that these monsters show no mercy. You will need to keep each other's back. Just remember, you do not have any wood with you that you can use to your advantage."

"When do we leave?" Karen asked.

"Let noon come. Then we will send you on your way. Be careful as they have a strong sense of smell. Rest outside here till we call you."

With that, the two Trainers went back into the building. The five of them unmerged and lay down on the grass. They wanted to rest their Guardians for as long as possible.

As they lay down and the silence became too uncomfortable for

Robert, he asked, "How bad do you think these Constries can be?"

Garon answered, "Considering how tough the Battois were, I would say that the Constries could be about twice as tough as them."

Clint laughed sarcastically and said, "Try ten times as strong."

"What makes you say that?"

"Think about it. They have two extra arms, which gives them extra support when needed. They also have a larger brain, which makes them process information much faster, making their reaction time consequently faster. Also, they can regenerate pretty much any part of their body, except the head. From what I read about them, getting to their head will be tough as they stand nearly nine feet tall. You might be the only one who could potentially decapitate them."

"Good enough. Where do you think they will send us this time?"

"No idea."

"You are going to the Schorl mines," James' voice came behind them.

Clint turned to see his fellow Covine, with his own Raven on his shoulder, standing against the wall of the palace. He twirled his shoulder-length hair with his finger, as if he had delivered news that would not affect the outcome of their encounter with the monsters.

Garon eyed James suspiciously.

"How long have you been here, James?"

"Not very long. I heard the Trainers talking about it sometime before. Just thought I would come and tell you about it. I actually wanted to tell Clint personally, but then I thought that I might tell you all. Anyway, I got to go back. They are expecting me to be eating breakfast now."

With that, James turned invisible, though his Raven did not. It flapped its wings and flew into the palace. Clint turned to the other four and said, "We got a problem. If what James is saying is true, then three of us our going to be more of liabilities to the group than assets. Karen, Edward, and I are those three. Karen, your merged form's frame will not be very useful in the tunnels of the mines. Also, your flames would become larger and more dangerous due to the methane in the tunnels. The same problem applies to Edward, though he should not have a problem moving around in the mines. I will not be able to use my wings to good effect down there. On the other hand, Vincent, Garon and Robert will have no problem."

Robert asked, "How? I grow a bit taller when merged. If the tunnel ceilings are anything lesser than seven feet, I am going to have a problem. And let us not forget about the stalagmites and stalactites that we might get there."

"They will not be there. I have been down there myself a few times. At some places, the ceiling gets a bit low, but otherwise we should be fine."

# CHAPTER 9

Raze hurried down the hallway. Xristos had summoned him for an urgent meeting. But he did not know what the meeting was for. He ran down the narrow corridor to reach the double oak doors that opened into the war room. As he entered, he saw that he was not alone.

In front of him, at a round table, sat six men, all dressed in civil attire. The table was meant to seat ten people, but three chairs were empty, not including his own. The two chairs on Raze's left were empty, as was the chair directly across the table from his. On the third chair from his left, Xristos sat, looking expectantly at him. On Xristos' left sat a man who looked like a beast in human form. His coat, made from lion skin, covered most of his body, except his face. He had green eyes, thin lips, and dark hair. He glanced at Raze and nodded curtly to him. The seat on that man's left was empty, as it was the seat opposite Raze. On the left of that seat sat a young man who was staring intently at his hand. As Raze looked properly, he realised that the youngster's hand was changing from the body part of one animal to another animal's. On his left was a man who was old enough to be Raze's grandfather. He smiled at Raze, and the smile was so infectious that even Raze smiled back without meaning to. To the old man's left was a man who looked like he had seen the worst of the battles he was in. His face was scarred in many places. His eyes flicked around from person to person, as if he did not trust anyone in the room. The last person, on Raze's right was a young man who looked a lot like the one on the right of the old man. He was holding a Transporter in his right hand and was moving the fingers of his left hand over it, in a hypnotic manner. Raze sat down and Xristos thumped the table. Around the table, everyone sat up straight and turned their attention to him.

Xristos started off, "Thank you all for coming. I have called this meeting because we have finally begun the first stage of awakening King Yedgal."

The old man spoke up, cutting off Xristos, "How many?"

Xristos looked pointedly at Raze. Raze got up and addressed the old man, "I have captured one Equine. His name is Dan. His power is to sense the emotions of any animal or human."

The old man, seemingly satisfied, sat down, and motioned for Xristos to continue. Xristos said, "Before I say anything, I would like to introduce you all to Raze. Raze, I want you to meet the others of the council I was telling you about. This man on my left is Sabre, King Yedgal's cousin and right-hand man. The seat next to him is for the King himself. Next is Bryan, King Yedgal's older son. His younger twin, Byron is sitting next to you. The old man over there is Giriod, King Yedgal's uncle. Next to him is Shane, King Yedgal's brother and navy commander. The seat next to you is meant for Listro, but owing to an unforeseen problem he will not be able to attend today's meeting." Raze thought that he saw Xristos glare at Byron when saying the last statement.

"The seat on my right is for my right-hand man, Karan. He will not be attending this meeting as well, because he is trying to shore up the defences of the fortress as we speak. Therefore, it is just the seven of us in this meeting."

Raze nodded. Apart from Listro, Karan and Xristos, he had not met any of the others in front of him. He noticed that there was a small line running from his right-hand side of the table, all the way to the centre of the table. There was another coming out from between Xristos and Karan's chairs, as well as from between Giriod and Shane's chairs. A fourth line came out from the right of Yedgal's chair. The four lines did not meet at the centre, but formed a square at the centre, inside which was a spiral design.

Raze refocused his attention on Xristos as the latter was saying, "Which brings us to the most pressing issue at the moment."

Byron put his palms down on the table and stood up saying, "Which is why I keep saying, as soon as one of them is captured, we take them to the cell and kill them, reducing the chances of them escaping down to nothing. But for some reason, my brother always negates me."

Raze turned his attention to Bryan, who was almost across the table from him. Bryan got up and said, "Byron, do you remember nothing of what father taught us as princes? He always said that we should not disrespect or dishonour any woman, girl, or lady. Neither should we kill any prisoner unless that person has a weapon on themselves."

"Did you not see that he has a weapon with him?"

Raze decided that he needed to speak up.

"With all due respect Prince Byron, while I may be inclined to agree with your point of view, your brother is correct. We are not to kill Dan unless absolutely necessary."

Xristos coughed and said, "He has an arrowhead with him. I hardly think that it counts as a weapon."

"Fine! I call for a vote. Should we kill Dan and the other five who are brought in? All in favour raise your hand."

Raze, Bryan, Xristos abstained from voting in favour of the motion. Giriod shook his head. That meant that Byron, Shane, and Sabre were outvoted. Byron glared at his brother and grunted, "Fine."

Xristos said, "Since Listro is not here to tell us what information his top spy has brought us, I will read them out."

He brought out a piece of parchment that looked like the writer was in hurry to give information to them.

Xristos read out, "The main six are being sent to the Schorl mines to train with Constries. Not our own. Training simulation. Three Trainers going. Do not attempt anything now. They will be sent to the Districts to try and scout out our location. Let them come. Attack then."

Bryan said, "Should we try and stop their progress into the mountains, or do we wait till they are literally outside the fortress?"

Shane answered, "No, nephew. If we attack them from the moment they set foot on the mountains, they will fall back to the nearest city, where there no doubt be help waiting for them. If we can cut off their escape routes by circling around them and hitting them hard from the back, then we will have another two or three people to revive your father. We already have one, thanks to Raze here."

"But that one is not the correct person. So, the way I see it, you have not brought in anyone." Byron interjected, glaring at Raze accusingly. Raze ignored him, though he was seething inside. He was very tempted to give Byron a piece of his mind, but as Byron was a prince and Raze himself was the captain of the King's private guard, he kept shut.

Soon, the meeting was over. Raze got up and walked out in his own hallway. Thinking about something that Xristos had told him, he came back to the room where he had brought Dan to Xristos. Glancing at the tunnel he had just come through to make sure no one was coming, he lifted his cape, where a red colour potion in a sealed vial was hidden. Taking a swig of the stampede, he counted till five and ran out the nearest exit from the mountain side. As he shot out into the sky, he changed into a winged Unicorn, a little variation of the original stampede potion made by Byron.

His bronze skin and wings matched the colour of the sky perfectly, and soon he was flying in the direction of Equis. He planned to land in the Isle of the Pegasi so that he could mingle within the Unicorns themselves. From there, he left the rest in the hands of destiny.

He used his great wings to get above the clouds. Every once in a while, he dived below the clouds to pick up speed, and then climbed above the clouds again. He flew over the Dividing Mountains and soon crossed over the strait of the Equine Gulf and started to veer east towards the Isle. He reached the Isle after sunset, so he managed to land in the midst of the animals without much of a hassle.

He started to wonder why Xristos had sent him all the way to Equis. There was nothing there to see. It was the slowest progressing District out of all the six. The only economy they had was their Rhodonite gems. These gems were the only gem that did not come out from the earth white in colour. The other five Districts had their gems come out without a bit of colour, which were later sent to licenced people in the capital to finish colouring and were then sent off throughout the District. Due to the special feature of the Rhodonite gems, and the small amount of money needed to extract them, the other Districts were ready to pay for a bulk amount, and as a result, Equis flourished.

The second and last contributing factor for Equis' small economy was the tourism. Sure, it was not like Tauris, which got a heavy income form the Games alone. The Rhodonite Hills were not very high, so people of all ages could climb them, with or without guides, and stop at any camp that was made in the Hills, to see the natural splendorous view and climb down later. The Equine Gulf was a body of clear water that was good for overnight cruises. If one stuck close to the shore and did one round of the Gulf, it would take about three days and three nights. Despite being not a very well-off District, Equis had a strong army as well as navy. They were the only District never to have lost a naval battle. Whenever a District got a new Lord, the first action that the new Lord normally took was to annex a neighbouring District. Leonis had tried to annex Equis six times before, but always got beaten back in spite of having a numerically superior army. No District could think of annexing Equis from the west, as the Rhodonite Hills came in the way. There was a small passage called the Unicorn Pass in the Hills, but it would reduce the chances of a large army getting an advantage over Equis' army. In the east of the District, there were no cities as it was a small desert. It was not a very large one, but it would take one month for an army to cross through, being laboured with food, weapons, and armour. The only thing that could cross the desert faster than an army was a Strawberry Roan Horse. They were fleet-footed Horses which were supposed to be the fastest herbivores in Lasgalan. They had a great amount of stamina and could maintain a consistent pace no matter how far they had to travel. They were the preferred mode of transport but were expensive to maintain due to the amount of food they ate to maintain their speed.

Raze remembered what Xristos had told him after he told him of his folly of bringing in Dan to be used to revive Yedgal. Xristos had told him that since he was the general of the Yedgal's army, he would get a District of his choice to rule over, and he wanted Equis. Raze did not know why Xristos wanted to rule a near stagnant District, but he did not voice his opinion at that time.

All Raze had to do was wait for a person of the Pegasi Tribe to come near him, then he would bring them to Xristos. After that, he did not want to know what happened to them.

Raze locked his knees and drooped his head a bit so that he could go to sleep. He shut his eyes and gave one final grunt.

# CHAPTER 10

Karen was waiting for the Trainers to transport the five boys and herself to Covis. They had not told them that they knew where they were supposed to be going. While they were waiting, she had seen Clint keep to himself. He had gone on his knees and was saying something under his breath. Karen assumed that he was saying some prayer to help him in the mines. She had gone up to him later and asked him what he was doing. He told her that he was praying for Edward's recovery.

Karen knew that he was lying; the tone of his voice was evidence enough. She decided to confront him later. Soon, Sens came to them and made them eat a hearty lunch. He then made them hold hands and teleported them, with their Guardians, to an entrance of a mine. He told them, "I want you to go down this mine and come out the other end. But be warned, there are Constries down there. You must kill them to get to the other side."

Karen asked, "Where is Edward?"

Sens replied, "In recovery. He will not be with you this time."

So saying, Sens teleported out of sight. Clint levelled his weapon and said, "Alright, listen up. The further down we go into these mines, the methane concentration is going to build up and the air will become harder to breathe. Remember, no wasted movements once the sunlight is out of sight. Do not doubt yourselves. Just keep moving forward. If you find a Constry, get behind it and slash as high up as possible. If you can decapitate it, do so without hesitation. If you want to merge now, do it. But be warned, you may not have time to merge once deep inside the mine. Let us go."

Clint, Garon and Robert instantly merged and entered the mine. Karen reluctantly merged with her Poison Bull, Qezre and followed. The last person in was Vincent, who did not produce a sound with each step he took.

As soon as Vincent was in, a rock rolled in front of the entrance and blocked off the sunlight. Clint cursed and said, "Well, risks are meant to be taken. Karen, flames please."

Karen took a deep breath and breathed out gently. Soon, they could see the walls around them, with now-lit torches hanging on holders in the walls. They each picked up one torch and headed for the far wall, where the wall had six tunnels branching off. Vincent grunted and said, "Six tunnels, five of us."

Clint shrugged and said, "Every one, pick one tunnel and stick to it."

They each took one tunnel, leaving the extreme left tunnel alone. Karen's tunnel was a dead end, so she took Clint's tunnel. She treaded quietly and suddenly felt a hand on her mouth. She was about to breathe out from her mouth, when she realised that it was a boy's hand. She turned to face Clint, who asked her, "Why are you here?"

"My tunnel was a dead end, so I decided to follow you."

Clint nodded. He looked ahead, where Karen could hear faint grinding noises. She looked at Clint, but he had already guessed her question.

"The ghosts of the mine are active. Come on."

"Ghosts?" If there was one thing that scared Karen, it was ghosts. She was hesitant to take another step. Then, from behind her, came a loud shriek.

Clint whirled around, almost impaling Karen with his spear. He lifted his wing, allowing Karen to slip under. He looked the way they had come and told Karen, "Run now. The tunnel gets narrow to the point of turning sideways to slip through. Do not stop, just run. The force you generate might be able to break some space in the tunnel. If you see a Constry, flame it."

"I am not leaving you."

"No. You are leaving." Clint swatted Karen with his wing, hard enough to propel her a good distance further into the tunnel, but gently enough so as to not break her bones. He steadied himself for a charge, but nothing came at him. Feeling something wrong, he tossed his torch ahead of himself, hoping to get a glimpse of what awaited him. All his army training could not have prepared him for what he saw just a few metres ahead of himself.

The first thing Clint saw was a long snout of green leathery skin, complete with glistening white teeth. As the creature stepped into view, Clint considered running away, but he was not made that way. He stood his ground and spread his wings, the tunnel giving him enough space. He considered letting Cyrus take over, but then realised that there was no one to knock him out of that state and that he did not have any sweenet with him. He saw more of the monster in the light of the torch. Four arms stretched out on the two sides of the creature. Its black eyes looked only at him and occasionally flicked to his quindent. The legs looked like solid miniaturised pillars and the arms were the same, each of the five fingers on the arms tipped with sharp claws. Clint did not want to know what would happen if those claws touched him. He crouched and extended the quindent to maximum length. Then, the Constry jumped onto the ceiling and crawled menacingly towards Clint, just out of range of the weapon.

Clint wondered how he was going to get the Constry impaled so that he could get on with his life. The monster regarded him with a cold look before trying to jump right onto him. This made things easy for Clint. He turned his weapon back into a spear and thrust it into the monster's throat. He opened it and ripped the throat of the monster open. The death was instant. Clint did not stop to admire his handiwork. He ran down the tunnel, looking for Karen. He came to a fork and cursed his luck. Assuming that he had not hit her directly into one of the tunnels, he did not know which one she would have taken. He could see that both the tunnels did not narrow down, so Karen would have fitted through either. Then he saw a blue flame coming towards him from the one on the left. He used his wings to shield himself, and charged into the flames. They only tickled him, but the heat was becoming a bit too much for him. He charged out of the flames and saw a dreadful sight.

Karen was being held against the wall of the tunnel by a Constry about one and a half times the size the one Clint had fought. It had got Karen's neck in one hand, her two wrists in another, and her stomach in a third. Karen was bleeding badly on her right side. The fourth arm of the Constry was red in colour, contrasting its green skin. Karen was trying to get her horns or nails to touch the monster, but she was losing blood and strength too fast. The Constry was evidently stronger than her and was going to go for the kill. Clint decided that Karen would not die that day and his vision went red. He slammed into the Constry and sent it flying, while at the same time freeing Karen from the grip of the monster. He stood in front of her and growled at the monster. The Constry tried to circle its way around Clint, but the latter again spread his wings to whatever space the tunnel allowed him, forcing the Constry to face him head on.

The Constry snarled at Clint, and lunged for him. With two extra hands, it could deal more damage to Clint than the other way around. At the last minute, it slid onto the ground, as if trying to fell Clint. But the young man was smart to see the move. He neatly step sided the monster and impaled it right through the heart. The Constry stopped moving, but Clint was not about to take chances. He removed his weapon and removed the head the same way he had done the previous one. He crouched next to Karen and tried to get her talk. When that did not work, he started beating his wings in order to give her some cool air, thinking that it might help her. She gasped a bit, but did not give another indication that she was okay. But that was enough for Clint to feel relieved. But just then, Clint heard a very loud shriek. He glanced up and realised that there was not a lot light in the tunnel, only the torch that Karen had was providing light. He slipped it under his wing to shield the light. He covered Karen so that she would not be seen from either side, and waited for the monster to come. It never came, so he managed to get Karen up, but she was dead weight in his arms. He finally managed to hold her in one arm and his quindent and torch in the other. It was a bit of a struggle holding the two objects in three fingers, but he managed to get his act together. He was not sure whether Karen had any life left in her, or her Bull. He virtually had the lives of two beings in his hands. Karen may have been lighter than him before merging, but now she was easily his weight. He heard sounds of a fight down the tunnel and headed that way. He was aware that if Karen woke up and thought that she was on a Constry's back, she would instinctively jam her claws into him. So, he started talking softly to her. He could not tell if she still had breath in her. Then he came to the end of the tunnel and nearly lost his breath.

He was on the edge of a cliff overlooking a massive cavern where Garon, Vincent and Robert were fighting for survival. There were holes all over the cavern walls, from where Constries just pouring into the cavern. It was a thirty-metre drop form where he was, onto the sloping surface below him. The cavern was almost a perfect sphere, and at its bottom most point were the three boys. Clint, using his quindent as a lever, brought the ceiling down on his tunnel, behind him, so that no Constry could come that way. He propped up Karen against the wall, out of view of anyone down in the cavern. He wanted to get down in the fight, but his father's words echoed in his mind. "Never leave a woman, lady or girl at the cruel hands of fate."

He knew that he had to keep her alive, so he gave her mouth-to-mouth resuscitation. When she did not respond after six attempts, Clint started to feel a fire burn within himself. He was about to jump down into the cavern and slaughter each of the monsters, when light streaming into his tunnel was shut off. He turned and saw a Constry looking at him. He glared at it and, suddenly, it got thrown back. Clint took a second to register what had happened. He saw Garon in the place of the monster, with the head of the Constry in his hand. Clint immediately relayed instructions to him, "Karen may or may not be alive. She took a beating and is bleeding from the right side. Keep talking to her, try stemming the bleeding, though it has slowed down a bit. Do whatever you can."

Garon nodded and switched places with Clint, before asking, "What are you going to do?"

Clint gave look back that made Garon shiver. "I am going to make sure these monsters know my name when they die."

Clint launched himself into the air and started to slay Constries before they hit the ground. He also started to block off all the tunnels around the cavern. He helped Vincent and Robert fend off the Constries, but the monsters ran for the only available tunnel, the one which had Garon and Karen. Clint yelled at the top of his lungs, "Garon!"

The first Constry jumped into the tunnel and Clint's heart froze. If Garon was caught unawares, it was all over for the two of them. Then, the monster was thrown out with such force, that it slammed into the floor of the cavern, creating an indentation in it. Clint glanced up and saw Garon emerge at the entrance. Garon had a green aura that emanated around him. He roared in defiance at the remaining monsters, who started climbing the rock face towards him. Garon flicked his palms open and his claws sprang to full size. His aura solidified into a Wolf, the same as the morning, when they had fought Edward. His eyes lengthened out and he barred his teeth. As the Constries came at him, he sent them back to the trio on the ground, who proceeded to rip the monsters' heads off. When they were done, bodies were littered everywhere and Clint flew up to the tunnel. Garon was standing guard over Karen's still motion-less body. His eyes were still filled green and he looked like he was ready to take Clint one-on-one. The aura was gone though.

Then, to Clint's shock, the green colour in Garon's eyes started to fade until his original eyes were seen. He shuddered a bit, but managed to stand up. Clint put his hand on Garon's shoulder, just to remind him that they were there for him. Garon looked at Karen and asked, "What do we do now? All the tunnels leading away from the cavern are gone."

"We create our own tunnel. Keep her here till we tell you to bring her out."

"How do you intend to do that? We still have one more threat to eliminate."

"What threat? All Constries are dead."

"No. The big, bad one is left. Just like our test with the Battois."

Clint gave Garon a hard look and said, "We will deal with that when it comes."

Just then, Robert shouted, "Clint! We need you down here."

Clint looked over and saw that Garon was right. The big, bad Constry had arrived. Robert had got the attention of it, while Vincent, silent as ever, was running behind it along the rock face, trying to get on top of it. But even his superior grip did not get him to the required height above the Constry. There were only two people who could make the required height to get the jump on the monster, Clint and Garon. Clint motioned for Garon to stay where he was, before turning to him and saying, "You better be there for me, buddy."

Clint closed his eyes and flipped over the edge. He opened his wings and shot down the cavern wall, headed right for the Constry's head. He opened his eyes, which were an indication for Robert to get out of the way, fast. But because he moved away, the monster figured that something was up. It turned, and Clint was forced to gain some height. He landed some distance from the monster. The monster saw the red eyes of the boy, and charged. Clint used his spear as a pole and vaulted over the Constry, hoping to buy time for Robert and Vincent to find an opening to strike the monster down. He kept light on his feet and kept darting from place to place, forcing the Constry to keep facing him. He could see Vincent trying to get close to the monster, so he kept his face only in front. Vincent lunged from almost behind the monster, but one hand shot out and grabbed him by the neck. The claws were almost touching Vincent's skin, but he managed to prise the fingers open and drew back from the Constry. Clint started to push the Constry back underneath Garon's tunnel, where the latter was waiting to get a shot at the kill.

Clint levelled his quindent and rushed the Constry, which was slow to react. It had not thought that Clint would be so suicidal. Clint impaled it right in the heart, before dragging it up the slope, to give Garon the final kill. As they neared the tunnel, Garon lunged out and ripped the Constry's head clean off the body. Clint got a good hit from Robert to subdue Cyrus. Clint motioned for the two boys below to find a way out of the cavern, hopefully through one of the tunnels that he himself had brought down. Meanwhile, Garon and he tried to get Karen to wake. When nothing worked, Clint put his head down in shame. He had failed to save someone, the first in his military career. He tried one last desperate attempt and yelled, "Karen!"

Karen seemed to jerk a bit, which gave Clint some relief. But the air down in the tunnel would be getting toxic for Karen. He stepped out of the tunnel and glanced at the top of the cavern. In a crazy move, he swooped down and snatched up Vincent's javelin, which he had dropped in the heat of the battle. He circled near the base of the cavern a few times, and suddenly shot up for the ceiling. He held one weapon in each hand and slammed both into the ceiling, embedding them both nearly a foot into the rock. He tried to get his spear to expand, but it did not. Clint did not give up. He pushed with full strength, and the quindent sprung to full size, pushing the rock apart. But there was only one problem.

The ceiling started to crumble and rocks started to rain down. Clint grabbed both weapons and shot towards the tunnel. He glanced at the two boys, who were not running for any cover, but jumping from rock to rock gracefully, evading them with ease, as if they had practised the technique before. Clint was wondering where they got the time to react, but he was more shocked that Robert, with an elongated Horse body, was not getting even one rock on it. Once the shower of rocks had stopped, Clint and Garon hoisted Karen up on their shoulders and with Robert's help, got her under the open sky, which flooded the cavern with sunlight through the hole in its ceiling that Clint had made. They set her down in the sun, while they themselves sat around her, discussing how to get her out from the cavern. Clint sat next to her and from time to time, checked her breath and heart rate. The bleeding had stopped, but he wanted to get back to Talis to be sure. Just then Vincent, in a shaky tone, said, "Guys, I do not think we are alone."

Garon turned back to the tunnel, but nothing was there. Clint saw a shadow move on Karen's face and glanced up. There was one more Constry staring right at Karen. It bared its teeth and started to climb down the wall farthest from them. Vincent picked up his javelin and aimed it right at the head of the monster. He claimed that he was very accurate at this distance, so Clint did not expect him to miss. But when Vincent threw the javelin, the Constry swatted it away like it was nothing. Vincent growled and ran for it. The Constry ignored him, as he was too low, but had not seen Garon run up the wall and charge for him from above. Clint was sure that they would get it, so he stood over Karen's body, determined to be the last line of defence for her. He and Robert stayed still, even though they saw, within a few minutes, Garon and Vincent in the hands of the Constry. Robert too charged, but got caught. He tried to kick with his hooves and break the monster's arm, but the arm was like rock. Unmovable.

Clint tried to stab the monster in the heart, but was caught as well. The hands of the Constry were full. It tried to get to Karen, but the four of them each grabbed onto a rock and held firm. They would not be able to hold him back forever, so Vincent decided to call on some help. He roared loud and clear. The sound must have awakened Qezre, because Karen got up with a start and first saw the situation in front of her. She started to back away, but Clint shouted, "Get closer and flame the monster!"

"I cannot. You may die as well."

Garon yelled, "We can take it. Trust us."

Karen shook her head adamantly. Clint realised that she was going to need more persuasion, so he let his head droop down, as if dead. He heard Karen shout, "No!"

He could feel the heat coming towards him, so he spread his wings as much as he could to cover the other three. He felt the heat singe his face and wings, but kept his wings up. After what seemed like a few days, he felt something across his face. He did not have the strength to open his eyes, but he could hear people talking in the background. He drifted off into a world of darkness.

When he next opened his eyes, he saw that he was in the palace hospital room. He could not see anyone else in the room, apart from two doctors who were with a patient on a bed across his. He saw one of the doctors shake his head and go back into conversation with the other. He made a small sound and got their attention. Giving one last uneasy look at the person on the other bed, they came over to him and helped him up. He went to see who was on the other bed. On seeing who it was, he felt guilt rushing through him.

Karen lay in front of him, as still as when he had tried to revive her in the mines. The doctors said that she was in a coma. They had been brought back by two Dragons. Robert, Garon and Vincent had escaped with minor burns and bruises. Clint had been out for nearly two days, while Karen was in a coma. They had tried various potions on her, but her body rejected them all, including sweenet, sapphire potion and carmine. There was one method that, in theory would work, but practically very risky for Karen. Clint did not understand. If potions did not work on her, what else was going to?

The doctors sent a message to bring the final solution. Edward arrived a few minutes later. Then Clint understood what they were attempting to do. Edward would have to transfer his own strength and stamina to her, in order to get her back from the brink. But the side-effects on Karen would be unknown until she opened her eyes. Clint looked at Edward, back at Karen and asked, without taking his eyes off her, "Will you be able to get her back?"

Edward responded, "Hopefully, if I can reverse the process I used on Robert."

"Then do it. I have faith in you."

The doctors backed away from Edward as he burst into flames. He looked at Clint and said, "If anything goes wrong, prise my hand out of hers and give me a beat down. No second thoughts. Her life is more precious and valuable to me than my own at this point."

Clint nodded and asked the doctors for his weapon. When he was ready, Edward clasped Karen's hand in his and closed his eyes in concentration. The flames stretched from his hand and onto Karen. Soon, she was enveloped in flames, though it did not look like she was being affected. Clint could see beads of sweat on Edward's cheeks, but did not try to stop him. He could see that the flames were getting smaller and smaller, as if they were seeping into Karen's body. With a final bit of energy, Edward shut his flames off and let the rest of the fire seep into Karen.

He collapsed onto the floor and Clint helped him onto the bed. Edward told the doctors to get ready with carmine, in case Karen woke up with shock. For a few moments, nothing happened. Then, they heard Karen breathe. Both the boys sighed in relief, as it was even and not forced breathing. Karen opened her eyes and looked around. When she was brought up to speed with what had happened, she smiled.

Clint then asked, “I do not suppose you forgive me?”

“What are you talking about? What do I have to forgive you for?”

“Because I asked you to burn the Constry. You expended whatever energy you had left. It was wrong on my part because I did not take into consideration what you had already gone through. Then, when you did not do it, I faked my death, assuming an emotional trigger would set it off. It worked, but nearly at the cost of your life. Saying that I am sorry does not even make up for what I put you through, but I am sorry.” Clint bowed his head, not even making eye contact with Karen.

Karen laughed. “Look at me, Clint. I am alright. Besides, you said that you and Gonth would be putting us through a lot, so I just take this as another lesson. Being a teacher and being a friend are not as different as you may think.”

Edward interjected. “Also, I just want to tell you guys that, in these two days, you have had a lot of visitors, but some stayed by your side most of the time, only leaving for food and training.”

Clint was puzzled. He did not expect anyone except people from his own District. He asked, “Who?”

Edward said, “Karen had most of the girls, though one would come to your side from time to time.”

Clint did not even ask who it was, he straightaway said, “Anne.”

“Yes. Also, Garon, Chris and James. They were not allowed to do anything to you. When you guys arrived, you two were the only two unconscious ones. They made you have a tablet that forced the Guardians out of you. Your Raven was at the windowsill all the time, from dawn to dusk. I would have tried what I did on Karen, on you as well, but because you were in a state to feel everything, it was too risky to try.”

“So can we leave now?” Karen asked the doctors.

One of them wringed his hands and said, “Ideally, we would like to run some more tests to make sure you are alright, but your Trainers might not like it. They were not sure you would want tests to be run as you are, as it is, very precious."

Clint was confused by their cryptic reply. "What do you mean?"

"We would want you not to engage in any strenuous physical activity. But you will lose out on training. So we will let you go."

Once they were out of sight from the guards patrolling the corridors, Edward told them, "Come with me."

He took them up some flights of steps near their rooms, to a balcony where they could see most of the city below them. Looking down they could see that most of the houses' occupants were asleep. Near the wall, people were still awake. Karen asked, "Why did you bring us here?"

"See the mountains there? We are going there soon. Our Trainers will not let us fight Yoknies and Jides. We will be sent soon into various Districts. Just remember, those mountains are not forgiving. I actually managed to smuggle our Guardians up here. Do you want to check out the mountains now? If so, they are right behind that door." He pointed to a closed door behind them.

Clint asked, "How is Karen supposed to come?"

"I will carry her."

"Sorry boys. I will not agree to it. You just do not want to explore the mountains, do you Edward?" Karen struck.

"You got me there. I actually want to find Dan and bust him out from wherever he is being kept."

Clint said, "You know that if we attempt that, we will be giving his captors a free gift of three very powerful youngsters?"

"Yes." Edward sighed. "But we cannot go back to our room now. We might as well just stay here. We head down in the morning."

"Fine by me." Karen replied.

# CHAPTER 11

Xristos and Byron walked down the rows of cells present under the fortress. They came to one filled with only one person. Byron looked at Xristos and said, "You sure you want me to do this?"

Xristos nodded. Byron opened his palms, where purple ovals of light were floating. He entered the cell and opened both his palms towards the prisoner. He said, "Listro, by my power, I claim you into the army of Yedgal."

The ovals shot out of his palms and wrapped around Listro. They touched him and he screamed in pain. They sank into his body and he stood up. Opening his eyes, Byron could see that the spell had worked. Listro's eyes had gone red all over, save his pupil and iris. He bowed to Byron and asked, "What task would you have me do, my Lord?"

"Go to Logder, to Bloodhound Mountain and retrieve as many Sapphire Roses as you can. Your services will be rewarded greatly."

Listro bowed again and left, acknowledging Xristos on the way out. Xristos drew in a long breath and said, "That one is too strong-willed. It would be a grave danger to have him in the battle."

"I know. But strong-willed people can also be manipulated the easiest. Once you have got them to your side, it takes a lot for them to be converted."

Byron could see that Xristos did not agree with him, but did not say so. They marched out and Byron suddenly stopped. He turned and asked Xristos, "Why did you support my father, even though there was no one at that time?"

"Prince, I have taken a vow in the name of Sorenth not to speak about my time joining your father."

Byron sucked in a quick breath. He knew that an oath in the name of Sorenth, the God of war, was punishable by instant death. If Xristos ever broke his vow, he would die at that very spot. Byron had to know all the oaths of Lasgalan, spells performed in Lasgalan, and the other related bits to them. He was the only one in his father's forces to know sorcery. It was thanks to his sorcery that his father's uncle, Giriod, was alive. If Byron stopped using his spells on him, he would die. The only case where Giriod would die was if Byron died.

He nodded and turned back on his way. He asked, "How would you like to rule over a District, when my father returns?"

"I would indeed welcome and embrace the opportunity. I just want you to have your father back first."

"What was it like, leaving your family and joining my father?"

Xristos eyed Byron before answering, "Do you remember the enchantment I asked you to place on me?"

"Yes. It always confused me as to why you wanted that enchantment, and not one which made you invulnerable or very fast."

"Well, I want to die, but only by someone who was my equal, mentally."

Byron read between the lines. "You mean to say that you…"

"Yes. I will always be ready for my death, since it has no fear in attacking. I will answer for my crimes, but only when I face my equal."

"Xristos!" Bryan came into view. He looked like he had had an encounter with a ghost.

"What happened, Bryan?" Xristos asked.

"You better see for yourself."

He led them to the throne room, where Xristos would normally sit.

Xristos did not recognise the room itself. After nearly two decades of waiting, the room was now reconstructing itself, as if preparing for the arrival of a king. There were mirages of people moving around, doing chores such as heaving thrones in for the people to sit, cleaning the floor, and other things. But Bryan was not stopping for that. He marched up the steps which Xristos normally sat on, walked to the covered object, and threw it off.

Xristos blinked twice to check if he was seeing things. The throne for the king was originally made from black obsidian and had six gems, one from each District of Lasgalan, stuck just above the king's head. Now, the red Rhodonite gem was glowing like never before. Its bright glow stood out in contrast to the dark background. The other five were not. Xristos knew it was only a matter of time before that though.

Byran turned to him and said, "It has started."

"Yes it has. I never thought that I would live to see this day." Xristos nearly shed a tear, but remembered his mission. There was no time for emotion to be shown. He bowed his head to the throne before walking out of the room.

Once he was gone, Bryan turned to his younger brother and hugged him. Byron whispered, "We will not be alone for much longer."

"No. We will make him proud of us."

"We could start with interrogations. Raze is coming soon with one of the Pegasi Tribe members. We will interrogate them."

"Yes. Let us go and see how Dan is doing."

"Thought you would never say that."

The duo made it to Dan's cell, where they were greeted by a boy who tried to jab Byron with an arrowhead. Bryan saw the movement and grabbed Dan's wrist. He turned his hand into a lion's paw and squeezed Dan's wrist. Dan screamed and dropped the arrowhead, which Byron picked up. Bryan was not done with him yet though. He twisted Dan's hand as much as he could, and then put his wrist through another bar, leaving his arm, from shoulder to wrist, outside the cell. Dan tried to remove his hand, but Bryan took some rope from one of the guards and tied Dan's wrist firmly to the bar. Dan yelled in agony, but the guards did not move. Bryan looked Dan dead in the eyes before saying, "Next time you try to attack someone, make sure that they are alone."

Dan spoke in a voice that showed how little scared he was, "I will repeat those same words to you when I kill you. Trust me, I always make it a point to repay my debts."

"We will see about that later. Right now, the only debt you have to repay is making sure that our father lives again."

Dan growled at him. Bryan shrugged his shoulders and walked away. Byron smirked at Dan and said, "And here, my brother wanted to keep you alive. I see that he nearly went back on his word. The irony of it all." He laughed before jogging a bit to catch up to his elder brother. The guards went back to their positions. Dan could withstand a lot of pain, but even he could feel his muscles getting stretched more than normal. He was starting not to feel his wrist and realised that soon all he would be feeling in that arm would be his shoulder. He closed his fist and calmly told the guards, "If you want to live, run."

One guard laughed and said, "You can't get out. Remember the bars are designed to keep you from bending them or punching them. They are your bane."

"I don't intend to punch my way out of this."

One person realised what he was planning to do. He shouted, "Tell..."

The rest of his sentence was cut short by the sound iron rods breaking. Dan's cell had been designed in order that he not break out from the inside. He assumed that it did not count for outside his cell. His assumption had paid off well, as he saw two out of the four guards get pierced by rod fragments. All he had done was flex his muscles and dug into all his berserker strength. Even he did not expect the result to be so lovely. The other two guards backed up nervously from him, as he emerged. He punched them both to the ground as they tried to run from him. He picked up one guard's spear and a sword and shield from the other. As they tried to get up, he knocked them both out permanently with one hit each from the shield. He slung the sword on his back. He managed to find his way out from the corridors lining the place. He came out to the room he had first been in. He saw that there were ghostly figures moving around the room. He did not stop for all that. He looked up at a shaft of sunlight coming in through the wall. He jumped up and grabbed a small hand hold. He climbed up to the hole and looked down on the other side. There were ledges going down all the way to the ground. He jumped down slowly but surely and reached the bottom in no time. He walked down the slope and kept moving from the shadow of one tree to another. He knew that he was not going to be seen, but he could not afford to be seen. He had almost reached flat land, when he heard a voice next to him, "Did you really think that you would escape that easily?"

He spun his spear in a full circle, but no one was there. He heard a laugh and started to worry. If he could not see his opponent, he was at a big disadvantage. He tried to make a run for it, but his feet would not move. Looking down, he saw that his legs had sunk into the ground, all the way up to his knees. He heard footsteps from behind him, so he dropped the spear and drew his sword. He saw Byron walk around him, inspecting him like a hunter that captures his prey. His hands were encased in golden light.

Byron laughed and said, "My father had a big objection about killing prisoners without weapons. The way I see things, you are neither our prisoner at the moment, nor are you without weapons. So I think I will just kill you now, and secure my father's return."

Dan spat at Byron and said, "Over my dead body."

Byron smiled, "Of course over your dead body. Did Raze not tell you that?"

"Byron." Bryan's commanding voice came from the side of the clearing. Dan saw him leaning against a tree, looking disapprovingly at Byron.

"What? He fulfils neither of the conditions our father laid down. Let me just kill him already."

"No." Bryan said, with the tone of the final decision.

He walked over and knocked Dan out, but not before Dan yelling, "Frea!"

# CHAPTER 12

Jacob and James were with their Guardians when Frea started acting skittish. The Blue Roan stallion started to neigh and buck up and down, sending the Horses into an aggressive stance against him.

As the two of them watched, Frea started to snort at them. Years of being with a Lion had taught Jacob many things, one of which was to get out of the way of a snorting animal. He pulled James out of Frea's way, just before the hooves of the Horse slammed into the hard marble of the floor. He kicked open the door of the room, and sped out.

James and Jacob made split-second decisions and merged, James flying after Frea, Jacob running to tell the Trainers and catch up with Frea later.

Frea had charged out of the city, causing a bit of helter-skelter among the citizens in his path. James flew over the trees, keeping Frea's blue form in sight, occasionally swooping in for a closer look to make sure that he was not losing track of the stallion. He wondered what had caused Frea to suddenly charge out like that.

He glanced back and saw Chris behind him. Chris pointed below him, where James assumed Jacob was running. He concentrated back to Frea, who was not being hindered by the trees. He was charging north, heading towards Leonis' border. James knew from experience that the guards at Leonis had expert aim with bow and arrow. He would be able to dodge three arrows at most, before he would get hit. He decided to turn invisible till he was well across the border. He glanced back and motioned for Chris to turn back to the capital, though the second Covine adamantly shook his head and hefted his metal mace.

James knew that Jacob would not have a problem getting into Leonis, though the guards would have a few questions as to why he was accompanying a Horse into Leonis, where they had restrictions, especially with food and other Districts' animals. James decided to use himself as a distraction. He got low enough for the guards to spot him and let them aim arrows at him. While he could have turned invisible and elude the arrows, he still had physical substance, which meant that he could be hit by an arrow or spear. He kept the fire focused on himself, while allowing Chris to shoot over him into Leonis. He heard Frea galloping fiercely through the gate and onto the other side of the border. Once he was sure that he had bought Chris enough time, he got clear of the range of the missiles aimed at him and shot into Leonis.

He saw Jacob race into his own District in hot pursuit of Frea. All James and Chris could do was give him support from the air.

They had been chasing Frea for two hours when Frea started to slow down. Chris saw a clearing up ahead and went right for it. Frea entered it and stopped. James and Jacob came in from behind Frea and watched as the Horse turned in one spot, neighing in distress and rearing up.

Chris turned and told the two others, "Dan was here."

Jacob sniffed the air and said, "I cannot get a scent. He might have been here a long time ago, maybe hours. I could try to search the surroundings, but I will not guarantee any good results."

James put his hand up to stop Jacob. "We got bigger problems. Leonis' forces are coming."

He pointed behind Chris, where the boys could see people in armour moving quickly towards them. Jacob roared loudly. The movement stopped for a moment before it started again. The three boys needed to get Frea out of the sight of the armed forces. Chris increased his muscle size and picked up the now still Frea, who was watching the advancement of the troops. James did not ask Jacob; he picked him up and shot into the sky, following Chris.

James was about to smile with relief, when he heard a string getting drawn. He should not have been worried, but he recognised the sound. They were heading right into a trap. James closed his wings around Jacob and himself and dived into the trees. He heard the weighted net being shot into the sky. He glanced up and saw Chris and Frea get entangled in the net. They landed in the shadow of tall pine trees and heard Frea neighing in desperation. Suddenly, he stopped neighing.

James and Jacob exchanged worried glances before heading in the direction where Frea and Chris had landed. They saw a golden light illuminate through the trees before shutting off. They came to a waterfall, but there was no sign of anyone there. Jacob went around sniffing the rocks and trees, but shook his head. James was really starting to get worried. Chris was a good fighter and never went down without a fight. If he was taken so easily, there was only one explanation. The second Chosen One had been taken by Yedgal's forces. Jacob clenched his fists and said, "I cannot believe that I acted like a coward."

James tried to console him, "You would never have reached in time to save them."

"No. You do not understand. I could smell whoever it was that took them. I should have acted faster."

"Look, we cannot undo what has been done. We can prevent it from happening again. Now, let us get back to Talis. We can inform the Trainers of what happened."

Jacob was about to nod, when he saw something sparkle in the water. He looked in that direction. In the water, stuck between two rocks, was a red Rhodonite gem.

Jacob picked it up and showed it to James. "Frea is dead."

"How did those people miss this? Unless Frea and Chris landed in the river, the impact killing Frea on spot…"

"Forget about it. Right now, our priority is getting this gem back to Talis. Dan is pretty much powerless without it. Give me a lift please."

James nodded. He grabbed Jacob and launched himself into the sky, making sure that he got enough height before heading for the border. He kept himself above the cloud level, swooping down occasionally to pick up speed.

They reached the capital and were greeted by two Trainers. When Jacob showed the Rhodonite gem to them, they understood what had happened. They said that since Jacob was the one who had found the gem, he would have to keep it with him till they found Dan. Until then, the gem was his responsibility.

Jacob realised how big the responsibility was, so he slipped the gem into his shirt and headed to the field after unmerging. He could see Clint and Vincent sparring away. He knew that he would never reach a power level like theirs, but he could improve his own.

He waited till the two had finished, and then challenged them. They both had long weapons, but that would not hinder Jacob. He placed his knuckledusters on his fingers and faced them. Vincent and Clint exchanged mischievous grins, levelled their weapons, and charged Jacob.

Jacob waited till he could swat their weapons away, but they evidently knew that he was waiting for that. Vincent turned his javelin at the last moment, smacking Jacob with the flat end of the javelin. Jacob saw it coming but could not stop it. He hit the ground and saw Clint coming at him with his spear. Jacob rolled and the spear hit the ground where he had been a second ago. He grabbed Vincent's javelin as it came towards him. He and Vincent tried wresting it from each other's grip, while Clint said, "Jacob, I could have already stabbed you five times. You are already dead."

Jacob left the javelin and turned to Clint. Clint twirled his spear and thrust it at Jacob's heart. Jacob was never a slow person, but this quick movement was something he had not seen before. He caught the tip of the spear a few inches from his heart. Normally he would catch any missile with his hands stretched out to full length. This was like an embarrassment for him. He scowled and let go of the spear. He turned and walked back into the palace.

Clint looked at Vincent and asked, "What happened to him? That was a pretty good catch."

"He can catch faster. You threw him off his guard." A new voice came.

Vincent did not have to turn to know who this person was. He had lived with him for nearly seventeen years.

Vincent said, "Clint, meet my fight-happy brother, Patrick."

Clint shook Patrick's hand and asked, "What makes you say I threw Jacob off-guard?"

"I have seen Jacob in action. While you guys were away in the mines, he was teaching everyone how to sharpen their reflexes when it came to catching objects. I have never seen anyone catch an arrow like him. Put this into perspective. Ake can fire as many as twelve to twenty arrows a minute, from a yew bow, a fast one. Jacob had enough time to catch the arrows, one by one, get to the ground to put the arrow down and come up again, ready for the next arrow. That, even for you guys, is insanely fast."

"Quiet. Here he comes." Vincent pointed to Jacob coming out, looking at Clint like he was on some menu for Jacob's dinner. Clint realised that Jacob had merged with his Guardian. His eyes were yellow, and his mane was showing. He fitted his knuckledusters onto his fingers and starting sparring with a wooden dummy that was movable on all of its six levels, save the bottom. Jacob kicked it into action and showed some interesting moves, some that Vincent had never seen performed by a tall person. He knew those moves, but even he had problems trying to do them. Then he realised what was happening. Every time the dummy's arms were about to hit Jacob, he bent his knees, keeping every part of his body above the knees in one line. It should not have been possible, but Jacob made it seem like child's play. Vincent realised the main factor governing all of Jacob's movements.

Jacob was doing a near impossible thing by keeping his body's centre of gravity out of his body itself. Vincent knew that it was possible if one flipped over a horizontal pole kept at a height. It was a test that all Leonids wanting to participate in the Games had to undergo. He had just about cleared that test, but Jacob was exceptional at that time.

If there was one thing at which Jacob outclassed the seventeen others, not including the six powerful teenagers, it was his ability to move agilely during close-quarter fighting. He got so much into the rhythm of fighting with the dummy that he forgot that it was not a person he was sparring with. His right hand smashed into the midsection of the dummy, breaking it into its various levels. One piece nearly hit Patrick, but he grabbed it before that.

He tossed it back to Jacob, who was reassembling the dummy. As soon as it was back in one piece, Jacob started off again. But he used a different method for blocking himself. He faced the attacks openly and used his legs as blockers as well.

Clint could see that Jacob was tiring out from the exercise, and wanted to tell him to stop. The amount of hits that Jacob was able to block was only about half the hits that came to him in total. The other half of the hits was enough to cause cuts along the skin, where there was no bone to protect Jacob. Clint saw that Jacob's aim was mainly that. He was purposely not using his bones to protect himself. Nevertheless, he wanted Jacob to stop harming himself. He was about to tell Jacob to stop, when he felt Gonth place his hand on him.

He turned and saw the Taurian looking up at him.

"What happened?"

"The Trainers want the five of you to teach us to fight Constries. They said that we would be going to the mountains behind the Backlash River. We leave in a few hours. Once we finish there, we will be sorted into groups and sent to the Districts the Trainers choose for us."

"Right. Get the others out. We will teach you right here, right now."

Within five minutes, Gonth had brought everyone, including the Guardians. Clint faced the crowd and started off by saying, "When you face a Constry, remember that you are facing a monster that can, and will, kill you in a matter of seconds. If you want to live, you will have to make sure you are fast, agile, and above all, close to its head. The four arms of this monster are hard and strong. As it has four arms, it can fend you off with one, while killing you with the other three. It does not matter how strong your skin is, how fast you can heal, or how powerful you are, it can still pierce you with claws. They can climb on any surface, whether vertical or horizontal, upside down or not, smooth surface or rough. Just bear in mind that they pack quite a punch. As we have no Constries here, we will have to show you how they fight, and trust me, they fight dirty."

They divided the group into six. For the next hour, Clint put down Gonth, Ake and Elesa. Jacob was the only one who could potentially survive a surprise attack by a Constry, Clint observed. He knew that they could never be truly prepared for an attack by Constries. He decided to let the Trainers know that they were ready to go. But one question sprung to his mind. Before the attack on the first base, their Trainers were helping them. Now it was like they were not there at all.

Clint was about to go to the throne room, when he saw a shadow on the floor above him. He knew that the only way he could see a shadow at that particular time of the day, was if someone was planning to sneak into the palace. He silently bounded up to the floor and climbed the outside of the palace wall. He reached the roof and saw a man whose back was to him. The man made no indication that he heard Clint coming towards him. As Clint got within six feet, he turned and stood up. Clint recognised him.

"What are you doing here, Jax?"

"Well, I wanted to meet with you guys to ask what your next step was. I could be of some help, you know."

Clint narrowed his eyes. "You could just walk in through the gates."

"They will not let an outsider meet you."

Clint flicked his eyes to Jax's right hand, which was behind his back.

"What do you have in your hands, Jax?" Clint asked carefully.

Jax laughed and said, "Nothing of consequence. At least not for me."

Jax lunged at Clint and tried to throw him off-balance. Clint moved to the side and grabbed his hand, twisting it in the process so that he dropped the Argentic Transporter Jax had in his hand.

Clint dragged a struggling Jax to Lord Veryu, who was in deep discussion with Sens. On seeing what the situation was, Sens ordered Jax into the jail, but Clint said, "Let me kill him. He is a spy for Yedgal."

"You have no proof about that, Clint." Veryu said.

"Actually, I do." Clint put his fingers on the top and bottom of Jax's eyes and opened his eyes even more. Both Sens and Veryu could see Jax's eyes' blood lines wider than normal.

Clint asked Sens, "Look familiar?"

"Yes." Sens looked at Veryu, asking a silent question. Veryu pointed to the dining room, which was indication enough for Clint.

He closed the doors behind him and, two minutes later, he walked out wiping his spear. He looked at Sens and said, "We are ready to leave."

Sens nodded his head and, bowing to Veryu, walked out with Clint.

Once again, the group of now twenty-two youngsters were transported to the mountains of Backlash River. This time however, they were left as one group. The last time they were on the mountains, they had their Guardians. This time, no such luck.

Clint got everyone together and said, "As we are exposed in this valley, we can fend off the Constries more easily than if we head for the trees. Karen, Ake, Edward, you are our first line of defence. If you tire out, the next line, comprising James, Garon and I take over. After that, well, whoever wants to go can go."

The group circled up. For a few tense moments, nothing happened. Then the screams of Constries were heard. They charged out of the trees on either side of the valley by the dozens, heading straight for the small group. Edward waited for the last moment before flaming the monsters. He created a small fire tornado and sent it through the Constry ranks. Ake used his gem and busted out two green, double-bladed axes. He sliced and diced the Constries, going only for the head. Following Edward's example, Patrick took Karen's place and sent out his own fire tornado.

Those Constries which made it through the three defences, found themselves on the receiving end of the club of Emmanuel, or the sharp points of Clint's quindent and Vincent's javelin. Soon, Clint could see that everyone was taking the Constries one-on-one. Karen and Elesa were working like a team, one throwing a Constry to the other to finish off. They had each other's backs. Robert was wrestling the monsters to the ground and taking their heads off. Victoria could not do much, but she managed to use a Constry to defend her from its brethren. Clint felt as if the team was coming together nicely. Just then, he heard Anne scream. He whipped his head around and saw Gonth standing over her, fending them off with his sword and shield. He ran to Gonth and saw Anne had a Constry claw embedded in her side. Gonth defended him while he pulled out the claw. Anne gasped as he applied some blocker on the wound. He helped her up and she got back into the thick of the action. James and Garon were playing a deadly game of close-quarter combat with the monsters, but were holding their own. Jacob was moving through the Constry ranks fast and efficiently, felling them with one punch of his knuckledusters. Clint realised that he had fixed claws on his knuckledusters, which explained why, every time he punched them, their heads went off. As he was one of the shorter ones in their group, he used the bodies of fallen Constries as leverage to jump high enough to get to the heads of the monsters still alive. Trest did not have much of a problem with the monsters, as she healed fast. But the monsters kept their attention focussed on her. She started to back away from the group, which was a bad move.

The Constries that kept pouring into the valley split into two groups, most of them going for the lone fighter. Edward saw what was happening. He controlled his flames and formed a shell around himself. He charged towards Trest and knocked away some of the monsters.

The Ring-bearers were using the Rings to full effect. Hasha produced a wall of ice to trap the Constries. She then used a sword made of ice to decapitate them. Vesper and Patrick worked well to keep the monsters defensive with their flames, while Adrian and Adriana came up from behind them and relieved their bodies of their heads. Thomas was using his Ring to fire gusts of wind to get the monsters off-balance. Once the monsters lost their footing, he went in for the kill. Even Clint could see that they were gaining the upper hand on the monsters. The only problem was that there were more of them coming into the valley by the minute. The group was tiring out but not giving up.

Suddenly, for a moment, the Constries stopped coming. This gave Clint a moment of clarity and he thought a plan up. He shared it with Gonth, their leader according to the Talons. Gonth agreed and they set up a new formation. Ake stood outside the circle, axe in each hand.

The next line of defence was Vesper, Patrick, and Edward. Behind them were Clint and Vincent. Next were Jacob, Robert. On the other side of the circle were Elesa, Victoria, Karen, and Anne. James, Garon, Gonth and Isabella made up the centre of the circle.

They got ready for another charge. Adriana, Hasha, Thomas and Adrian formed their own circle with Emmanuel being their first line of defence. Clint saw that the Ring-bearers were getting tired with the effort they were putting in using the Rings.

The screams of the Constries resumed and the two groups steeled themselves for the second wave. The Constries that charged out this time looked quite strong, and Clint wondered if the two groups could stand an impact from this wave. He watched as the monsters drew closer. He waited till the last second before giving Ake permission to slice and dice the monsters. The monsters that were able to avoid the axes were caught in the flames of Vesper, Patrick, and Edward. But Clint had not forgotten about the other group, which was also being attacked. He saw Emmanuel knocking the Constries' heads clean off their bodies. Those that evaded him were engulfed in walls of ice produced by Hasha. They were easy pickings for Adriana and Adrian. Meanwhile, James had gone invisible and taking out Constries where they could not see him. However, Clint remembered that James would not stay hidden long if a Constry caught him by surprise. He kept piercing the monsters, until he felt as if there were no more reinforcements left for them. He cut down the last Constry on his path and allowed the group to recover. He ordered them together and did a head count. Twenty-two of them had arrived at this valley, and twenty-two would leave the valley.

He walked around the group, checking for any damage they might have sustained, but no one betrayed any signs of hurt. It was only when he checked Emmanuel and Garon, did they complain of pain in their arms. Clint touched their arms and they went down in pain.

Clint quickly poured sweenet down their throats and waited for their arms to heal, while checking others for injuries. By the time the entire group was ready to go, the two of them were healed and ready. Clint looked around but did not see anyone coming for them. He did a quick look around. No one was there.

He said, "Thomas, get above the tree tops and see if anything is coming our way."

Thomas propelled himself up through the air and hovered there. He came back down and said, "Nothing to report."

Clint furrowed his eyebrows. They had killed all the monsters. So why was no one ready to receive them?

Clint did not want to, but he started walking towards the trees. He was about to step into the tree line, when a dagger hit the tree on his side. Clint glanced back at Garon, who shook his head, before running up to him and retrieving the blade. He said, "Do not even think about entering the woods. We are safer outside in the open, where nothing will get the jump on us."

"What is in here?" Clint gestured inside the woods.

"Something deadly. I can't see clearly, but something is waiting for you to enter the trees. Don't do that."

Clint glanced back into the woods before heading back to the group with Garon. He did not understand why they were stranded the way they were. He saw the Constry bodies littered around them and came up with a crazy idea.

He called them towards him and said, "We are stranded here for a reason. We do not know what it is, but I promise to get you guys back to the capital intact. For now, we will have to use these Constry bodies to our advantage."

Anne asked, "How do we do that?"

"First, I want all the bodies brought to the centre. Ake, in the meantime, I want you to get some trees from that side." He gestured to the forest line on the side opposite to the one he had just come from.

"Gonth and Robert will help you. I will send others soon."

Soon, everyone had been assigned duties. Garon pulled Clint aside and asked, "Did you see what was written on the ground?"

"You mean what was burnt into the grass?"

"Yes."

"You want to let anyone know?"

When Garon had thrown that dagger to stop Clint, he had not seen something inside the woods, but rather, near Clint's feet. It was a message burnt into the ground that said, "No one is coming for two days. Survive on your own."

"Would you want that happening?"

"No. Sometimes ignorance is bliss."

"Not ignorance about one's safety. You do realise that we can be attacked anytime by anything, right?"

Clint did not say anything. He wanted their shelter to be built before nightfall. He saw Ake slice through three tall trees. As the trees fell, Elesa and Robert caught hold of one, as Gonth and Anne caught the other one. Ake used clamps to slow the fall of the third one. While the two duos got behind their respective trees on either side of Ake, he used ropes formed by his gem and pulled all three fallen trees, with the four others assisting him. Once he brought them to where Clint asked him to, he dropped the ropes, while Jacob, Emmanuel and James started to break the trees down with the five of them, for building fortifications. Isabella was making her traps in the trench that Adrian and Adriana had created as a second defence for any attack that might happen. She was getting ropes, the main part of her traps, made by Hasha and Patrick, who used their Rings to create the ropes. Garon and Clint were overseeing the entire operation. Thomas was doing guard duty with Trest and Edward. Karen was working with Vincent to sharpen the points of the pieces that Jacob and the others were giving them. Hasha was working on their first defensive structure, which she was using her ring to create. Clint speculated that if a raging fire had caught in a blizzard and instantly froze, it could not be far from what Hasha was creating. And he was not wrong. Pointed spikes protruded at all possible angles from a seemingly flat part of an iced incline. Victoria was helping in all fields, from the making of traps with Isabella, to the breaking of the trees with Jacob's team. She brought in the last few Constry bodies and asked Clint what to do with them.

Being a military man, Clint said that, once the fortifications were complete, he would tell her. He had made sure that, when he walked away from the message, that he wiped it clean so that no one else would see.

From his higher vantage point, he could see that, in less than a month, the team was growing to work together in cohesion. He knew that they were missing two people, and he vowed to save them when he could. His only concern at the moment was that they would not be finished with the fortifications by nightfall. But the eight of them were working tirelessly to break down the three trees, which Clint thought would be more than enough to build a protective structure for themselves. Garon asked, "What exactly is your defensive plan?"

"First is Hasha's ice wall. Next we have the trench lined with Isabella's traps. Next will be the wooden wall itself. If somehow, monsters get past these three defences, we unleash Ake. If we still do not stand a chance, we get out from a path I will ask Patrick or Edward to make once the wooden wall is up. We escape while Ake holds them off. Once we cover enough ground, we set up a new base. We have only two days, so we may just get by."

"You want to sacrifice Ake, who is right now our heaviest hitter, and the reason the trees are down?"

"It will not come down to that, trust me." Clint sounded like he was trying to convince himself, but Garon did not say anything. He could see that Hasha was tiring out from building her wall, but was almost finished with it. He headed down to meet her once she finished. He gave her water that he had got from the Backlash River, which he had found on exploring the area a bit. He told Clint about shifting to there, but Clint vetoed him, saying that they were well protected out here between the mountains, whereas the place Garon was suggesting had a mountain on one side and a cliff on the other. As the sun began to set, one wall had been finished and the trench had been lined with traps on all sides. Clint and Garon had also joined in the construction, and soon two more walls were up. As they started the fourth wall, a long and loud howl was heard, echoing off the mountains. The team stopped for a moment, before continuing with the construction. The last few touches to the wall were made and everyone was inside. Clint looked around to admire their handiwork.

Ten-feet-tall wooden spikes stuck out of the ground, some vertically, for the perimeter walls, and some at angles, on the inside, in case the attacker decided to jump the perimeter and land inside. In front of the perimeter was a trench covered with leaves that also had angled spikes and ropes to capture the attacker and make it an easy picking for the ones within the structure.

The howl sounded again; this time much closer. Clint made sure that the wall spikes were firmly embedded in the ground. He could see fear on some people's faces, including his brother, Thomas. Ake suddenly had a sword in one hand and a shield in the other. Seeing Clint's confused expression, he said, "Something is charging this way."

Clint could not hear anything, but since hearing was Ake's strong point, he decided to believe him. Glancing at the many Constry bodies, Clint said, "Gonth, Elesa, Edward, pick up the bodies and come with me."

The trio followed him to the bodies and picked up two each. They came back to where they could now hear the growling of an unknown animal outside the wall. Clint said, "I want you guys to throw the bodies one at a time, across the wall. Edward, I want you to flame them once they cross the wall."

Edward looked at him sceptically, but nodded.

Gonth threw his pair first. Edward waited and then hit them with red-hot flames. As soon as they heard the two bodies hit the ground, the growling stopped, before flesh could be heard being rendered from bone.

Karen sounded a bit concerned when she turned to Clint and asked, "Another Constry?"

Clint shook his head. He had a suspicion on what the creature outside was, but did not want to shock the others by voicing his thoughts. He was from the army, which made a lot of people in his group take his word for anything he said. He glanced at Gonth, who was putting up a poor show of masking his fear. Just then, there was a loud sound of a bone snapping. With quick reflexes, everyone crouched and readied their weapons. The Ring-bearers too got ready, but instead of weapons, they produced ropes. Clint raised an eyebrow questioningly at Thomas, who snapped his wrist quickly up and down, producing a sharp sound in the air. Clint understood. To prevent themselves from tiring out faster, the six of them had produced a basic weapon, the whip.

Ake's focus had not shifted from the wall in front of him. He had a shield on one arm and an axe in the other. He waited patiently for something to happen.

A few quick howls were heard again from the outside, which made Clint make up his mind. He motioned for Edward to get ready to burn them a pathway out. Edward took his place by the back wall, while Ake got ready for a breach in the wall. There was scratching sounds coming from outside, and the wood started to bend. Ake looked back at Clint, who motioned for Edward to burn a hole for their escape. Once that was done, Ake screamed at the top of his lungs and charged the wall, slicing it open like a hot knife through butter. Clint made the others get out fast, being the last one to exit their shelter. He looked at Ake and the creature Ake was facing. His fears were confirmed.

Ake was going up against an Underworld Hound. It was five feet tall, making it more than a foot shorter than Ake. But it was a huge beast, at least six feet long. Clint did not see how Ake was walking away from that fight without incurring serious damage to himself. But his duty was to get everyone to safety. Ake would have to hold his own for a few minutes, which Clint doubted Ake had.

Nevertheless, Clint herded the rest of the group into the woods. As he did a head count, he realised something.

"Where's Hasha?"

Garon spun around to look back in the direction of Ake, where he could see him about to get assistance. Hasha was charging in with her ice whip, but Garon could tell, she was way out of her depth. The Hound turned its head in her direction for a second, which was all Ake needed. He dropped the shield projection and used both hands to slice the axe at the beast's jugular.

The axe made contact with the beast, but ricocheted off, much to Ake's surprise. The Hound turned back to him and bared its teeth, each of which looked like four inches of pain to whatever they bit into. They were glistening white, about to become red with Ake's blood.

Ake started to back away from the Hound, leading it away from the group. But Hasha was like Ake. She got close to the Hound and tried to whip it from the back, only to have the whip bounce back at her. The Hound turned and snarled at her, evidently irritated by the arrival of another person. Ake did not want his sister to be the monster's meal. He formed a bow and quiver full of arrows and fired at the monster, trying to get the latter's attention. The Hound was now facing a two-pronged attack, with Hasha and her whip on one side and Ake and his arrows on the other side.

Ake shouted at his sister, "Go back. I can handle this."

"Not happening little brother. Who will look after you and make sure you don't run into trouble?"

"I don't run into trouble; trouble runs into me." Ake protested, laughing. The Hound growled fiercely, not backing down. Ake was not sure what could penetrate its hide, if his own gem's projections and Hadver's strength could not. Maybe if he dropped his weapons and went hand-to-paw with the Hound, it would prove to yield promising results.

He crouched and faced the Hound, giving Hasha a few seconds to back away, which, like any loving sister, she did not. She still had a whip in hand, but seemed unsure on how to use it.

Ake's sharp ears picked up another howl, whose source seemed to be moving rapidly towards their position. He did not want another Hound on him when he could not figure out how to kill one standing in front of him. Just then, Hasha had a brilliant idea.

She snapped her whip around the Hound's neck, forcing it to rear up and turn towards her. But as the whip was flexible, the Hound charged Hasha before she could turn the whip to rigid ice. It pounced on her, freezing Ake in his position as the Hound placed its paw on Hasha's neck. The look in the Hound's eyes was one of self-assured victory. Ake did not dare move, in case the Hound decided to put its full weight on his sister's neck.

Then, before Ake could register what was happening, a blur of fur shot past from behind him and latched onto the Hound, dragging it away from Hasha and wrestling it to the ground, where the Underworld Hound breathed its last.

Ake was stunned, but he gathered his wits and stood guard over his sister, watching as the new animal ate away the dead Hound's flesh. When it turned to face the brother-sister duo, Ake put his hand on Hasha's Ring, as she was ready to blast it with a wall of ice or water from it. Ake raised his hands so that the animal could see that there was no weapon in his hand. The animal seemed to be no larger than Hadver, which Ake found disturbing. Nevertheless, Ake stretched out his hand, a peaceful way, in Logder, to befriend a Wolf.

The animal came to Ake and looked at him with a piercing gaze. Ake did not waver, but kept his hand outstretched, waiting to see what the animal would do. It put his head under Ake's palm and sniffed his arm-guard, the one where Ake had put his gem. Ake flicked his eyes quickly to the rest of the group, where he could see Clint ready to charge the animal if things went wrong with Ake or Hasha.

Ake shook his head slowly, indicating to Clint not to do anything. When the animal finished with Ake, it glanced back at the group, as if it had known it was there the entire time. It grunted at the twenty of them, before heading back the way it had come.

Clint and Garon quickly got Ake and Hasha into the group. As they journeyed through the woods, Ake told the others that the animal which had brought down the Underworld Hound was like his late Wolf, Hadver. He was sure that it was an Acid Hound, as it was the only animal in Lasgalan that could bring down an Underworld Hound. As they journeyed on, Clint and Gonth had a soft conversation ahead of the others.

A crack of a branch above them was heard and the entire group froze, to see a large branch coming down, straight down to James and Thomas. Ake ran and summoned a sword, three time the size he normally used, and pushed the branch away from them. He inspected the branch and realised one thing.

The branch was too small and too light to fall under its own weight. Something heavy must have sat on it, causing it to fall. Ake looked up, but saw nothing. Just then, Garon yelled, "Weapons!"

Ake ran to him and looked in the direction Garon was facing. He could see nothing at first, but then saw what the problem was.

A single Jide was heading for them. It had a wingspan of about five feet, which Ake thought was small for a monster of its reputation. But then, the Jide opened its mouth, revealing two rows of teeth that looked like miniature daggers. Ake had presence of mind and yelled for Edward. They had reached the end of the tree line and were looking out to a massive spread of land in front of them. There were trees on the opposite side of a stream that flowed in front of them. The distance between the two tree lines was about three hundred metres.

Edward appeared at his side, assessed the problem, and sent a blast of fire at the Jide as a warning to stay away from them. The Jide climbed and circled them, like a predator watching the prey caught in a trap.

It came at them once again, only to be shot through the head by Clint's spear, thrown by Vincent. The Jide spun towards the ground and landed in front of Ake, where he decapitated it with a sword.

Before the decapitation happened, however, the Jide managed to get a screech out of its lungs. As soon as Ake took the monster's head off and tossed Clint's spear back to him, a number of Jide-like screams were heard from the opposite tree line.

Ake shut his ears before he could become deaf from hearing such high-pitched noises. Clint took a split-second decision and said, "Everyone, head back. Now!"

Ake turned and started running, bringing up the rear of their group. He turned and saw a number of Jides rising from above the trees and heading their way. Patrick and Edward fell back to him and sent a few flames up, in no particular direction, to dissuade the Jides from following them. They ran in no specific direction, but just away from the stream. Then, they came across a cave which looked as if it had not been used in some time.

Creepers had grown around it and the trees on the sides camouflaged it almost perfectly. A few bushes were at the mouth of the cave, but it looked accessible. Clint and Gonth herded everyone inside, and entered last themselves. They covered up the entrance of the cave with some branches they found on the ground, and waited with utmost silence for the danger to pass. They heard the Jides pass by the cave a few times, but did not do anything. When Ake said he thought the danger had passed, and Garon said the same, Gonth allowed for some light to be created, courtesy of Edward and Patrick. As it was night, and the cave was nearly pitch-dark, this was very welcome.

Ake and Garon volunteered to take watch for the night, in case they were discovered. Vincent stayed up with them as well. Isabella, Clint and Gonth searched the inside of the cave, but came to a dead end. That meant that they would not be surprised from the back in the night. But it also meant that they would not have any escape route out of the cave in the same scenario. Once everyone was asleep, except the flame providers and the three watchers, Vincent broke the uncomfortable silence.

"This is crazy."

Garon looked over at him and asked, "What are you talking about?"

"We came here to battle Constries and get out of here. But instead, we have no help, Jides on our tail and no food for tomorrow, not even our Guardians. How are we supposed to get out of this?"

"We can try and capture a few Jides, cook them and eat them." Edward said.

Ake smiled and sarcastically asked, "I suppose you eat Jides for breakfast, then."

"Come on, it should not be that hard. Fire is their weakness. We can take them out easily."

Patrick spoke up.

"In case you have not noticed, Edward, their teeth are very sharp. We have only two sources of light in this cave, and neither of us can keep this up all night long. Ake can hear the best, which is why he is not sleeping. Same with Garon, for his eyes. Vincent is our expert marksman, for advance protection. Also, we have no idea where the Jides could be at this point. Even if we did, we cannot risk more than two of us going out together. But not one of us can survive without the others at this point."

Silence followed Patrick's speech. Ake kept his ears strained to hear for anything coming from the outside. Garon too, was using his eyes to look beyond the cave walls. Ake nudged him and asked, "Can you not try to look for the heat of a Jide, while at the same time, look beyond the wall?"

"I could try, but the last time I did so, looking for you and James, I got a headache."

"Try it again, please."

Garon obliged his younger friend, but as expected, got a headache. But to his credit, he refused any rest and stayed up. He peered through a gap in the branches and tried to see the heat given off by anything outside. He saw mostly blue, but no yellow or red, the colour he saw when the object gave off heat. He went to a corner of the cave for a lie-down, and only woke up when he felt a strong hand clamp his mouth shut.

# CHAPTER 13

Chris was forced to walk down a corridor lined with jail cells. He walked past one which held an unconscious Dan. He grabbed the bars of the cell and shouted, "Dan!"

But Dan did not respond. He just lay sprawled on the floor, and a horrible thought occurred to him. Chris spun around to face his captor.

"You didn't…"

"We have not killed him, if that is what you are asking." His captor was a young man who seemed to have no problem moving around, despite the fact that he had more armour around his abdomen than any other part of his body. His hands were thick, and he wore a cloth on his head, as if to keep his hair from showing. His legs were average size, which was very peculiar. The only weapon that he sported was a double-bladed sword, much like the one Gonth had used in some of their practises. How the man wielded it was a mystery to Chris.

The man put his hand on the scabbard to make sure Chris kept moving along to a cell. Once Chris was inside, his captor said, in a very calm yet fractured voice, "You may be the wrong choice for capturing, but I am sure you will suffice till the end."

Chris knew how to deal with bullies. He had dealt with them all his life. But this man seemed different. He did not strike Chris as a coward, but a brave person. He had confiscated Chris' mace and had two guards watch over him. As soon as he left, another young man walked in.

He looked as if he was in very bad shape. His left hand was a Lion's paw, his right hand looked like a Horse's leg. Chris would have felt sorry for him, had he not seen guards snap to attention for him. Chris put his face as close to the bars as possible, to get into the man's face. As soon as he could, Chris growled and tried to grab the man's neck, but the newcomer sidestepped him and made a lunge for Chris' hand. Chris was forced to pull his hand back inside.

He regarded the man with cold, menacing eyes, but the man was not interested in any show of strength, apparently. He started off, "My name is Bryan, King Yedgal's first born son and heir to the throne. You will help in bringing my father back to life, perhaps at the cost of your own life, but it will not be in vain. You will be remembered by all."

"Listen carefully to me. I would rather be remembered in life than in death. I do not care who you are, or what your father will do, but know this. I will not allow myself to be used in some sort of experiment. If half the things I have heard about your father are true, I will never help him. If he wants Lasgalan, he is not getting my help."

Bryan did not say anything for a few seconds. Then he said, "I hope you will be comfortable here. Just a word of advice. Do not try and escape. The cells are specifically designed to inhibit your powers. If you do manage to escape, your fate might be worse than your friend's."

Chris clenched his fists and growled. Bryan didn't do anything. He just shrugged and turned to go. Then suddenly, he turned and roared like a Lion in Chris' face. Chris, caught off-guard, backed up till he reached the back of his cell.

Bryan walked away from the cell, leaving Chris to contemplate different ways of getting out. Dan had done it, but had been captured again. Bryan had said that the cell was designed to inhibit his powers. Chris thought he was bluffing. However, when he tried to use his powers, he realised that Bryan was not bluffing. He did not have any weapons, he own powers would not work, he could not trick the guards into opening the cell. He definitely did not want to sit around in the cell doing nothing. In anger, he punched the bars of the cell. The guards did not move, leaving Chris no option but to stay put. His plan had been to make the guards turn to see what he was doing. Then, if they were close enough, he would pull one of them close to himself to grab a weapon, thereby forcing them to open the cell. He would then try and overpower them, grab Dan and make a run for it. He glanced around his cell to see what could make a formidable weapon to use in case he managed to escape. But the cell was bare. The walls were made out of solid earth. Only the back wall of his cell was softer than the others.

Chris pressed his thumb against the wall, and it created a small indentation in the wall. Chris started formulating a plan. He started scraping away at the wall near his foot, so he could cover his work with his body when anyone checked in on him. He needed to just roll out from the hole he planned to create. Soon, he had got the hang of it. He had scraped out about seven inches of the wall, when he got a strong smell coming out from it. He recognised it: chloroform. Doctors used it on patients so that they did not feel any pain during operations. The smell was not strong enough to knock him out, but Chris took no chances. He ripped off his sleeve and wrapped it around his nose and mouth. He did not want to inhale any of the chloroform.

The cell door had bars, which meant that the smell would not stay in his cell. It would diffuse outside. Chris continued till he had scraped out a foot of the wall. He looked at the amount of earth he had got out, and had an idea. He covered his hands with a thin layer of earth. Just then, he heard one of the guards say, "Look, the first captive is awake. Should we take him to Lord Byron for the sacrifice?"

The guard sounded dead serious, so Chris put more earth on his hands. He got to his feet, went to the door of his cell, and waited for a guard to pass him. As soon as he got a chance, he caught a guard's face and forced him to breathe the gas. The guard slumped against the door, while Chris grabbed the keys and sword from his belt. He heard guards running to his side and was relieved when he saw the remaining three guards in front of his door. That meant that Dan could make a run for it. A sword was never Chris' favourite choice of weapon, but he had to make do for the time being. He stayed out of the sword reach of the guards, knowing that they would dare not enter his cell. Then he remembered an old tradition of Covis, where a prisoner could challenge his captor to single combat within the jail cell. He was taking a chance as to whether any of the guards were from Covis. He levelled his sword at one guard, who laughed and said, "None of us are from Covis, kid. Put the sword down before you hurt yourself."

The guard barely had time to finish his sentence, than he got tossed like a sack of rocks onto his two comrades. Chris glanced at them, before going to the door of the cell. Dan stood at the gate of his own cell, breathing heavily. He walked up to Chris' cell and said, "Get to the side."

Chris moved away from the door, which Dan slammed into with his body. The door went flying into the back wall and got stuck in it. Chris got out of the cell, and told Dan, "Thanks for the save."

"Don't thank me yet. We need to get out of here fast. From what I can tell, one prince can tell where we are, as long as we remain in a certain vicinity of this place. But I have no idea where we are."

"We are somewhere in the Diving Mountains, in Leonis. Frea led us here."

"Then we better get out of the District as well."

Chris glanced at the guards. He grabbed a sword from one and tossed one to Dan.

"Let's get out of here. You need to catch up on some news."

Dan and Chris raced out of the corridor. After a few twists and turns, they came into the room which Dan had been to twice before. Chris glanced in awe at the architecture that was forming before his eyes.

White columns rose out of the ground, each forty feet high. They had a golden base and black top.

Chris had time to see just that, when Dan shook his shoulder and pointed in front of them. Chris shifted his attention to the man facing them. He was the same man who had put Chris in his cell. Chris spoke up.

"Where is my Raven?"

"You should worry about your own safety first. The necessary precautions have been taken."

"Necessary precautions?"

Dan spoke in a soft voice, "They killed him."

Chris was puzzled. He turned back to his captor and asked, "Is this true?"

The man looked at him with solemn eyes and opened his palm, revealing a Schrol. Chris felt something inside him snap.

Without thinking, he ran at full speed to the man, who brought out his own sword, this time with only one blade, and swung it at Chris' neck. Chris dodged, ducked, and slid on the smooth marble floor. While the man was turning, he slashed the sword across the back of both his knees. Blood splattered out, but the man turned and swung his sword again, as if he had not been cut across his knees.

Dan charged in from behind, wanting to stab the man in the back. To his surprise, the second blade jutted out from the hilt, forcing him to move away. He and Chris glanced momentarily at each other as the man casually twirled his sword around himself, sending a clear message to the two of them to get back.

Dan wishfully said, "Frea would be really useful right about now."

The man laughed and said, "Sadly, both your Guardians have met the same fate."

Dan's calm face became a face of rage. He roared loudly and charged the man, much to the latter's shock. He was slow in raising his sword for defence, a result of which saw him getting backed into a wall. Dan dropped his sword and grabbed him by the abdomen armour he was wearing. Dan spun him twice before throwing into a wall, fifteen feet above the ground. The wall did not crack, but the man got back to his feet unsteadily and grabbed his sword which was near him. He glanced at the gem near Dan's foot. Dan picked it up and tossed it to Chris, saying, "I don't know what good it will do, but keep it and run."

Chris got up and shook his head adamantly.

"I don't run from a fight. We will get out of here, together."

He passed the gem over one arm-guard and let it melt into the metal. He felt Cronder back in his mind and felt his wings ready to open. He opened them and took a few steps forward to get to Dan. He said, "Cover your ears."

Dan plugged his ears with his fingers. Clint took a deep breath and screeched loudly. The man covered his ears and dropped to his knees. Chris kept at it, moving closer to him. When Chris was close enough, he swatted him with his wings, until the man dropped unconscious. Dan whistled appreciatively and asked, "Can you go higher?"

"Let's not test that now. I just alerted everyone in this place to our jail break. Can you find us an escape route?"

"Already got one." Dan pointed up at a hole from where sunlight flooded in.

Chris flew him up to the hole, where Dan slipped through first, before helping him out as well. Soon they were flying south, towards Talis and away from the mountains.

# CHAPTER 14

The sun shone straight into Dan's eyes as Chris gained more height, with Dan firmly caught in his claws. Dan could not do anything, so he closed his eyes and waited for Chris to land.

Soon after, he could feel Chris slowing down and dropping in height. He opened his eyes and saw Chris coming in for a landing near a river. He said, "Drop me in the water and get to the bank."

Chris readily obliged and dropped Dan in the water, ten feet up. Fortunately, the river was shallow, so Dan got wet up to his knees. He came ashore and sat down next to Chris, who had folded his wings away and was drinking the water of the river like there was no tomorrow. Dan did the same, though he drank slowly. When they were both refreshed, they compared notes on what had happened in the time Dan was missing. When Chris got to the part of Frea leading him to Leonis, he cast his eyes down and said,

"Frea's death is on me. I'm sorry I could not get him to safety sooner."

Dan skipped a stone across the water before saying, "I could blame you if I wanted to. But sometimes, anger must give way to forgiveness."

"You forgive me?"

"Not entirely. But considering what you said about Ake and Hadver, where is my gem?"

"It fell into the river where I was down. James and Jacob must have found it."

"It didn't get washed away?"

"The last I saw, it got wedged between two rocks. They would have seen it."

"Right. And these potions you spoke about?"

"You will get your share. First, we need to get back to Talis and you need your gem."

"Before that, you might want to DUCK!" Dan pulled Chris to the ground as a spear flew past them, nailing itself to a tree behind them. Dan got up first and saw that they were in an ambush.

Twenty people, all in armour, stood around them in a wide arc. Some had crossbows ready and aimed at their chest. Others had spears in their hands. Chris too got up and stood with his back to Dan's.

"Dan, you think we can take them?"

"Before a fatal blow is landed on one of us? No way."

"Then I suggest you get ready for another screech."

"Ready when you are."

"Now!"

Dan shut his ears as Chris let loose another screech, even louder than the last one. Arrows went flying in every direction, some narrowly missing the duo. Spears fell out of their owners hands, and Dan made a run for two of them. Chris stopped and grabbed one spear from Dan. He looked exhausted, which Dan was not surprised by. He could feel anger and sadness in Chris, along with fatigue. It would not be long before Chris needed help. He was pushing his Guardian to the limit. Dan readied himself as the people around them got up and aimed weapons at them again.

Just then, a commanding voice shouted, "Hold your fire."

Dan and Chris exchanged worried looks. If they had been found again by the people they managed to escape, there would be no mercy. However, they did not have to worry.

A short man walked towards them, crossbow on his back. He took off his cloak, revealing an armour unique to Logder. The duo heaved a sigh of relief. The District Lord of Logder himself, Lord Huy, was facing them. Both the boys looked uncertainly at each other, before kneeling before Lord Huy.

"Rise, please. Now, at ease men."

The other men surrounding the three of them lowered their weapons and spread around them in a loose circle, far enough to be out of earshot but close enough to move in at a moment's notice in case of a surprise attack on the group.

Huy sat down on the ground, leaving the two of them with no choice but to follow suit.

Huy started off, "What brings a Covian and an Equine to Logder?"

Dan spoke up, "We came here for a little adventure and to get away from the hustle and bustle of city life back home."

Huy allowed a faint smile and removed his crossbow. He looked into both the boys' eyes.

"When will you learn to trust anyone, especially someone who is ready to help you?"

"What are you talking about?"

"The home you are talking about is in Talis. You two were captured by Yedgal's forces and were on your way to Talis. But your companion here, went east instead of west, so that it would throw your pursuers off your scent. I must say, it did work."

Chris and Dan shot up from where they were sitting. Chris levelled his spear at Huy's chest, but Huy did not seem fazed. He just sighed.

"You think I'm here to capture you. Fair enough. After what you have been through, I don't expect you to trust me. Ever since you boys disappeared, all six Districts have been sending out search parties looking for you. None know your name, only your description. We gave simple orders: find the boys and send them back to Talis with adequate supplies. Now that I have found you, I can send out a message to the others to stop looking for you."

"Why should we trust you?"

"If I wanted to kill you, I would have told you before I did so. We Logdans may not be perfect, but we strive to be as honest as possible. You will find that with most of our citizens."

Dan relaxed a little bit, but Chris stayed stiff. He asked, "What do you want us to do?"

"You need to understand that not everything has a price. However, since you asked, I would like you to give something to your Trainers."

"Good joke. We can't call them Trainers anymore. They stick mostly to the side and only give us advice when we stumble."

"Their logic is: "why mess up a system that is functioning the way you want it to?" You two need to give them this."

Huy brought out a wooden casket about one and a half feet long. He opened it, revealing a white piece of metal that looked like an arm bone, hollow in the centre. He took it out and said, "Give this to your Trainers, it is a new type of armour we have developed in Logder. It is almost as strong as your skeleton and can pack quite the punch."

Dan laughed loudly, causing a few warriors to turn and look at him with confused looks.

Chris on the other hand, was still sceptical. He asked, "How do we know it will work?" He still had not lowered his spear.

"Well, it is not for you. It is for someone in your group, from Talis himself."

Dan understood. But he asked, "How does this armour work?"

Huy rolled his eyes and asked, "Can you have a little faith, please?"

Huy stood up and opened the piece. He closed it over his right arm, though it looked a bit too big for the width of his hand. And, before the boys' eyes, the piece contracted to fit his hand.

From the metal piece, more metal came out and enveloped his entire hand. Then, the entire right side of his body was shrouded in white metal. It continued till only Huy's face was visible.

Chris finally lowered the spear in his hand. He walked around Huy twice, before asking, "How much power behind a punch?"

"Well, it's basically your own power, twice over." To demonstrate, Huy asked for the two spears. The first one was shot at a tree fifteen metres away, without Huy using the armour. The spear got embedded only up to the end of the tip. The second one, thrown with armour on, got stuck in the tree with two feet of the shaft inside it.

Dan asked, "How did you manage to fit so much metal into such a small space."

Huy smiled secretly and said, "Trans-dimensional warping."

Chris froze in his tracks. He looked as if someone had told him that the sun would rise in the west the next day.

Dan asked, "Chris, have you heard about this before?"

Chris nodded slowly. "My father always used to talk about that. I never believed in any such thing. He said he was close to cracking the code to it. But he died, and took all his knowledge with him."

Huy looked carefully into Chris' eyes and asked, "What was your father's name?"

"Ikol."

Huy got up and put his hand on Chris' shoulder and said, "Ikol was Logder's foremost scientists on this kind of armour. We used whatever notes he left us and the result is this armour. When the war against Yedgal is over, your father would have not died in vain."

Chris looked at Huy with confusion written all over his face. He then said, "Your face is still visible. Our friend will not be safe."

"That is where you are wrong." Huy tilted his head slightly forward and the metal under it enclosed over his face.

Huy removed the armour and placed it back into the casket. He handed it to Chris and said, "The armour works in sync with your nervous system. Whatever you think, it will happen. Tell your friend this."

"That's all?" Dan asked.

"That's all." Huy confirmed.

Dan looked at the case and back at Chris, "I will carry it for you, if you want."

"That would be better. Once I decide to fly, I will lose my two fingers."

Chris gave Dan the casket.

He turned to Huy and said, "When this war is over, I will burn this armour to ash."

Dan did not understand, but apparently Huy did. The latter nodded and said, "Do what you feel you must. I wish you a safe journey to Talis."

Chris spread his wings, which looked like ghostly black mirages. He lifted off the ground with two mighty flaps of the wings and caught Dan by the shoulders.

With a last nod to Huy, Chris shot into the sky, heading west across the mountains, Dan in tow. After two hours, they hit the Dividing Mountains and Dan decided to break the silence between them.

"You want to talk about what happened?"

"If you mean about my dad, no."

"Fair enough. What exactly is trans-dimensional warping?"

"It is the use of magic to keep matter in another dimension, but in the same space."

"That sounds contradictory."

"That's even what I thought. But the difference is that another dimension refers to another level of reality, what our eyes cannot perceive, unless we enter that reality. Space refers to a three-dimensional part of a place, that is irrespective of the reality."

"So how does this armour work on that basis?"

"I'm just speculating here. Logder's scientists created a full armour, then enchanted it to contract into the piece we have. Obviously, it could not accommodate so much matter, so they warped it. Warping means the use of magic to transfer matter from one dimension to the other, and then call on that matter when needed."

"My head hurts from hearing that. Could you explain it in a simpler way?"

"Ha. There exists, in another dimension, an armour exactly identically to the one we have. But it contains all the matter of the armour, which ours does not."

"Right. That is easier to remember."

"I suppose it is." Chris spoke in a tone which sounded like he was trying to remember something.

Dan did not want to, but he asked, "Do you mind if I..."

"Do it. You can't access my memories, so I am not worried."

"Thanks."

Dan focussed his mind and got into Chris' mind. The emotions he felt were, surprisingly, not sadness or longing, but rage. Dan was a bit confused. But he did not ask questions. He knew that if he stayed inside someone too long, they would eventually sense his intrusion. The same applied if he tried to concentrate into someone's mind using all his power.

Just then, Chris screamed in pain, forcing Dan to leave his mind to avoid pain. Along with sensing another's emotions, he could also feel what else went through their minds, to a small extent, but enough to disorient him.

Chris started to drop in height. It was not a fast drop, but the tops of mountains were coming into view. Chris needed to pull up or slow his descent, or else there would be a lot of broken bones, and Dan knew that they would not be his. He glanced up at Chris, whose eyes were open, but the focus in them was fading. His claws had not gone back to being feet, so he was still aware of his surroundings. Unknowingly, Chris had tucked his wings in, so they were not pulling up fast.

Dan saw that they were no more than a thousand feet above the nearest surface, so he opened the casket and got out the armour. He had to put it onto any of Chris' limbs, so he slid it onto Chris' left hand.

As soon as the metal started to emerge, Dan shook himself from Chris' grip, and free-fell to the ground. He saw Chris also falling towards him, but he was not in control of his fall. Dan knew he could withstand the impact of the rocks. He sped to the ground and braced for impact by curling up into a ball.

He hit the ground hard, but did not suffer broken bones. A few cuts here and there, but he was otherwise fine. He glanced up and saw the armour heading right at him. He smiled and got ready to receive Chris, but froze upon looking up at him. The armour was being chased by ten large birds.

Dan had never seen birds of such size, so he understood that they were not going to help Chris down to the ground. He grabbed a rock by his side, and, using all his strength, threw it at the birds. He was hoping to distract the birds at the least, so that they stayed away from Chris. He would have liked to hit the birds, but he wanted Chris to be away from the birds. He managed to knock out one bird, causing the others to shift their attention towards him. Chris slammed into the ground next to Dan. Dan tried to prise the armour off him, but it would not work.

Dan stood up to face the birds, assessing the situation. Nine birds were heading towards him, each with a wingspan of five feet and a lot of teeth. Dan knew he could not keep them all at bay. He grabbed a small rock, no bigger than four feet across. He kept his eyes fixed on the approaching birds, who were slow in descending.

Dan summoned some of his berserker strength. He picked the rock up, spun around twice and launched the rock towards the birds. Two went down. The rest hovered above the duo, now quite wary of Dan. Just then, Chris gasped.

Dan turned to face him. The armour around his face had gone back, allowing him to see what was going on. Chris asked, "Care to help me up?"

"What happened to you?"

"No idea. Probably exhausted the gem's power. Don't think I did, but perhaps."

"We got bigger problems." Dan gestured to the seven hovering birds.

Chris thought for a moment and asked, "Think you can muster enough strength to get me to their level?"

"I just threw a rock to that height. You will be piece of cake."

"Then do it."

Dan grabbed Chris' hand, looked him in the eye and said, "Get down here without damaging yourself."

"No problem." Chris let the armour cover his face.

Dan threw Chris towards the birds. Chris waited till he was close enough, and extended his wings. He summoned two maces from the gem, knocking out one bird with each. The five birds left turned their full attention to him. Chris shot away from Dan, allowing them to give him chase. As they got closer, he morphed the maces into swords, right before he started climbing to do a full vertical loop, coming up right behind the birds and slicing all of them up.

He landed back next to Dan, who laughed and said, "Well done, you show-off. Now let's get back to Talis. I want to see what power I get from my gem."

Chris smiled beneath the armour and said, "Fine by me."

# CHAPTER 15

Ake placed his hand on Garon's mouth to prevent him from waking up and speaking. When Garon understood, he nodded. Ake quickly conveyed a message in quick sign language, "Our Trainers have gone overboard with training us. Have a quick peep outside."

Garon got up from his place, registering that everyone else was awake. He peeped through some branches, getting a good view of his opponents.

Battois and Constries stood about two hundred metres away from the entrance of the cave, as if waiting for the entire group to emerge. Jides were perched on trees nearby, while some were circling the sky above. Garon quickly pulled himself from the entrance and did a quick search outside the cave, using his eyes to see through the walls. No opponents were waiting to strike them from behind. It did not provide any relief for Garon though. The group was outnumbered and completely out of their depth. Not even Ake could slaughter a substantial number of monsters for them to stand even a remote chance against the remainder.

Just then, Clint said, "Everyone listen closely. I have a plan of attack, but we all need to be quick on our feet. We go out altogether, so that we can overwhelm the monsters and cut a path right through their ranks. Then we run as fast as possible."

Gonth stopped Clint and said, "There is no way we make it out of this alive, at least not with Clint's plan. I got another plan. We send out Ake first. He creates a disturbance in their ranks. If they all decide to converge on him, they get packed together, making them easy pickings for the rest of us, who can hit them from outside. Facing a two-pronged attack, we should be able to win."

Clint sighed and asked, "What about the Jides?"

Vincent spoke up, "Edward and I will handle them."

Clint raised his hands, signalling that he had no better alternative.

"Very well. Ready yourselves. All hell will break loose soon. We are just twenty-two, they must be twenty-two hundred. But I made a promise never to leave one of you behind. Let's go show our Trainers that we can work together, as a team."

Ake took his position at the mouth of the cave, with two axes in his hands. He gestured to Edward to burn the bushes in front of him, giving him some element of surprise against the monsters.

He charged through the smoke, screaming to try and scare the Battois, but it did not work. As he got close enough to the thick of the group, he started to spin, getting Constry and Battos blood on himself. But he would not survive long. He dropped his axes and summoned shields to protect himself from the Battois' fire. Then, the rest of his group burst forth and threw themselves at the monsters. Edward sent his flames at the Jides, forcing them off to get away from the cave.

Vincent had got a spear made by Hasha, which he used to take down the Jides that Edward was scaring away. He did not have a strategist's mind, but he knew that they were not making much progress through the monsters' ranks. Soon, a hit would be scored by the monsters. They needed a higher kill frequency, which did not seem to be coming.

Then it happened. Like a miracle. A shadow fell over the battleground. Vincent glanced up in time to see a large bird, or so he thought, drop a large ball over Ake. The "ball" glanced off his shields, and Dan announced himself in the battle by ripping through Constries, even though he did not know how to kill them. Vincent heard Jacob shout out for Dan.

A red gem was thrown from Jacob to Dan. Dan caught it and within seconds, the battle seemed to turn in the direction of the youth. Ake, happy with the support he had got switched from defence to offense. Dan did not hold back. He went berserk, using a red mace with one hand, and a red sword with the other. Looking up, Vincent saw that Chris was taking care of the Jides. He was using a black bow and quiver to take them out, hitting them right in the brain. When his duty in the air was over, he turned his bow downwards and picked his targets off at an easy pace.

The arrival of the duo was much appreciated by Clint, as now all two dozen of them were working together, without slipping up. As Dan did not manage to take the heads off the Contries' bodies, Garon was doing it for him. Dan would fell a Constry, Garon would proceed to rip the head off.

When the monsters were reduced to nothing, Clint ordered everyone together. He first thanked Chris and Dan for showing up. When he asked where they had been, they just said, "We are not ready to go through that place again."

Clint nodded. He then addressed the entire group, "I'm glad to see that all of you worked like a team today. I want this performance to improve as we get closer to our target. Now that we have gained some momentum, let's not lose it."

Ake sarcastically shouted, "Hear our saviour please."

The entire group laughed away. Clint too had a smile across his face. But he knew something was wrong. He could not sense any immediate danger, but his military experience told him something was up. He felt the ground sink slightly under his feet, but he did not pay attention to it. He moved off the spot and scanned the area.

They were back at the river bank, open to attack. With three Guardians now dead, Clint was now getting worried. That meant that they had lost three fighters. He did not dare voice his opinion, not with everyone looking up to him. However, he told Gonth about his fears.

Gonth nodded and said, "I know. I feel the same way. But it will happen, to all of us, by the time we storm the palace."

"Let's see if we can avoid that, shall we?"

"You can't cheat destiny, Clint."

"Maybe, but everyone knows that their Guardians will die soon. What if we could change that?"

"I don't follow."

"We keep the Guardians locked in Talis and storm the palace itself."

"And get captured? We were supposed to split up to go to the six Districts in groups, remember?"

"I think that may not be required." Dan spoke up from behind Clint.

Clint glanced around to make sure no one else was listening in on them. He asked Dan, "You know where it is?"

Dan spoke in a hoarse whisper, "I think it is on the border of Leonis and Equis..."

"Inside the Dividing Mountains." Gonth completed his sentence.

"Yes. How do you know?"

"Lady Ara appeared in my dream and "favoured me", according to the Trainers. Clint and I are leading the group."

Dan's face lost a bit of colour.

"What's wrong?"

"Nothing."

Gonth understood that Dan was not telling him the whole truth, but he did not press Dan for answers. He nodded and said, "We should be going back now. Just wait for someone to pop up and then you can be given the run down on everything."

"I look forward to it."

Soon, Luca came and took them back to the capital. He showed the new armour that Dan and Chris had brought with them. Edward tried it on. To his surprise, his flames did not rage out of his control. Everyone had their round with the armour, but ultimately, it was given to Edward to use and give at his discretion.

Garon and Clint got together after lunch, in the field, and started planning the group dispersion.

Clint said, "I would first sort out the humans and send them to their own Districts."

Garon laughed, "Even we are humans, just enhanced ones."

Anne joined in on the conversation and suggested, "Would it not be better to include everyone in this, instead of them thinking that this is a dictatorship being run by the two of you?"

Garon said, "Perhaps, Anne."

"Not perhaps. Do it."

Clint laughed and asked, "You sure your power is not similar to Jacob's?"

"Very funny."

Garon said, "Anne's correct. If we are sending people to their Guardian's death, we might as well tell them the specifics of what will happen."

Clint glanced over to Anne and asked, "Could you please get the girls to the library? We will discuss the matter there."

"No problem, sentinel."

Clint's ears went a bit red. Garon did not need his powers to see that. He waited for Anne to go away, then asked Clint, "Sentinel?"

Clint shot him a glare. But Garon was not done with him. He smirked and said, "I will keep asking you this question. You better answer fast."

"Oh, shut up."

Clint and Garon got up and gathered the boys, who were rough-housing around in their rooms. Garon got them out and herded them to the library, where the girls were waiting.

Anne winked at Clint, which Garon found amusing. He knew that Clint was not the type who was into the know-how of everything considering that his being in the army sometimes made him be away from people for a long time.

Clint remained standing with Garon and Gonth, while everyone else took their seats.

Clint said, "We have called you here to tell you how we plan on finding Yedgal's palace. Now, what we are about to tell you may cause you to revolt against us, but we have no choice. There are six Districts in Lasgalan. There are two dozen of us. Four people a District. What I propose to do is simple. The normal humans will go to their respective District. Accompanying them will be two people who are not of that District, with either Garon, Karen, Vincent, Edward, Robert or myself with them, as the fourth person. None of the six of us will travel together."

Jacob asked, "How will we know when come across the palace?"

Dan stood up and answered.

"It will not be easy. But the more monsters you face as you head into the Dividing Mountains, the closer you must be getting to the palace. That's simple military strategy. Am I right, Clint?"

"Yes, Dan. You are correct. And to make sure that no one in the group gets left behind or is separated from their group, all four people will be from different Districts. So if you have already tried to fix your groups, I am sorry. If you will not listen to me, you have to listen to Gonth. He is the real leader here."

No one had any questions.

Garon took over from Clint and said, "We have devised a systematic way to get you sorted. As I call your name, please stand up and join your group. The first group, leaving from Equis, comprises Adriana, Vincent, James and Victoria. The second group, departing for Logder tomorrow will have Hasha, Clint, Dan and Jacob. Group three, heading for Covis, has Thomas, Edward, Elesa and Emmanuel. The fourth group, leaving Leonis, has Patrick, Karen, Chris and Isabella. The second last group, leaving from Tauris, contains Adrian, Anne, Trest and myself. The last group, leaving from here, will have Vesper, Gonth, Ake and Robert. Each group departs at dawn for the mountains. Our Trainers will give us our supplies before dawn. They will transport you to your respective Districts, from where you will be on your own. Remember, if you find the palace, fall back without engaging, contact the rest of us and wait for us to come. If one of you gets captured, please do not die fighting our enemies. Try to stay alive as long as possible. Every second that you are alive is a second closer to us being able to help you, and you being able to fight your way out. We'll try to train as much as possible for the rest of the day. Rest your Guardians well. They will be of great need in the days to come."

Before the group dispersed, Gonth made one final announcement, "We came into this as complete strangers. We leave tomorrow for the same cause, the cause that we were born for. We knew little about each other first. Now, I am as worried for each of you as I would be, if you were part of my family."

Everyone got up and started to leave the library. Only the six of the stronger ones stayed back.

Robert said, "Eventually, Yedgal will rise. We all know that. We cannot stop it, but we sure can make sure his reception into this world will be a painful one."

Clint nodded his head, "We are the only one who know when to let go. If Yedgal does come to life and make the others an offer they might not refuse, we may be the only ones to save them. But personally, I would like to be the one to land the final blow on Yedgal. He took away my family from me. I am going to give him the justice he deserves."

"You are not the only one." Garon interrupted. "He slaughtered the entire Wolf Tribe when I was but an infant. I don't know how many siblings of mine died, so that I can be here today. I too want revenge."

Karen sighed and said, "You boys only think of violence as the means to the end. Does it really justify the end?"

No one met her eyes, as expected. But Clint looked her dead in the eye and replied, "You do not drop to the ground knowing all sides of the story to pass a judgement. Sometimes, you have to make that instant decision, which could either make or break both the offender and the offended. Ask me, I know what it is like to go to sleep with that on my conscience."

Garon looked at Clint, finally grasping a bit at why Clint was called "sentinel" by Anne. But he kept quiet.

Edward said, "What if we are wrong? What if we go searching for this place, and end up getting captured ourselves? We are behaving as if we will not get caught, when in truth, Yedgal wants our powers."

Clint answered without batting an eyelid, "Simple military strategy. If the others get captured, they might be used as bait to lure us in and surrender our powers. If not, they get used in whatever Yedgal's forces are planning. Either way, they assume that we will come back for them."

Karen asked, "Which is what we will do, is it not?"

Once again, no one met her eyes, not even Clint.

"Oh! You would rather…?"

Robert spoke, "We will have to bail out the moment we might get captured. We will not be given any Transporters to use, should they fall into the wrong hands. Sacrifice has always been the cost of a great victory. Archers are always placed behind the infantry to soften up the enemy, but are normally the weakest fighters. Once their armies clash, they are left open from any side, whether to die or to live to fight another day."

Lord Veryu's voice came from above them.

"So, you have realised the outcome of what is to come."

Clint raised his eyes to see the Lord of Talis watching them closely.

"Indeed we have, Lord Veryu. None of us want this to happen, but it would appear we have no choice but to let the future unfold."

"Yes. I wanted to wish all of you the very best from my heart, but it seems as if you six will have my blessing. I must leave now. Your supplies are being made as we speak."

"Thank you."

Karen waited for Veryu to walk out of earshot before saying, "We need to come up with a better plan by dawn, if we want to save our friends."

Clint said, "Do not bother overthinking it. Gonth himself has tried to see versions of battle where we come out on top, but it was in vain."

"Fine. But what about the Guardians?"

"Well, the process of them dying has already begun."

"How?"

"Dan was kidnapped. Ake went to look for him and lost Hadver. Dan broke out of wherever he was. Frea sensed it and ran to meet him. Chris followed Frea. Both Frea and Cyrus died together. Now we just wait for the others to die as well."

Garon leant forward and asked, "How can you be so casual about this? Your Guardian is at risk as well."

"I know that. Sometimes, in order to reach a place, you don't change your route. Stick to it and change your route when you reach a checkpoint."

Garon laughed and said, "Well, at least we can agree on something. But we have not fought two monsters yet. Underworld Hounds and Yoknies. I would not be worried about the Yoknies as much as the Hounds, but the group heading to Equis will face problems, should there be Yoknies in the water. What do you think, Robert?"

Robert slumped his shoulders and said, "Let us just pray that they do not run into Yoknies. The last thing we need is three people gifted to Yedgal."

Edward put his hand up and said, "We keep this conversation under wraps. Karen, if you have better alternative to offer, let us know. Right now, I want some practise with Ontemp."

Garon got up as well, "I am coming with you. About time we tested the durability of your new armour."

The two of them went out together, leaving the other four alone. They mutually decided to go back to their room and relax.

# CHAPTER 16

Chris and Ake were having a friendly duel with their weapons, when Garon and Edward stepped into the field. Garon said, "Ake, Chris we need the field."

Ake wondered what had happened to Garon, who usually asked politely. Nevertheless, they obeyed Garon's order and went off the field.

Garon and Edward had both merged. Edward had scales all over his body while Garon did not seemed to have changed, but Ake knew that he had merged. His dark eyes were now green, and his nails had become claws.

In Edward's hand was his armour. He put it on himself, but kept his hands open, as well as his face. Garon glanced towards Ake and Chris and said, "If you think, at any point, we need to be put down, deliver a hard blow to us."

The two of them nodded, and Edward went ablaze. He concentrated until only his face and hands were enveloped in flames. He said, "I like this armour. Too bad you guys will not be able to wear it all the time."

Garon smiled and said, "Do not hold back."

"I will not."

Garon moved in quickly towards Edward, who started throwing fireballs at him. Garon comfortably dodged them, but was caught off-guard when Edward brought both his palms together and directed the blast of fire towards him. Garon had to restrain Edmund from trying to take over his mind.

Garon examined his new skin tan. He gave a thumbs up to Edward and said, "Now you come at me."

"You sure about that, Garon?"

Even Chris sounded concerned for Garon's health and safety. Garon flicked his palms open, ready to grab Edward once he came close.

Edward shrugged his shoulders and ran at Garon. Garon waited till the last second and grabbed Edward's hands. The heat was not uncomfortable, but Garon was taking no chances. He allowed Edmund to take control and let loose the beast within himself. He could stand the heat quite easily and forced Edward to unleash his inner beast as well.

The result was even better than Garon anticipated. An orange misty aura surrounded Edward. Garon waited for it to solidify, the way it had for the others. The aura solidified into a Dragon with its maw wide open, as if ready to swallow anything in its path. Edward's flames elevated him a few inches off the ground. Both of Edward's hands held miniature fireballs and the flames around his face illuminated his skull. He landed gently on the ground, his orange eyes filling the whites of his eyes and pupils lengthening out.

Garon was confident that he could take Edward, so he went all out in attacking him. Surprised by the flurry of attacks, Edward started to back away. But Garon kept coming at him. Out of nowhere, Edward grabbed both his hands and roared triumphantly.

Ake and Chris were watching safely from a distance, but now they ran towards the duo, axe and mace in hand. Before Edward could do anything to Garon, Chris smashed his metal mace into Edward's back. He expected the blow to be a distraction for Edward, not a strike that completely shut down Ontemp's power surge to Edward. Ake, meanwhile, had got Garon back to his senses with a hit of the flat of his blade.

Edward was given carmine and sweenet. When he came around, he was surprised that he was still merged. Chris advised both of them to stop fighting and give their Guardians sufficient rest for the days to follow.

Edward and Garon grinned like maniacs, but agreed to do so. Once they were back in their room, they discussed the final ends of the plan with the other four. All six headed down to the armoury to sharpen their weapons. Once that was done, they went back to the room to relax and told the others to not use their Guardians until the next day. The rest of the day went by slowly, as if time itself wanted the twenty-four of them to enjoy their lives for that day. Dinner was a near-silent one, though Veryu wished them well and tried to keep them calm.

Once they went to sleep, almost everyone had a fitful slumber. But Garon had the worst of it. He woke up almost every twenty minutes, causing the torch near his bed to flicker on and off. When he could not stand it any longer, he got out of his bed and walked out of the room. Thankfully, no other torch ignited. However, Garon realised that he was not alone in waking up and walking out of the room.

Ake and Hasha's voices could be heard by him. He walked till he reached the staircase that led down to the dining room, and saw that they were not alone. Even Elesa was there.

Ake saw Garon and chuckled softly.

"Seems as if all four of us had bad sleep. What brings you here Garon? And why do you have a dagger ready?"

Garon looked down to see that he did have a dagger in his hand, but he calmly said, "Safety precautions must be taken."

In truth, he wanted to use the dagger for not his own safety, but for another's safety, one who he loved close to his heart.

"What were you guys talking about, before I came here?"

Ake said, "Just before I lost Hadver, I had an encounter with a ghost."

"And..?"

"It was the ghost of our father, Garon. The one who got killed in the Wolf Tribe slaughter, a dozen years ago."

Garon steadied his breathing, "So I still have one sibling left." He smiled, "So I can still boss over you like an elder brother, then?"

"If you want."

"And what makes you to us, Elesa?" Garon asked.

"I honestly do not know. Just think of me as your friend." Elesa said.

Garon and Ake smirked.

"Very well. Friend it is, then." Ake said.

Garon then said, "We will not see each other for some time. Keep your eyes and ears sharp. I will not be able to protect all of you."

"Yes, brother. We can handle ourselves."

"Good. Now go back to sleep." Garon ordered.

Once they went into their rooms, Garon headed to the Guardian's room. He slowly opened the door and found his way to Edmund. His Guardian woke up on smelling him. No other Guardian moved. That made Garon's job easier. But he knew that he must finish it fast and cleanly.

Garon raised his dagger shakingly.

"I am sorry Edmund. I truly am. But I must protect you."

Edmund just watched Garon's face calmly, which made Garon perspire. He could not bring himself to kill Edmund. Edmund's gaze shifted slightly towards the dagger, as if it understood what Garon was planning.

Garon glanced back to see that no one had followed him. He looked back to Edmund and said, "I will keep you safe, you hear?"

Edmund seemed to smile at that statement. He lifted his head as much as he could, exposing most of his chest to Garon. Garon understood.

He was about to do something that would haunt him for however long he lived. Garon raised his dagger and drove it cleanly into Edmund's heart. The canine did not make a sound. He looked up at Garon with a look of satisfaction and trust on his face, and quietly fell to the ground. Garon looked at the fallen form of his Guardian, his tears ready to fall. Edmund's body dissolved into green vapour, leaving an Emerald behind.

Garon felt guilty lifting the Emerald, but he had made a promise to keep Edmund safe. He was not going to break that promise unless he died. He beheld the Emerald, its pulsating light, understanding the power that he had taken upon himself. He slipped out of the Guardian's room and went back to his own. Everyone was asleep, so he stayed outside for a few minutes. He remembered what Ake had told him about harnessing the gem's power.

The only emotion he had in himself at that moment was grief. He used that emotion and allowed the gem to pass into the arm-guard. His senses felt heightened, and he felt as if his powers had multiplied ten times. He got back into the room and fell asleep, this time a peaceful sleep.

# CHAPTER 17

Raze was awake, when he felt a gentle hand on his ribcage. He glanced behind to see a young girl, perhaps seven years of age, looking at him with probably the sweetest smile he had ever seen till then. His wings had disappeared overnight, so he was safe.

Raze gave a smile as well, which the girl giggled at. Then, a man who looked like her father strode towards them. He looked at Raze and said, "You look like a fine animal. I wonder how strong you are."

Raze could not respond. He was taken from the herd by the man, who allowed the girl to climb onto Raze's back. Raze stayed calm until he felt he had earned the man's trust. But he also knew what was expected of him. He remembered what Bryan had told Byron in front of him, and decided to use that to his advantage. The potion would be wearing off soon, so he started to buck wildly, forcing the man to take the girl off him and try and subdue Raze. Raze used his size and multiplied strength to get the man on the ground. Just then, he returned to normal human form. He whipped out his Argentic Transporter, and seemingly vanished into thin air with the man.

In a few seconds, he landed back into the main hall of the palace, surprising Xristos and Sabre. Xristos recovered from his shock and helped Raze subdue the man, gagging him with a chloroform cloth.

Xristos told Sabre, "Take him to my chambers. He will be interrogated later."

Sabre nodded and carried the man away. Xristos said, "Well, you have done well, again. I must ask you though, did anyone see you?"

"Yes."

"Who? We must leave no loose ends, you know that."

"I am sorry to say this, Lord Xristos. The person who saw me cannot be harmed in any way, either mentally or physically. I was seen by a girl, no more than seven years of age. And if King Yedgal came to know of what you were going to do, I am sure that he would not approve."

Xristos gave him a hard look before calmly saying, "Yes he would. Thank you for reminding me of the rules he had laid down."

Xristos did not sound sarcastic at all. Rather, he sounded a bit humbled.

Raze asked, "Lord Xristos. Once you are done with that man, what are you going to do with him?"

Xristos waited for a moment before answering, "I would not worry about that if I were you. Whatever information we get out of him will be reward for your troubles."

Raze was not happy with the way Xristos had framed his reply. But he still saluted Xristos and went away.

Xristos watched Raze's retreating form and said to himself, "It seems that we need to keep a close eye on you Raze, whether you like it or not."

Sabre returned to Xristos and said, "He is ready to be interrogated. Would you like me in there, in case he tries to escape?"

"No. Get the boys. I want them. If you wish, you can stay outside and be the last defence."

Sabre nodded. He went to fetch Bryan and Byron, who were arguing over something. As Sabre got close, his neck hair stood up as he understood what they were talking about.

Bryan asked Byron in a cold tone, "Would you be able to sleep knowing you had defied our father's orders?"

"At least then, we would still have those two with us, you thick-headed, law-abiding stickler!" Byron retorted angrily.

Sabre coughed loudly and addressed them, "My nephews. We can argue later, but right now, Xristos wants you both in his chambers for an interrogation."

Byron shot one last dirty look at his brother, before walking fast towards Xristos' chambers. Bryan was about to follow, when Sabre stopped him and asked, "What happened?"

Bryan said in a voice that scared his own uncle, "Both our prisoners have escaped. Karan tried to stop them, only to get his arm bones and back injured very badly."

"Very well. Is he in recovery?"

"Yes. He will pull through, but I am not sure till what extent."

"Fine. Let us go to Xristos now."

They walked up to Xristos' door, where Sabre took up his position. Bryan went inside and shut the door behind him.

Sitting on a chair, near the window, was their prisoner. He was a strong man about thirty years old, with a dark tan and a strong physique. Bryan had no doubt that he would be able to hold his own in a fight. The man did not look visibly afraid of the trio standing in front of him. He watched each of their movements carefully, as if he would suddenly try and make a run for it. He looked unharmed, though a bit drowsy. His posture was slightly relaxed, and he waited for one of the three people in front of him to say something.

Bryan started off by asking him, "Would you like some water?"

The man focussed his eyes on Bryan, with a gaze that looked as if he was reading Bryan's soul. He nodded. Xristos poured out water into an iron glass for the man and gave it to him.

Byron asked, "What is your name?"

"I am afraid that is a question that I cannot answer. Names have a lot of power, you know."

Xristos interjected, "Then answer this question. How much do you love your daughter?"

The man's eyes tightened, and he leapt out of the chair, as if ready to overcome all three of them with just an iron glass. Byron shot two silver disks to restrain his hands to the arms of the chair.

Xristos said, "Well, evidently, enough for him to try and kill us."

The man growled and said with icy certainty, "If you lay a finger on her, I will make you pay with more than just your life."

The silver disks started to tighten on the man's wrists. The smell of burnt skin started to fill the room. Bryan tapped his brother on the shoulder, ordering him to stop. Reluctantly, Byron obeyed.

Xristos said, "Look, we just want some information. We will then allow you to go back to your life, no questions asked."

"And what guarantee do I have that you will not harm me, or the people I love?"

Bryan realised that this man was going to be tough to crack, so he drew his sheathed sword. The man looked a little frightened, but Bryan was not interested in him. He walked to a small candle and sliced his palm slowly. Blood dripped out, one drop at a time, into the flame.

Once Bryan saw three drops hit the flame, he took a vow in the name of Sorenth, not to harm the man, or the people he loved. He knew that the people of Equis worshipped Sorenth. He was practically their God. They took vows under Sorenth seriously.

Xristos remembered his own vow as well. He waited for Bryan to finish and come back.

Bryan then asked the man, "Is that enough of a guarantee?"

"It would seem so. But I can only answer certain questions."

Byron asked, "How about every question we ask you?"

"You will not try and kill me, considering you already have me as your prisoner."

Xristos stopped their conversation and said, "You have a man in front of you, who took a vow in Sorenth's name. We do not wish to harm you. The sooner we get this over with, the sooner you get sent back. Now, how do you make stampede potion, in bulk quantity?"

"Ah. The stampede potion. I do not know myself how the potion is made. I take out blood from the Unicorn, send it away to a neutral location, then pick up the finished goods later at the same location."

Bryan studied the man's face and said, "He is being truthful. I can say that much."

Xristos stared hard at the man and said, "You are not helping your case. Well, where does the Tribe live?"

The man laughed and said, "I think you know that answer to that already."

Byron sighed, as if he was getting bored.

"Alright. It was fun and games until now. But here is where you answer truthfully."

Byron's left hand got encased in blue light. He caught the man's face and pushed it back slightly. The man screamed in agony as he felt the light streak into every opening on his head, weaving a path towards his brain.

Bryan pulled his brother's hand away, but the damage was already done. The man straightened up and looked around as if he was lost.

He asked, "What did you do to me?"

Byron laughed and said, "Answer our questions, your eyesight will be restored."

The man slumped his shoulders and said, "Ask away."

Xristos asked, "What position of power does the Pegasi Tribe hold in Equis and Lasgalan?"

"In Equis, we advise the Lord of the District. We are not his right-hand people, though. Our Tribe leader advises only the ruler of Lasgalan, mainly in terms of economy."

Bryan popped the next question, "How much influence and wealth does the Tribe have?"

"Enough wealth to sustain Equis for seventeen years, as of this moment. In terms of influence, we can be very influential. We can topple the Lord of the District with almost no effort at all."

Xristos and Byron exchanged worried glances. But Xristos regained his composure and said, "Give his sight back."

Byron held out his hand, and the blue light exited the man's eyes. He looked around, but saw only the three of them.

Xristos gave the man an Auric Transporter and said, "Once you reach your destination, throw the Transporter high into the air. It will be destroyed. No one will follow you."

The man took the Transporter and waited for the gold light to take him back to the Isle. When he came back to the Isle, he immediately threw the Transporter up.

Like his interrogator had said, it exploded, leaving no trace. The man smiled. He turned around and walked back towards the herd. He needed to get some facts straight, and he needed to pay a visit to an old friend. Maybe, just maybe, his friend could provide him with the answers he needed. Faldor knew a lot more than people assumed he let on.

# CHAPTER 18

Garon had slept peacefully after taking the life of his Guardian, which he still felt guilty about. The first thought he had after waking up was to go and check on Edmund, as had been his habit from childhood. But then he remembered the events of the previous night, and a shiver went down his spine. He pushed aside his guilt and was soon ready. The others in his room got up as well.

Soon, all the two dozen youngsters were having breakfast and a there was a murmur about the table. The Trainers were busy preparing their last-minute potions. Garon glanced around the table to try and make eye-contact with Clint, but Clint was in a deep discussion with Gonth and Lord Veryu. He glanced down at his hands, and imagined a small dagger. One green dagger appeared in his right hand. He closed his fist and looked up, only to see Ake looking at him across the table. Garon just smiled and went back to finishing his breakfast.

As they left the room, Garon went ahead to the Guardians' room and walked out again, leaving everyone to assume he had already merged. He grabbed his pack of potions from Reidan, who wished him well. Garon carried a bag with two sets of clothes, some daggers and he planned on keeping his potions inside as well, if needed. He went to the field and waited for the others to come out. Once they started to come out, he felt a bit more relaxed.

Chris, Dan, and Ake came out together, the last to get to the field. Garon and Clint quickly sorted them out, as the sun started to peep over the walls. Luca, Reidan, Latyu and Lucia transported four groups away, except Ake's group, which was going to leave from Talis itself.

The group that Garon was in was transported by Lucia, when she returned. She made them hold hands and transported them to the outskirts of a Taurian city.

She told them, “Fight well, fight hard and do not get captured.”

She got encased in golden light and disappeared into thin air. Garon took stock of their surroundings and asked Adrian, “Where are we?”

Adrian glanced at the city walls, the mountains ahead of them, as if judging the group’s position in Tauris and replied, “The city behind us is Askalien. It holds a special place in Tauris as the city that has not known famine, or any natural calamity that has affected Lasgalan or Tauris. This might be our city to fall back to. If we head north, our next city to fall back to will be Shodor. But we have a long way to go, before we get there.”

Anne looked at the mountains in the distance, as if they were something other than mountains. She said, “We will be able to get there within a few hours. But if the palace is not there…”

Garon completed her question, “What are we doing here?”

“Yes.”

“We may find small sections of his army here, as if under command to run into the District and subdue any resistance they may face. Or we could find monsters in there, waiting for an opportunity to strike. Don’t forget, monsters also marched in Yedgal’s ranks.”

Trest eyed Garon and said, “You know a lot more than what you are telling us, are you not?”

Garon smiled and said, “Too late to turn back now. Besides we cannot go into any city now. Not with you two merged. Trest, you can still pass for a human. Anne, no one is going to buy the story that you have a condition in which hair sprouts from your neck. You cannot even say that you are an actor.”

Anne nodded and said, “I guess that the only time I can go inside a city is when David is dead."

"David is your Guardian?"

"Yes. A Claw Lion."

"Very well. Let's head onwards."

Two hours later, the four of them got to the foothills of the mountain range. There was only one problem.

Anne and Trest looked back at Garon, asking him, "How are we supposed to climb up a vertical slope, one that is two hundred metres high?"

Garon knew that Trest was the only one who would have a problem climbing up. He tested the slope for some soft portions, but had no luck. He said, "I do not want to cause any problems here, but it seems that Trest will have to hold onto me while the three of us scale the slope."

Anne had no qualms about scaling the slope. She extended her nails, which became claws, almost like Garon's. She jumped as high as possible and started to ascend, picking the softest parts of the slope. Adrian followed her. He summoned two ropes from his Ring. He lashed one to the slope and pulled himself up, using the second one to get his second anchor point. Garon looked at Trest and said, "It is now or never."

She laughed and said, "Do not lose your grip on your way up there."

Garon summoned two daggers, allowed Trest to get onto his back and started stabbing his way to the top of the slope. He reached the top, where Anne and Adrian helped him up and got Trest off his back. Garon got up and said, "Well, I haven't been honest with you guys."

Adrian said, "You hid the fact that your Guardian is dead. Now you are even more powerful. That is all I need to know. I do not know about the others, but I will not ask for details."

Garon was happy at Adrian's reply. He backed away from the edge of the cliff he had just climbed up. Summoning two daggers he said, "The tree line starts from here. This is not another simulation by the Trainers. This is now a case of life or death. We do not get to come back here to correct our mistakes. We do not know what to expect, so keep your eyes up, ears sharp and powers at the ready."

Garon scanned the tree line for possible threats, but could not see any. So he used his heat-vision. That too gave him no positive result for threats. He approached the trees, leaving the others no choice but to follow. He knew that he was the most likely target for many reasons. He was playing the role of a leader here. If he was captured, the others would accept defeat easily. He also was the brightest object in the vicinity, with two green glowing daggers in his hands. Also, he was the most powerful one out of the four of them. Capturing him would be better than capturing Anne or Trest.

Edmund may not have been physically present, but Garon trusted that his Guardian's instincts would take over, should the time arrive when they were taken by surprise. They plunged into the trees, and soon Garon was the only source of light underneath the canopy. The trees were close together, making it difficult for sunlight to penetrate through the canopy. Adrian rubbed his Ring, as if having second thoughts about being in the group.

He had fallen a few steps behind them, so Trest too went back and asked him, "Something wrong?"

Adrian looked into her eyes, as if he was seeing a ghost. But he replied calmly, "No. I am fine. I'm just wondering about the other groups."

Garon glanced behind and said, "Hurry up, you two. I do not want anyone separated."

He turned and kept walking ahead. Anne, who was in his line, looked back at the duo and shrugged her shoulders, as if she did not know why Garon had suddenly become so blunt with them. The group came upon a smoking birch tree. It looked as if it had been stuck by lightning.

It was split down the middle, almost in perfect symmetry. Smoke was coming out from the split. Garon looked back to Adrian, who said, "Tauris' monsoon season went last month. This has to be a Battos' doing."

As if on cue, a roar sounded ahead of them. Garon instinctively readied his daggers. Anne stood where she was. Adrian produced a whip and stood next to Anne. Adrian said, "That is not a normal Bull."

Garon tensed up. He could feel the ground shaking slightly under his feet, but it was like minute, periodic tremors passing under him. He motioned for the others to stay where they were, while he went in an arc, to see what lay in front of them.

After a few minutes, when he did not return, Adrian got worried. But since there was no sound of a fight going on, he figured that Garon would be on his way back.

Just then, Garon's voice was heard. It was a scream so loud that birds on the trees above them flew up through the canopy. Adrian and Anne did not hesitate and charged the way Garon had gone.

Garon was going head-to-head with two Battois. Both were about seven feet tall, with muscles that looked too big for them. Garon still had his daggers, but seemed unsure as to how to use them. He could not get close enough to stab them, as they would grab him and crush him. He already had a burn mark across his chest, where his shirt had burnt off, absorbing most of the Battois' flames. He did not appear to be damaged, but he would be wearing out faster than the monsters. He did not appear to have seen the trio, but he put his hand out, signalling them to stay away. Adrian did not like the look of the fight, but he obeyed Garon. Just then, one of the Battois saw the trio and charged towards them.

Garon dashed into the monster's path, throwing it off balance. He managed to stab both the daggers into its stomach. He summoned another two, but before he could do anything with them, and before the group could come in close to help him, the Battos turned its head to look at Garon and blasted him with its fiery breath, straight from the mouth.

The trio stayed frozen as they heard Garon scream in agony. The blue flames had seemingly encased his body. There was no way he would be brought back from the dead, if there was a body to recover in the first place.

Suddenly, Garon's screams shut off. Anne gave a nervous glance to Trest, who had started to back away slowly. Then, a guttural roar was heard from within the flames, and Garon shot out of them, taking the Battos' head off with his nails. Garon faced the other Battos, which grunted in an angry way. Garon extended his nails and roared again. His green aura surrounded him, solidifying into a Wolf twice his size.

The Battos backed away from Garon, trying to get away, but Garon had other ideas. He lunged at the monster, catching it by the arms, sinking his teeth into its abdomen. The monster did not make another sound.

Garon turned around to face the three of them. Anne stepped ahead of Adrian and said, "Get some sweenet ready. He may need it."

She faced Garon, whose eyes were bright green. He smiled, which was creepy, but Anne did not back down. She was ready to run at him, but he shuddered and dropped to one knee. Anne was not sure what to make of it. Garon shook violently and fell face-first into the ground. Adrian brought out a vial of carmine instead of sweenet. Anne and Trest turned Garon over. They prised open his eyelids, to reveal eyes which were white again. Adrian did not hesitate and put a few drops of carmine into Garon's mouth. Being on ration, they could not afford to use a lot of their potions. They waited for Garon to come around, though it took him five minutes. He got up slowly, with help from Trest. He examined his chest wound and asked Trest, "Anything you can do, considering that you are the healer?"

Trest looked gravely at him and asked, "How much pain can you withstand?"

"I guess we will have to find out."

Anne asked Trest, "What are you planning to do?"

"Look, I read in the library that a Battos' flame, even if it grazes someone on unprotected skin, can turn to poison after a few days. We do not have the luxury of time, so I will have to get the burn marks off him, here and now."

"How are you going to do that? You will have to…" Realisation dawned on Anne's face and her eyes widened in shock.

Trest said, "I got no other option. Unless we take a chance and see whether he can withstand the poison."

Garon dropped on his back and looked at Trest.

"Do it. I have faith in you."

Trest ordered Anne and Adrian to restrain Garon's limbs. She got a vial of blocker only, much to the confusion of Garon. She brought out her scalpel and sliced off whatever was left of Garon's shirt, revealing his muscled chest and abdomen. She placed the edge of the blade against the join of his two skin tones, and slowly sliced through his burnt skin, taking it off and drawing blood.

Garon screamed as he felt the blade go over his ribs. His adrenaline infused blood did not help and came out of him at an alarming rate. Trest kept calm and continued with her surgery. Adrian and Anne looked concerned over Garon's condition, but did not say anything. Trest managed to get half the burnt skin off, revealing his red pectoral muscles.

The muscles did not show any signs of injury. Garon had stopped screaming, but his eyes showed all the pain that he was experiencing.

A few minutes later, Trest was done. She had applied as much blocker as she could risk, on Garon's exposed muscles. To prevent more bleeding, she had tied Garon's shirt strips around his chest.

Garon was breathing heavily now. But Trest knew that they could not stop so early. She hauled Garon to his feet and made him walk a few steps, first with some support. She then left him and made him walk on his own. Garon looked in bad shape. His eyes lacked a lot of the focus they had when the group had set out in the morning.

Anne asked him, "What did you do, that you got back to normal?"

Garon looked weakly up at her and said, "I still have some conscience left. But I use up all my willpower trying to rein in my Guardian."

"But can you fight, using him, again?"

"I don't know. I barely managed to rein in Edmund just now."

Trest said, "Well, you better know the answer soon. If the monsters showed up so early, we can be hit by anything. I do not mind healing you guys, but every stop is going to delay us."

Garon grimaced with pain and held his left shoulder. Anne rushed to hold him, and so did Adrian. They supported him as they headed up the slopes.

At one point, Trest turned and asked Adrian, "Have the peaks of the Dividing Mountains ever been scaled, in Tauris?"

"No. As far as I know, no peak has ever been scaled."

Garon gasped and said, "Guys, correct me if I am wrong, but are those Constries in front of us?"

Trest turned, but only saw more trees ahead of them. She said, "Garon, you might be hallucinating. You have lost a lot of blood. Your heart might be working overtime to compensate the loss of blood. It is possible that you are anticipating Constries."

Anne craned her neck and sniffed the air. She shook her head and said, "Garon is correct. I am not sure what, but something large and foul is beyond those trees. I can smell that. How come you cannot,

Trest?"

Trest furrowed her eyebrows. She readied her scalpel and gestured for the trio to follow her. They came to a plateaued clearing, where Garon said that he could walk on his own. At least out here, they would not be taken by surprise. Adrian used his Ring and constructed a small earth wall to keep any monsters approaching from land at bay. Garon looked at his chest, still red with all the blood stains on it. He sat with his back to the wall, looking alert despite being tired. Trest had to make sure Garon stayed alive as long as he was around her.

Meanwhile, Anne remained watchful and continued to look for any threats around them, though Trest could not see what she was being worried about. Then, they all heard the screams of Jides and Constries, coming fast towards them.

Adrian helped Garon up. Anne told the two of them, "Run. I will hold them off. Trest, you can stay if you want."

Anne tossed Garon's bag to him. He caught it and looked at Anne in confusion saying, "You sure you can hold them all off?"

Anne looked as if Garon had asked her a stupid question.

"Yes, of course."

"That is all well and good, but I am not running away from anything." Garon shrugged Adrian's hand off. He flicked his palms open and walked to Anne. Anne gave a look of worry to Trest, who shook her head. All four of them waited for the charge to come.

Constries broke into the clearing first, twenty of them. They had to cross Adrian's wall to get to the group, which was six feet tall. Garon knew that he could not ask Edmund for more power, because the result could be worse than the last time. Just then, Anne said, "Guys, I do not think I can hold my form much longer."

Adrian looked at Anne and sure enough, she looked like she was having trouble staying merged. Garon said, "How long can you hold it?"

"Few minutes, tops."

"Then let David out now. We could use the extra fighter."

Anne looked unsure, but agreed. Her Lion sprung onto the field, looking a bit worse for wear, but its presence was enough to keep the Constries at bay for a few seconds. Then they charged the youths together. Garon ditched the green daggers he was holding in his hand, and brought out a quiver of arrows, with a bow. He started picking his targets, which Trest took care of by decapitating them. Adrian sent a wave of earth into the path of the Constries, getting them off balance. David took care of those monsters.

Suddenly, there was no monster left alive. Garon almost laughed. But then he saw a Jide coming down at them. Before he could even decide what to do, David leapt in front of him. The Jide's mouth, into which Garon would have put a sword, closed around David's neck as the two beasts fought on the ground. David gave a roar and went limp. Garon, in a swift motion, sliced off the Jide's head and pulled it off David.

The Lion was still alive, though it was bleeding profusely. Trest was about to pour on some blocker onto David's neck, but Anne held her hand, shaking her head. There were tears in her eyes, Garon could see. He motioned for the two of them to give Anne a last moment with her Guardian, while he went back himself.

Anne stroked David's mane, saying something to him at the same time. She put her forehead against his, as the Lion's eyes closed. She watched as the Lion dissolved into yellow vapour, leaving behind a Fire Opal on the ground where he was a few seconds before. She did not pick it up though. It was as if she did not notice it. Adrian looked at Anne, who pointed at Garon and then to Anne. Garon understood the message.

He went up to Anne, whose eyes were closed while tears ran down her cheeks. He picked up the Fire Opal and placed it in Anne's palm. She opened her eyes and looked at Garon, as if seeing him for the first time. She looked down at the gem and slipped it inside her shirt. Garon stopped her.

"Put it over your arm-guard. Use the grief to let it give you power."

Anne looked doubtful, but did what he said. The gem melted in and she said, almost in a whisper, "Thank you."

Garon said, "I know what it is like. But at least you know now you cannot lose David again."

"So now, what can I do?"

"You are still Anne. But underneath, you have David, ready to help you at any time. I do not know what part of your merged power will show itself now, but you are stronger now, than you were before."

"I guess we will see when the time is right."

"Yes we will. Now, dry your eyes. Let's wreak havoc on anyone who tries to stop us."

Anne wiped her eyes and accepted Garon's hand. They made their way back to Adrian and Trest, both of whom offered their condolences to Anne. They left the clearing and headed up the slope again.

# CHAPTER 19

Emmanuel and Elesa finished off the last of the retreating Constries as the monsters tried to run for their lives. Elesa ripped off the last head and tossed it into the fire they had going, courtesy of Edward. Emmanuel put his club on his shoulder and walked towards the fire. His club was slick with blood, but he did not bother to clean it. None of them were injured at all. All had merged, which meant that they only had one extra fighter, Elesa's Wolf, Ketta. Edward had loaned his armour to Thomas, who had made sure it had not been damaged in any way. Edward himself had only flamed the Constries, letting them run helter-skelter while Elesa and Emmanuel took them apart.

As they watched the last head burn up, Thomas said, "Thanks for the armour, Edward. Though I doubt I will not be needing it again, hopefully, I think you better keep it with yourself."

Edward shook his head and said, "You are the most vulnerable one out us the four of us. You do not have anything that can give you an edge in battle, excluding what you have on your finger."

Thomas appreciated how Edward had called him "vulnerable" and not something like "weak." He knew that they had just started their journey into the mountains, and that they were going slower than they would have liked to. Thomas was the only one who did not have the endurance the other three did, and he knew that they knew it as well. The only good thing about his group was that they did not give him any grief about it. He had not used his Ring so far, but he knew that when push came to shove, he would have to.

Elesa crouched and examined the ground. She said, "I am no

tracker, but are these cart-tracks?"

Emmanuel crouched and saw where she was pointing. Two straight lines, perfectly parallel, not visible unless someone strained their eyes to the spot, were present, heading off into the direction they were planning to go.

Emmanuel said, "Could be a caravan."

Thomas laughed softly and said, "There is no entry point into Covis from the east, except for the Jet-Horn Pass. And we are quite south from there. The closest city, of Tauris, is Askalien. It is far south from Shodor, where we were taken from. Whoever made these tracks is not a friendly person. I can tell you that much with full confidence."

Elesa said, "We should head further up the slopes. Perhaps we will be lucky and then head north without much hindrance."

Edward replied, "No. The peaks of these mountains are very cold. We will be able to survive. Thomas may not be able to survive."

"That is why you are here, Edward. You can keep me warm with your fire."

"Sorry to break it to you, Thomas. I cannot keep my flames up permanently. I will be exhausting my own strength as well as my Guardian's."

"What if you turn your flames on only when I say I cannot handle the cold?"

"That could work."

Emmanuel was paying attention to their conversation, but also keeping a watchful eye on their surroundings. His horns were large, but not large enough to pass for a Bull. But his Guardian, Aral, was a Hump Bull, which meant that he had a high level of endurance and was a good powerhouse, if he had to defend the whole group singlehandedly. His fists were the size of miniature cannonballs, making him the physically strongest people in their entire group of twenty-four. But strength alone did not make a person superior to others, his father had once told him. It was the nature of one's character that made a person strong or weak. Emmanuel had always been brought up with that philosophy. He knew that he was strong, but he knew that there would come a time when he would have to step aside and let someone else take his place.

Just then, Ketta started snarling loudly. All four of them took up their positions. Thomas snuffed out the fire with a strong gust of wind. At first, no sound was heard. Then they heard trees getting pushed out of the way as something large headed towards them.

Emmanuel readied his club, facing the same direction as Ketta. He could make out something was charging towards them, but it looked too thin to be a Battois. Then he realised another thing. The creature heading their way was a quadruped. They had studied about only one type of monster like that. The Underworld Hound broke through the trees and faced the five of them.

Edward let his arms catch fire, to intimidate the Hound. The Hound looked at him, assessing the threat, but did not back away from them. Edward said, "You guys get clear. If I can use my full power, without Ontemp's help, and damage this thing badly, you go in for the kill."

Elesa said, "Not an option for any of us here, Edward. You know that you cannot kill it."

"I did not say I will kill it. I will damage it badly. Then you guys can deliver the final blow."

Emmanuel, keeping his eyes on the monster said, "We still will not be able to. Ake's weapons, which he produced after his Wolf died, could not penetrate the hide of the monster. How are we supposed to even make this one bleed?"

Thomas made his decision. He casually extended his right hand upwards, and brought it down quickly. In front of them, the Hound's legs gave way under it, and it got flattened against the ground.

Emmanuel did not need to ask what he was to do. He charged the Hound, now immobile, and started smashing his club all over its body. Edward glanced at Thomas, who was using a lot of concentration to keep the Hound pinned. Elesa and Ketta too were trying to damage the Hound, but Emmanuel was having more success, which was not saying much. The Hound was getting irritated, but it could not move.

Thomas was feeling the strain of keeping the Hound down, Edward could see. But Edward stood guard over Thomas, so that when Thomas stopped doing what he was doing, Edward could grab him and get him away from the Hound. He knew that Emmanuel and Elesa would be able to hold their own against the monster, but he did not know how long they would be able to fend it off.

Emmanuel could see that the Hound was slowly managing to get up. It had slid one foot underneath its body, as if ready to jump. He knew he could not kill the monster, but he sure could injure it. The Hound had its eyes on Thomas and Edward. Emmanuel knew that Elesa and he would only be hindering it, which is what they wanted.

Elesa and Ketta were not even annoying the Hound. Ketta was more of a threat for the Hound between the two, with her fangs and claws. However, they needed an Acid Hound to kill the Underworld Hound.

Thomas cursed as he felt his concentration wavering. He could only keep the air column above the Hound intact for a few more seconds. In desperation, he lifted it and tried to blast a tornado at the dazed Hound, only to see it fizzle out before it covered even half the distance between them.

The Hound roared loudly and charged towards Thomas and Edward. Emmanuel tried to tackle it to the ground, but the Hound kicked him away. Edward sent his flames at the monster, which had a positive effect and kept the monster from the duo. The Underworld Hound was cornered. It had three options. One was to run away from the group and attack later on. The second option was to run through the flames and fight the duo behind the flames. The last option was to face the trio behind it.

Emmanuel asked, "Anyone have an Acid Hound on call right about now? We could really use the help."

Elesa said, "I do not know about an Acid Hound, but we have a very strong Grey Wolf here."

Edward shouted, "It does not matter, we need to kill this thing now."

The Hound was still unsure which way to go. No one moved closer to it, which was good. Suddenly, it leapt through the flames, causing Emmanuel to freeze in his place. He heard the triumphant roar of the Hound, right before Edward's flames shut off, giving Elesa and Emmanuel a perfect view of what was in front of them.

Somehow, while diving through the flames, the Underworld Hound had managed to judge the distance of Thomas and Edward, and had them pinned to the ground with both its front paws on their sternums. Thomas' eyes were closed, and Emmanuel had a horrible thought. He looked at Elesa, who shook her head slightly, as if indicating to him not to attack the Hound.

Edward had both his palms underneath the Hound's paw, which it did not seem to have noticed. It was busy looking smugly at the trio while not paying attention to what was happening right beneath it. Edward locked eyes with Elesa and his eyes, including the whites, turned orange. The Hound did not notice anything, but when its paw started burning, it looked in surprise at Edward, who roared at it.

Edward grabbed the Hound with one hand, which he had pulled free. He then threw it off Thomas and himself. The Hound got back to its feet, unsure of what to make of Edward. Edward's aura formed a Dragon above him, this time successfully intimidating the Hound, which backed up slowly.

Meanwhile, Elesa ran to Thomas' side and dragged him away towards Emmanuel. Emmanuel checked Thomas' breathing, which was faint but steady. Emmanuel knew that he could not administer carmine to Thomas, in case the latter was in shock, which they could not tell at that moment. They just had to wait and see what would happen.

Edward was forcing the Hound back, but it was getting over its initial shock. It tried to look for an opening, which Edward was not giving. He had Ketta for assistance, who had decided that Elesa could take care of herself. After a few initial snaps from Ketta, the Hound backed off, and suddenly charged an unsuspecting Edward. Ketta saw the quick movement, and ran into its path. The Hound did not expect it and tried to get Ketta's throat within its jaws.

The Hound roared again at Ketta, as if telling her to stay out of its way. Another roar sounded from behind Emmanuel, though it must have been far away. Edward took advantage of the roar and roared himself. The Hound looked positively scared now. A blur of silver raced past Emmanuel and Elesa, seeking out the Hound. Before the Hound could do anything, it was pinned to the ground. The animal holding it in place was a majestic animal, with silver and black hair over its body, rippling muscles held together in a lean frame, dark eyes and very furry white tail.

The Underworld Hound tried to snap at the new animal, but the Wolf would not budge. It opened its mouth, to reveal two very large teeth, each three inches long. It closed its jaws around the Hound, killing it instantly.

The Acid Hound turned away from the corpse and walked away from the group, but not before running and slamming into Edward to knock him out of his beast form.

Edward got up and said, "I do not need anything. How is Thomas holding up?"

Emmanuel said, "Just about there. Not sure how long he will be knocked out. What happened to him?"

"The Hound leapt through the flames, catching me off-guard. It pinned me down and slammed Thomas into the ground with a lot more force than me. I did not hear any bones breaking, but the only thing we can give him is some blocker."

"He is not bleeding."

"Not that we can see, Emmanuel," Elesa said.

Edward said, "Maybe blocker can work on internal bleeding. We have to take a chance. That Ring will not be coming off, unless he gives it of his own free will. For now, the Ring is safe."

"Unlike the rest of you." A new voice sounded from in front of them. A man stood about fifty feet away from them. His coat looked like different animal pelts stitched together. He carried a stick which looked like an unfinished sword. He gripped what Elesa assumed was the hilt. From the hilt came a thin golden metal piece. It looked as if the man was holding a sword, but without any blades. The weapon would still be formidable if the man got too close for their comfort.

Ketta put herself between the four teenagers and the man, snarling loudly at him. The man sighed.

"Look. I will make this clear only once. I need your Ring Bearer and this one."

He pointed to Edward with his free hand.

Edward calmly asked the man, "And if we refuse?"

The man held his weapon at shoulder level and pressed a button on the hilt. Two blades emerged throughout the length of the thin metal piece. The man was holding a short broadsword. The blades were about three feet long and had an intricate design on them.

"I always get what I want. Do not test me."

Edward cracked his knuckles and said, "I hope you said goodbye to the blade because it is about to get melted right out of your hilt."

The man's eyes betrayed a sign of regret and he said, "You will be sorry about this."

"We will see."

Before Edward could hit the man with his flames, Ketta lunged at the man. He neatly sidestepped her and brought the hilt of his sword down on her head. Ketta hit the ground and did not move. Behind Edward, Elesa screamed in pain and anger. Edward understood that she must have felt Ketta's pain in her mind, as they were still merged. The man did not pay any attention to her as she ran behind him towards Ketta. Edward blasted red flames at the man, who made no attempt to dodge them. He got enveloped in flames. Out of nowhere, he appeared in front of Edward and swung the flat of his blade into Edward's stomach with so much force that Ontemp and Edward unmerged. Ontemp landed next to Emmanuel, but managed to get up again. He roared at the man, who simply looked up and grabbed an unconscious Edward by his shirt and stared down the Dragon. He pointed to Thomas, who was half-awake and said, "I will be back for him soon. Turn around and go back home while you still can."

The man disappeared in a flash of golden light, leaving Emmanuel, Thomas and Ontemp facing a broken Elesa. They walked ran towards her, only to see her holding an Emerald in her hand. She was very still, which unnerved Emmanuel. She asked, "Edward has been taken?"

Emmanuel had never been a person who liked to intrude into someone's personal space, but he put his arm around Elesa and said, "Yes."

Elesa turned to look at him, determination written in her eyes. She passed the Emerald into her arm-guard. She gripped her sword tightly and said, "We need to make sure that Edward gets his Citrine, fast."

"Yes. But first, we need to get to safety."

Elesa surprised him by saying, in an almost threatening manner, "There is no safety! They can find us, if they search systematically, don't you get it? We just need to push harder and find the palace."

Emmanuel said, “I get your point. But how are we supposed to hide a big Dragon like Ontemp? He is not exactly a stealth machine.”

Ontemp, in the meantime, was laying waste to all the trees he could find, torching them with his breath and trampling them underfoot. Elesa looked at him and said, “Give me two minutes, and we will not have to bother about that.”

Emmanuel realised what she wanted to do. He asked, “Are you thinking straight? Ontemp will easily squash you or fly out of your sword range.”

“No, he will not.” Elesa said it with such conviction that Emmanuel nearly believed her. Thomas looked at Ontemp, who was eyeing the approaching Elesa with a careful eye.

Elesa had her regular sword in her hand, which Emmanuel was sure would break on contact with Ontemp’s scales. However, Elesa stabbed her sword into the ground and took five steps forward towards Ontemp, producing her own green sword, fifteen feet tall. She slashed it a few times in the air, with Ontemp betraying no sign of fear. She shouted at Ontemp, “Get over here, Ontemp. NOW!”

Emmanuel watched her as Ontemp moved towards her, one eye on her and one eye on her sword. Emmanuel would not have had the guts to do anything like Elesa, not when he had to face something that could make short work of him without touching him.

Meanwhile, Elesa was saying, “You will help Edward, you hear me? Now, stay still. Your use as an animal is nearing its end. Your true use will be coming soon. Thank you, for taking care of Edward.”

Ontemp tilted his head. He towered over Elesa by twenty metres, his head just five metres above the tip of her sword. He lowered his head and without hesitation, Elesa swung her sword in a deadly arc.

Emmanuel expected Ontemp’s head to get separated from his body, but the moment the sword connected with his skin, there was a flash of orange and green light. When the light cleared, Emmanuel could see Elesa holding a Citrine gem in her palm. She turned to Emmanuel and Thomas, who were staring at her in disbelief.

She looked at them and asked in a surprised voice, "What happened to you guys? Are we going to move on ahead or not?"

Thomas smirked and said, "Well, we do not have any other plans for today."

Emmanuel was about to move along with them, but a thought struck him.

"Elesa, if we keep heading up, we play right into our enemies' hands. The only way to stop that is to head back to the closest city for cover."

"Then you take Thomas and run for cover. I do not do the whole "cover" thing. Make your choice. I have made mine."

Elesa gave him a look of defiance. She crossed her arms, waiting for Emmanuel to make up his mind.

Emmanuel shook his head and said, "You are crazy. Unfortunately, so am I."

Emmanuel and Aral unmerged. Aral did not look tired at all. Emmanuel told Thomas, "Get up."

"Why?"

"It could be the fact that you have exhausted yourself to a great extent and that we want you to stay alert at all times. Now, if you would please get up on him, we will be able to get on with our lives." Emmanuel replied dryly.

Thomas nodded and got onto Aral. The Bull did not seem to mind and they were on their way soon.

After an hour of climbing a gentle slope, they encountered a waterfall. It was about fifty metres high and came cascading down to a small lake.

The lake itself must have been about hundred metres across, if not more. They could not tell how deep it was. The water was fresh, as Aral had no problem drinking it. They decided to stop there for some time.

Elesa watched Thomas very closely, making sure that he did not disappear anywhere. However, Emmanuel and she would be requiring food to sustain themselves soon. They did not have any predator with them that they could have used to fetch food. Just then, Thomas screamed from the shore of the lake. Emmanuel and Elesa charged down to see what was going on.

Thomas was lying flat on the ground, Aral standing over him. Thomas' eyes were open wide, as if he had been stunned. There was nothing around them that could have been a threat. Aral saw Emmanuel coming towards him and bellowed and pointed his horns towards the water.

Emmanuel did not turn his back to the water, in case he was attacked. He waded a good five feet into the lake, where the water came to the level of his ankles. He took his club and brought it down with full force into the water. As expected, he hit solid rock. He mustered some more courage and waded five more feet into the lake. Here, the water was coming to the level of his knees. He brought his club down again. This time the club hit something not as hard as rock and stayed stuck to it, as if the club was inside a crack. What happened next was proof that Emmanuel could respond faster to life-threatening situations than he originally thought he could.

As he tried to get his club out of the crack, he felt something graze against his leg. He could see a dark shape moving towards him. He again tried to pull his club free. In desperation, he put his head underwater to see why his club was not coming free. All he could see in the dim light was a circle of black, enclosed in a ring of green. His club was stuck one foot from the edge of the ring. Emmanuel shot his head out of the water, just in time to see the dark shape emerge from the water. He knew that he was doomed.

The Yoknie was the very personification of power. Its head was about five feet back to front. The eyes were the size of dinner plates. The neck was twenty feet long, connecting the head to a body that Emmanuel would have thought difficult to manoeuvre. The body was probably fifty feet all the way around, but that did not matter. It could have easily body-slammed Emmanuel into the water and killed him, but Emmanuel ran to the shore for all he was worth, registering everything within two seconds. Elesa stopped him from running away from them, turned him around and asked, "Any idea on how to kill these things?"

Emmanuel shook his head and said, "There are two of them. One we can see. The other is right below my club. We do not have the strength of numbers. We are safe here, as they cannot come onto dry land and get back into water. Those bodies may be easy to move underwater, with water buoying them up. But on land, with no water, they are subject to gravity."

"I did not ask for an explanation on their limits. I asked for a way to kill them."

"We cannot kill them. We would have to get close to them, which means that we risk making contact with their skin. I only waded out ten feet and by then, I had knee level water. I do not know how deep this lake is, and I am not anxious to be dragged underwater to find out."

"So, if we can't touch them, I suggest we prod them."

"What do you mean by that?"

Thomas had taken the safety of the shrubs around to hide himself from the monsters, not that it did him any good.

Elesa said, "If we can injure them from the shore, maybe they will die from their wounds."

Twin green swords were produced in her hands. Emmanuel laughed at them and said, "You might need a bow and arrows for pulling off your little stunt. My club is stuck over there." He pointed to where he thought his club was, only to see a second Yoknie emerge from the water. This one was a copy of the first and both the monsters eyed the objects on the beach. Emmanuel's club was nowhere to be seen near the eyes of the second Yoknie, which meant that Emmanuel was without a weapon.

Elesa looked at her swords and said, "If they cannot come onto land, we have to get into the water."

Thomas spoke from behind them, "I can help you with that."

Both Elesa and Emmanuel asked, "How?"

"I can hover Elesa above the lake. From there, keep attacking them with any missile weapon. They may not register your gem-produced weapons as physical weapons."

Emmanuel shrugged his shoulders and said, "Could you give me a club?"

"Sure."

Emmanuel stood guard over Thomas as he attempted to levitate Elesa above the lake, with her shouting directions at him. The heads of the monsters were visible above the surface of the water. Emmanuel made sure that Elesa was at least thirty feet above the water, to get her out of the Yoknies' attacking range.

Once Elesa was aligned, she started producing javelins and spears, hurling them at the monsters. As expected, the weapons either adhered to their skin or glanced off harmlessly. Elesa gestured at Thomas to get her closer to the surface, but Emmanuel forbade him from doing that. He was not sure how deep the lake was, for the monsters to make a dive and then shoot out of the water to get Elesa in their jaws.

Just then, one of the Yoknies roared loudly, causing Emmanuel's eardrums to beg for mercy. Thomas got the worse end of it. He fell to the ground, keeping Elesa in the air, but he could not focus on blocking his ears as well as keep her afloat in the air. The roar sounded like a Lion's roar, mixed with a Bull's bellow and a Wolf's howl.

Emmanuel stood up after the roar subsided, his legs shaking a bit. It was as if the roar had gone through his entire body, leaving his muscles a bit shaken. He hauled Thomas to his feet. They looked up to where Elesa was supposed to be, only to see an empty space above the water.

Thomas looked absolutely gutted. Emmanuel turned to chew him out and saw that Thomas was not ready to forgive himself. Emmanuel calmed himself down and said, "Look, she would not have gone down easily. She has strong survival instincts. We have to trust that she is not dead."

Just then, one Yoknie jumped out of the water, heading right for the trio. Emmanuel backed up, dragging Thomas with him. The Yoknie beached itself. They waited for something to happen to the body. Then, from the stomach of the monster, two green sword blades sliced out and Elesa walked out of the hole she had created in the belly of the beast. She had a few cuts on her face, but was relatively unharmed. She pointed one sword at the other monster and said, "We need to kill that one. As long as it is alive in the water, we will not be able to have peace in this area."

Emmanuel said, "Perhaps we could bait it to come closer to the shore and beach itself."

Thomas spoke, "Their heads are pretty big. I suppose they have brains that size, which help in deciding whether to commit suicide or not."

"Thomas, cut the sarcasm. Elesa, step aside please."

Elesa was confused as to what Emmanuel was going to do, but stepped aside. Emmanuel caught the Yoknie's neck joint and started to pull it ashore. Elesa and Thomas understood what he wanted to do and helped him bring the body out of the water. Thomas asked Emmanuel, "What do you plan to do with this fellow?"

He gestured towards the dead monster body.

"Elesa, would you be kind as to dice up this fellow? Preferably into bite size pieces that we can store in our bags."

Elesa understood what Emmanuel wanted to do. She brought out two long and thin swords. Emmanuel gathered twigs from the ground and got a fire going soon. Elesa worked hard and cleaved flesh from bone very cleanly. She tossed the meat to the boys, who had a skewer ready for the meat. Some meat she stuffed into their bags.

Meanwhile, Aral stood guard over them, facing the way they had come. All the fat that Elesa found in the body went into the bags without any second thought. Some meat was thrown into the water. Maybe it was to feed the second Yoknie in the water, or maybe Elesa was doing it out of spite. Emmanuel was not about to question a girl with two deadly swords in her hands.

After about an hour, Elesa tossed the last of the meat into the water. She was sweating a lot, so Emmanuel suggested that she clean and freshen up in the lake, just wading out two feet into it. Elesa gave him a deadpan expression, but did what he suggested anyway. The three of them sat near the fire and ate the cooked Yoknie meat.

Thomas was apprehensive at first, but he ate his share quietly. Aral was watching over them, grazing on the grass close to them. They heard the Yoknie coming above the water and moaning sadly. But they did not pay it any attention.

Thomas asked, "Elesa, what was it like in the Yoknie's body? I do not want to experience it, though. Just tell us."

Elesa brought out a sword. For a moment, Emmanuel thought that she might use it on them, but Elesa let it vanish.

She said, "I saw the monster coming up from way below the surface. You lost your concentration and I fell down into its' mouth as it shot out of the water. At the last moment, I summoned a spear and went through the neck, right down to the stomach. I took my chances that the monster was a mammal, which paid off, as it came up to breathe as it was dying. Now we know how to kill these things. The stomach itself was not very big, though I had enough space to move around. I could hardly see any acid in the stomach, though there must have been."

Emmanuel said, "Let us just hope you do not have to do anymore of these suicide missions."

Behind them, Aral let out a low bellow. Emmanuel understood.

"Come on guys. We cannot stay here too long. We have to keep moving. We need to find the palace, fall back, summon the others, and then storm the palace."

Elesa swallowed the last of her meat and tossed her skewer into the fire. She stood up and glanced towards the water. The pieces of meat were not visible, which meant that the Yoknie must have eaten them.

Emmanuel walked over to Aral and patted his head.

"Time to merge, Aral. We got to stick with each other from here on."

Aral gave Emmanuel a look of boredom, as if he had heard those words many times over. Nevertheless, Emmanuel was soon bulked up, with horns coming out of his head and his club on his shoulder.

Thomas stayed between Elesa and Emmanuel. He was the most wanted person out of the three of them. He had to make sure he was not captured.

Over the next two hours, Emmanuel and Elesa took the three of them higher up into the mountains. By now, snow was taking over the ground. First, it was in small patches. Then an entire plateau of snow revealed itself. They rested themselves there, on Emmanuel's command. Thomas immediately flung himself onto the ground and started to make a snow angel. Emmanuel chuckled, but then he glanced back at Elesa, who looked as if she was going to be sick. She was standing just two feet from the edge of the plateau, and her swaying motion made Emmanuel rush to her side and pull her away from the edge. Thomas saw what happened and shot up from his snow angel. Emmanuel lay Elesa down on the ground while Thomas forced more air into her lungs. Elesa gasped and her pupils dilated and constricted violently and erratically, causing both the boys to panic. Thomas asked, “Is this normal for you guys? I thought that you could survive extremes.”

Emmanuel studied Elesa’s eyes and said, “I am speculating here. This is not a problem related to how well we function. This might be an internal problem of hers that we do not know about. Whether she knows about it or not, we will have to wait and ask her.”

Thomas did not know what else he could do to ease Elesa’s pain. They could have tried carmine on her, but Elesa was not in shock, so giving carmine to her could have negative effects on her systems. He took off his coat and put it on Elesa, to provide her with some warmth. Emmanuel was sitting cross-legged, next to her. His horns were almost straight, but they curved backwards towards the top. They were twisted throughout their length, making them look like a type of corkscrew. He did not seem to have any problem with the cold, though sometimes he hugged himself tightly, as if to prevent the warmth from leaving his body.

Thomas watched as Elesa started shivering, despite the coat being on her. Her left eye slammed shut and she turned uncontrollably onto her left side. Emmanuel did not hesitate.

He grabbed Elesa and put his arms under hers, bringing his hands to her face level, where he held her by the neck and jaws. Thomas thought that Emmanuel had lost his sanity, and produced a whip. He snapped it once on the ground, as a warning. But Emmanuel said, “No! I have to do this, to ensure that nobody gets hurt.”

“You will break her bones!”

“I will not! Trust me, this is something I have dealt with before, though never this extreme.”

Thomas nodded, but kept his whip ready. Elesa stopped shivering after what seems like a long time. Thomas waited for Emmanuel to release her, which he did not. Instead, he did something that Thomas thought would have earned him a death sentence by Elesa, who had made it clear to them that she did not like being touched.

Emmanuel let go of Elesa's head and let it drop down slowly. He put his hands around her chest, as if giving her a hug. Elesa looked almost dead, but Emmanuel did not think so. He held her for five minutes, while signalling Thomas to provide some warmth. Thomas did not know what to do. The plateau was not protected by natural elements, and the wind was piercing through him. He needed a fire, or something equivalent to it. He decided on something that Clint had once told him many years back, though he did not believe it would work.

He held his Ring out and concentrated on the air particles around Emmanuel and Elesa. He willed them to stop. Once he was sure that he was on the right track, he got them to move slowly across only Emmanuel's skin, picking up speed by and by. He wanted Emmanuel to tell him if he could feel any heat from the wind that he was producing. Emmanuel could not figure out what Thomas was doing. He furrowed his eyebrows at Thomas, but Thomas kept at it. When Emmanuel figured out Thomas' plan, he nodded, signalling that he could feel the heat. Thomas then concentrated that same wind onto Elesa's body. He could not tell if she was getting the warmth or not, but he kept at it. Emmanuel nodded encouragement to him, as if he could tell whether Elesa was getting warmer. When Thomas could take no more, he stopped the wind altogether and threw his coat over Elesa, to keep whatever little warmth she had, near her body.

Emmanuel spread out his own coat on the snow-covered ground and put Elesa on it. She was breathing, though it sounded almost forced. Emmanuel took Thomas aside and said, "What Elesa had was an epileptic fit. I realised that the moment she started to shiver under your coat."

"Then why did you catch her the way you did?"

"When you have a fit, or an "attack," as we sometimes say, you tend to lose control of your body. Your brain enters into a different state and you yourself do not know what you are doing. A lot of energy is expended by the body, more than what would normally be used to do those actions that you are performing during the attack. All inhibitors in the brain are shut down. That's where all the power comes from. A normal epileptic attack lasts for a maximum of a minute. For your main question, I held her the way I did, because her head was in danger of twisting her neck muscles beyond repair. The head and neck are always the first to get the extra energy boost. Now, we have to wait for her to wake up. The energy expended by her body will take its toll. She will not be waking up highly energised. She will still feel tired. So that means that we will be on this plateau for a while."

"How do you think she got this? She was perfectly fine till this point."

Emmanuel glanced back to make sure Elesa was still where they had kept her.

"I have a few theories. One is that her attack was natural. I have had it as well, when I was younger. It passes on, and you soon forget about it, but there is no telling when it can occur again. Another theory is that her Guardian is trying to fight her for complete dominance of her mind, and that struggle is being brought to the surface. A third theory is there, but it seems like the least likely."

"What is that?"

"Her Guardian died while she was still merged to it, right? So maybe that last bit of pain that she felt in her mind caused her to snap."

Thomas noticed that Emmanuel was sounding as if he was trying to convince himself that the last theory was plain wrong.

They spent the better part of half an hour waiting for Elesa to wake up, sparring with each other, careful not to let anything happen to her. When Elesa woke up, she gasped for breath, as if she had stopped breathing altogether. Emmanuel and Thomas helped her slowly sit up, using their bags as backrests. Emmanuel made her eat some Yoknie meat, to get her energised.

Through bites, she asked, "Did we stop here to nap, or to wait for monsters?"

Thomas exchanged dark looks with Emmanuel. He asked Elesa, "What do you remember, before you went to sleep?"

"Well, I was feeling a bit dizzy. Then, if I am not wrong, Emmanuel helped me lie down. How long was I out for?"

Emmanuel looked Elesa dead in the eye and said, "You were out for about half an hour. The thing is you did not go to sleep. You were swaying at the edge of the plateau, as you were dizzy."

Then Emmanuel recounted the incident to Elesa, who took it quite calmly. She said, "Well, I have heard of epileptic attacks, though I have never had one myself, until today as you just said. As for your theories, well, I can say that the third one is probably the most valid one. If we are what the Trainers said we are, a problem such as epilepsy should not be hindering us or our bodies. So I am not exactly buying your first theory."

Emmanuel said, "You are taking this news better than I expected. I guess this kind of makes you the tougher one in our little group."

Elesa laughed, "I suppose it does."

Thomas was half listening to their conversation, while half listening for monsters. As they were on an open plateau, only Jides would get the jump on them. But there were no screams to be heard. Only silence was around him, save for the duo talking behind him. He glanced back, where Emmanuel was saying something to Elesa, his hand half-outstretched, as if he was unsure whether to touch her or not, to reassure her that she was alright.

Elesa had no such inhibitions. She grabbed Emmanuel's hand and placed it on her shoulder. Emmanuel looked almost mortified, as if he had thought Elesa was never going to let him touch her again. But Elesa seemed chilled about it. Thomas wondered where the palace of Yedgal was, and when they would come across it. Thomas let his thoughts wander out to Clint and the others. Apart from Clint, Chris and James, he never let himself be emotionally involved with anyone in their group of two dozen teenagers. He considered it dangerous to do so. If something were to happen to anyone, and he were emotionally involved with that person, he would get emotionally compromised. In his place, he could not afford to get emotionally compromised.

Elesa seemed to be breaking down his normally unbreakable resolve, without meaning to. He couldn't help feeling an urge to tell her to stop being herself. But he got rudely distracted by a Constry which tried to sneak up on him.

It was not as if he had spotted the monster. He saw Emmanuel lock eyes onto something behind him, and throw his club at him. Thomas instinctively ducked and rolled to his right. As he glanced up to see what had happened, he saw the club stuck half way through the skull of the Constry, with the latter trying to get a grip on the club. Elesa did not waste a second. She leapt at the four handed creature, producing a green sword, seven feet long. The Constry's head rolled across the snow and came to a stop near Thomas' feet. He kicked it away and asked, sarcastically, "Are we going to cook this fellow as well, or leave the body here to rot away?"

Elesa just rolled her eyes at Thomas. Her sword vanished and her nails extended. Thomas was afraid that she might use her nails on him, but she used them to rip through the chest cavity of the monster. She pulled out its heart and threw it down the side of the plateau. Thomas had seen worse stuff than a heart being exposed, but the way Elesa did it was another level altogether. Thomas would not be getting that image out of his mind any time soon. He was thankful that he did not have a memory like Emmanuel or Clint. The body was thrown down as well, courtesy Emmanuel. The trio glanced up at the rugged mountainside in front of them.

Pointed rocks were jutting out like piercing needles. Thick white mist curled across the ground, obscuring their view in places. The white snow created a great contrast against the dark ground. The tree line stopped abruptly about one kilometre above them, as if the trees had come to a mutual agreement to not go any further. The enormity of their mission had already made an impression on Thomas. But he only just realised how drastic the consequences would be, if they failed.

There was a moment of silence that surrounded the trio. Emmanuel broke the silence and said, "Well, I guess we start finding a way to and above the mountains."

Elesa nodded. She shouldered her bag, which contained their food. Emmanuel had taken over Thomas' bag of potions and Edward's armour and had kept everything in his own bag. Only Edward's bag was not there, as they had lost it in the heat of the battle with the Constries before Edward was kidnapped. Thomas hoped that it would be lost forever, never to be recovered by anyone. In the wrong hands, that bag would be very dangerous. In the hands of someone who did not know what they were, the potions would do worse than just kill that person. Emmanuel made no effort to hide his horns under his hood, now that they were far from any town.

Elesa sniffed the air and said, "Up there, we will have to watch each other's backs. I hope I do not have to save you many times."

Thomas said, "No need for you to do that. I got eyes at the back of my head."

Elesa laughed, but Emmanuel remained stoic.

"I hope you are right. We have wasted enough time here. Let's keep moving."

# CHAPTER 20

Vincent slashed and tore through the Battois that were in his way. He used his sharp claws to rip through their major muscle groups, where all their crucial veins and arteries were. He had studied animal physiology well, and was using his knowledge to great effect. He could not afford to go back to finish the job, lest he get caught off-guard and get hit with their fiery breath. He had not needed to go into his beast mode yet, and he preferred it to remain that way. Meanwhile, Adriana was hurling rock after rock at the monsters, trying to stay away from them as much as possible. But out of every ten rocks she hurled, eight got blasted with fire, yielding no result. The other two rocks only seemed to stun the Battois, not kill them.

James was having a bit of trouble in the air, keeping the Jides away from the ground and focussed on himself. His knife throwing prowess was second to none, except probably Garon's dagger throwing skills. James had first sported three toes on each foot and the same number of fingers per hand, when he first came to Equis with his group. He had white wings that were so feathery, Victoria had joked that they could use his wings as warm blankets for when they went to sleep. Now, however, James looked like a normal person, with five fingers and five toes per limb, although he now sported black, mirage-like wings and his knives were the same colour. James was getting closer and closer to the ground, almost as if he was luring the Jides towards the Battois, hoping that the Battois would aim their fire at the Jides.

Victoria was the first to notice this. She threw the dead bodies of Battois towards the ones still alive, in an attempt to distract them and make a run for it. She managed to keep at it, but one Battos got smart and lunged for her, grabbing her hand. Victoria barely had time to use her powers on the monster, when it threw her into the air straight towards James, knocking him out of the air. He instinctively grabbed Victoria by her stomach, wrapped his wings around her and fell like a stone towards the ground. He yelled in pain as his wings made contact with the ground. Victoria understood that the pain in his wings must have felt the same as in his arms, if his arms had hit the ground in the same manner. To James' credit, he did not let the pain stop him.

He furled in his wings, and they disappeared behind his back. Two jet-black swords formed in his hands. He took a step away from Victoria and surveyed the group of seven Battois and many Jides closing in on them. The Jides did not seem interested on getting close to the Battois, due to the latter's flames. That was fine by James. One less threat to deal with. He remembered what Chris had told him, when Chris had first lost his Guardian.

James said, "Victoria, shut your ears."

Without waiting for a response, James screeched as loud as he could, going as high as he could dare. The Battois in front of him and some around him clutched their ears and bellowed. Some of the monsters faced downwards, their breath setting the field on fire. Some faced upwards and did the same, killing most of the Jides. The ones that did not help in James' cause, he started swinging his swords at. There was no quarter given by James. Vincent on the other hand, was almost toying with his set of Battois. He was roaring at them, and taking small steps towards them, though in a circular fashion, almost menacingly. James wondered why beasts, nearly twice Vincent's size, were backing away from the latter. Then he saw it.

Vincent's eyes were glowing yellow, which was nomal, as he was merged with his Guardian. The problem was, it was not just his iris that was yellow. Both his eyes were yellow, with a thin slit of black running across their length. As the trio watched on, some of the

Battois ran away from him, being smart enough to understand what their fate would be if they stuck around. The stupider Battois, however, stood their ground. They roared right back at Vincent, sending a huge wall of flames towards him. When the flames shut off, Vincent was nowhere to be seen. Only a flaming area of grass was visible. James' heart was in his mouth, as he saw the monsters turn to face Victoria, Adriana, and himself. He readied his two swords while the girls got into fighting stances. As the two groups regarded each other, a roar sounded from behind the trio. It was louder than James' screech.

Vincent leapt in front of them, roaring in defiance. A yellow aura emanated from his body, solidifying into the figure of a roaring Lion. His claws elongated and he charged the Battois alone, without waiting for backup. He moved so swiftly; James had trouble following his movements. Within seconds, a group of about twenty Battois had been reduced to dead bodies. James saw Vincent coming towards them, his eyes still lit up. James put his swords away and said, "Adriana, make sure that he stays where he is. I need to bring him back to normal."

Adriana pointed her Ring at Vincent's feet, where the ground rose up halfway to his knees. Vincent tried to move, but was stuck. James produced a club, walked up to Vincent and hit him in the stomach. The yellow glow subsided from Vincent's eyes, after four or five direct hits.

He caught James' shoulders for support, saying, "That was insane!" He grinned like a madman, causing James to laugh as well. James gestured to Adriana to let Vincent go, which she did. Vincent was a bit heavier than James, but James managed to support him and got him on the ground, where he waved away both carmine and sweenet. James recounted the incident, and Vincent listened with full attention.

Vincent said, "I remember unleashing carnage, though my view was quite crazy."

Adriana patted him on the back and laughed.

"We live in a world of crazy, Vincent. What did you see?"

"Well, until I let Nilesh take over control, I had normal vision. When I unleashed him, it was as if I had got tunnel vision. I saw no friends, no enemies. I saw only threats. My first instinct was to go for the bigger threats, so you guys got saved. I guess the Guardians do not see people as threats, even ones with their own Guardians. No offence, though."

Victoria examined her arms, showing off her scales. She said, "I wonder whether we too can do the same. Unleash our Guardians and wreak havoc, and all that, I mean."

James glanced at Vincent, wondering whether he would tell the truth or not. But Vincent did not know that James had been on the field, the night the six of them were spoken to confidentially by the Trainers. Vincent sat up straight and said, "Perhaps you could. I am not sure. Maybe one day we will find out."

James raised an eyebrow and said, nonchalantly, "You do not sound so confident about that, my friend."

Vincent shrugged his shoulders, evidently wanting to get off the topic. He nodded towards the south, where clouds obscured their view of the only west-facing port of Equis, Cylinx. They were a few leagues from the city, but only two leagues above sea level. The main problem was that they were about three leagues from it, if they were on the ground. That gave them a direct distance of about three and a half leagues to cover, if they decided to jump off the mountain they were on, assuming the winds would carry them safely. Practically, only James would be able to make that move. The others would have to traverse five leagues of rough terrain to make it to the port.

Vincent asked, "Anyone ever been to Cylinx?"

Adriana said, "I know the port. That's my hometown. I am giving you a heads-up from now. That city is one of the few cities of Lasgalan where you have to fight for everything. Being so far away from every other city, it developed a different personality. You might find it strange to see little to no military power there, but the citizens guard the city with all their heart. Let me do the talking, and you may survive."

Vincent did not like the way she said the word "may". But he nodded. Below them was their first stop. He knew that he would have to come up with an excuse as to why he had hair sprouting from his neck, by the time they reached the port. James also realised this. He tossed his own cloak to Vincent, saying, "Use this as a cover-up. They might mistake it for a fur coat you are wearing."

Adriana looked over the side of a cliff, as if gauging how far down they could jump in one go, without breaking their bones. She said, "In order to make sure that we do not lose sight, or feel of each other, we will have to descend down the side of this mountain tied together. James, if you want, you can fly solo, but remain close to us. You may be able to see us better at a distance, through the clouds. You can also help guide us to spots on the mountainside, where we can rest for a while."

James looked up at the sun, which was nearing its zenith. After their breakfast, they had survived only on small game like rabbits and baby deer. But Vincent and Victoria were soon going to be running on fumes, as their Guardians, being predators were going to be asking for more energy to stay merged with them. How they were staying merged was a mystery to James. He did not have to worry about getting separated from Riyo, who had died taking a Battos flame to himself, in order to protect Vincent, who had been knocked unconscious by another Battos. James had unmerged, and given Riyo instructions to protect Vincent. James was happy that he did not have a merging like that of Elesa or Ake, with a telepathic link. The last thing he wanted was Riyo's last thoughts to be permanently stuck in his head.

Vincent glanced at Adriana and asked, "You sure you may not get us killed?"

"Ha! I grew up over there. I know how the system works. Besides, you are important to our plan. We cannot afford to lose you."

Vincent said, “I’m sold. Let’s do this.”

Victoria brought out some rope from her bag. She said, “This rope is not two leagues long, so we will have to be close to each other as we head down.”

Vincent took one end of the rope and tied it around himself. He waited while the girls tied it around themselves. Vincent volunteered to stay as their anchor on the top, until they found a place to stop or when the rope would be extended as much as possible, whichever one came first. He let the girls go down, while he used some of his Guardian’s strength to stay steady. James unfurled his wings and dropped off the cliff, watching the girls go down slowly. He watched as they came in and out of his view, courtesy the clouds in his way. He waited for the rope to suddenly become tense, so that he could see where the girls had ended up and tell Vincent to plan his descent accordingly.

Vincent, on the other hand, hated his role. His javelin was strapped to his back, with his bag on his shoulders. He wanted to be at the girl’s side to protect them. But he had learned the hard way, that the males of, at least Leonis, if not Lasgalan, were the ones who had to step aside and let the women do what they wished. His mother was a hard woman to please. She was mostly the reason that Vincent was who he was. He was constantly pushing himself to his limits, to find out whether he could go beyond his current power level. Once, he had tried to break an army record of the longest accurate javelin throw. The record was one kilometre. He trained for six months before the main event. On that day, he had walked up to the javelin, picked it up and threw it with so much power, that he ended up tearing both his hamstrings, dislocating his right shoulder and breaking two ribs, almost puncturing his right lung. Six months of slow recovery and eight surgeries got him back on his feet. His throw had gone accurately for half a league, breaking the army record by a little more than a full kilometre. He thought that his mother would now be pleased, but all he got was a hint of a smile. The few times that he did get a proper smile was when he did something that was rare or unheard of. Patrick was not his biological brother. His parents made sure that he knew that. By a law in Leonis, an adopted child inherited equal part of the family's fortunes, as did the child's sibling or siblings. But, if the biological child of the parents could prove that the former was not related by blood to the parents, the adopted sibling would gain nothing, unless by discretion of the biological sibling. The problem was, Vincent and Patrick were the same age, sixteen. They did not share the same birthday, but that did not stop them from pretending to be twins.

Just then, Vincent felt the rope starting to tighten around his waist. He grabbed the rope with both hands and stood his ground. He waited for James to come and tell him what to do while descending, but heard a scream instead. It was definitely James. Vincent did not hesitate. He roared and jumped off the cliff, headfirst. He could smell all three of his friends, but he smelt a lot of smoke as well. That could not be good news. He waited till the last second, before raking his claws against the rocky surface. He came to a stop two feet from Adriana, who was holding on for dear life to the side of the mountain. James was fastened to the side of the mountain by iron clips. Then Vincent understood what was wrong.

"Where is Victoria?"

Adriana gestured weakly towards the ground. Vincent knew that he could not be in two places at the same time. He wanted to release Nilesh to follow Victoria's scent. But they were still too high for Nilesh to survive the fall. Vincent cursed his luck. He carefully made his way to James. He ripped off the iron clips from his hands. James fell through the clouds, but levelled out and came back to them. Vincent came back to Victoria's position and grabbed her end of the rope.

He asked, "What happened?"

James said, "They came out of nowhere. They rode up the slope, as if it was no big deal. Straight out of the clouds. I did not even see them coming. It was as if they were…" Whatever he was about to say, Vincent realised, was best not said out loud.

Adriana said, "I have never seen horses so fast, so agile. I tried to rip out sections of the slope to slow them down, at least. They just skirted around the rubble, as if it was nothing."

Vincent said, "James, I need you to go ahead of us and try to track these people. Kill them if you can. But make sure that Victoria is not touched, harmed or dishonoured in any way."

"No problem. But how are you going to catch up to me? You still have to scale down this mountain. Then cross Unicorn pass, if those people have made it that far. It is not one of the safest places in Lasgalan for an attack to be launched, even I can tell you that much."

Vincent smirked and said, "An attack by a large army is different from an attack by me."

"Yes, it is. You will die faster." James said coldly.

Vincent faced Adriana and asked, "Do you trust me?"

"With my life? At this point, I would say yes. But given what your nature is, not really."

Vincent shrugged his shoulders and said, "Fair enough."

James launched himself from the rocks and disappeared into the clouds. Vincent bundled up the rope, grabbed Adriana's waist and let go of the mountainside. They fell fast, and Adriana was sure that they would break their bones on impact with the ground. Vincent evidently did not think so. He kept scraping his claws against the rocks, but they were not slowing down at all. As the ground came into view, they could see that the ground had suddenly become a slope that they could use to come to a gentle stop. Vincent suddenly kicked his legs against the rocks, and they got propelled forward. They hit the ground, and Vincent felt his knees get a bad shock. He dropped Adriana and rolled onto the ground, hugging his knees. The pain was not excruciating, but he knew that he would not be able to walk ahead, forget run, properly and without pain.

Adriana, meanwhile, had dug into her bag, and produced sweenet. She gave Vincent some, and he could feel his knees popping back into position. He gingerly tested his weight on his legs. He walked slowly, Adriana next to him.

Adriana said, “We have managed to get down here. But how do we track James?”

Vincent closed his eyes and concentrated on the sounds around him. He did not have Ake's hearing abilities, but he knew sounds. He knew that James would be somewhere ahead of them, which served his purpose well. He knew that in Equis, low snorts of Horses were common, not loud roars of Lions.

He roared loud and clear. It was a good thing that there was no snow-covered hill around them, or else there could have been an avalanche. He waited for the sound to die out, as it was echoing off the mountain that they had just descended. They waited. No sound was heard. Vincent did not get worried. He did it again. Again, no response.

Adriana said, “Vincent, he may be too far away from us to hear you. Let's just move ahead. He knows our destination. We will meet up there.”

Vincent scanned their surroundings. Trees started ahead of them. But the problem was that Vincent needed food to sustain his Guardian. He took two steps and instantly felt his entire orientation with the ground change. He flipped around in the trap, trying to align himself properly. He was in a net, suspended fifteen feet above the ground by a rope that was wound around a branch of the nearest tree. He heard a rush of people coming towards him, from behind the trees. He saw that Adriana had hidden herself from plain view. He could smell her. He smiled. If she could evade capture, she could follow his captors and get him out from their grasp.

He stood in the net as a group of ten young men and seven young women approached him, spears in hand and swords strapped to their waists. He did not see any other threats, so he growled softly. They did not pay any heed to him as they proceeded to cut the branch that the trap was attached to. Vincent waited until he was being carried away. He flicked one claw against the net, in a casual manner. The claw barely managed to make a mark on the net. This shocked Vincent. He retracted his claw and kept still. He knew that his movements were being watched. He hoped that Adriana was following him. He could feel Nilesh wanting to break out and struggled to restrain him. One woman was walking in line with him. She glanced at Vincent's neck hair and asked, "I have heard of and seen men getting a lot of facial hair, if they let it grow out of control. Where did you get so much hair from? You cannot be more than seventeen years old."

Vincent replied in a menacing voice, "Let me out of this trap. Then I'll tell you my secret."

"Thanks for the offer. But I think I will wait till you are properly locked up before asking again." She replied with a wink.

Vincent did not realise that they had come to a stop. He was thrown, net and all, against a ten-foot-tall rock. He braced himself as he slammed into it. Luckily, only his hand hit the rock, saving him broken bones. Nilesh nearly took over control of his body.

Vincent waited while everyone settled down and had a fire going. He tried to see as much around him as possible without drawing attention to himself. He could not see Adriana anywhere, but then his eyes fell on a sack from which had a hand popping out of it. He blinked twice to check if he was seeing things.

The hand had reddish-orange lines crisscrossing, producing almost diamond like patterns on the hand. Vincent saw two women getting ready to leave. He watched as they picked up the sack and pushed the hand inside.

Almost instantly, the hand grabbed one woman's neck, causing both the women to drop the sack. Victoria emerged from the sack, with the look of a cornered animal in her eyes. Her orange eyes did a quick sweep of the small group. As no one had long range weapons that would kill her, Victoria had an advantage. She choked her victim a bit more, as if enjoying what she was doing. Vincent could not allow that to drag on. He roared as loud as he could, hoping to get Victoria's attention. It worked.

Victoria threw her victim to the ground, ran over to Vincent and ripped the net apart. Both of them stood with their backs to the rock, facing their captors. Vincent said, "I'll give you a boost over the rock. Run for all you are worth. I will find you later."

"The thing is," a voice came from above them. "You won't have to."

James landed on the ground in front of them. He spread his wings as much as he could and said, "You guys take a break. I will handle them."

The stench of fear coming off the group was a lot. Vincent could smell it. Having a predator with him was always good. He put his hand on James' shoulder, signalling him to stand down.

Vincent spoke to the group, "Look, we do not want trouble. Just give us some food, point us in the direction of Cylinx and we will not bother each other again. Fair deal?"

The woman Vincent had spoken to earlier said, "And what if we say no?"

James produced an extra-large mace, just to show them who was dictating the terms. He arched an eyebrow and casually said, "We could always agree to disagree. Here is what would happen: you say no, we fight. The three of us kill all of you, take your supplies and pretend that we never saw you."

Vincent did not like the way that James spoke. The men exchanged scared looks and said, "Fine. What do you require?"

"Half the quantity of meat that you have right now, along with one bag."

Vincent ate some of the meat to test if it was alright. He nodded to James, who got up, ready to take flight. Just then, Vincent felt all his body systems shutting down. He barely heard someone shout, before he fell unconscious, "Catch them!"

He woke up, chained to two wooden poles with iron fetters holding his wrists. His legs were also shackled in the same manner. He heard the murmur of a crowd in front of him and looked up. He was in a city, though it looked as if the city had been shaken by an earthquake. Walls rose in front of him, but Vincent could see entire sections of walls were absent, some full walls had holes large enough for a Bull to pass through. The day had almost come to an end. The last rays of sunlight created a silhouette of the walls, falling onto Vincent's face. The crowd in front of him looked normal enough, but looked older than they probably would have been. Everyone carried a weapon, whether it was a child, a teenager, an adult or an old person. Battle scars and tattoos covered their bodies. Vincent saw nothing but mistrust in the people's eyes.

"Welcome to Cylinx."

James was on Vincent's right, tied up in a similar manner. His face was bruised badly, and one of his eyes was swollen shut. Vincent figured he could not be worse off, when he realised two things.

"Where is Victoria? Where are our bags?"

"Victoria and our bags are safe together. As you fell, I grabbed and tossed her over the rock behind us. She ran off. They knocked me out, but could not find her. I heard them talking about it as they brought us here. I was only pretending to be knocked out. But you have something else to worry about."

"What?"

James looked at Vincent's neck pointedly. Vincent's eyes widened in realisation.

"What did they do to my Guardian?" Vincent's voice was eerily calm and even.

"I do not know. But he is alive. Even I can vouch for that."

Vincent struggled against his chains. An old man walked up to him and inspected him. He signalled to a younger man standing nearby. The latter was about thirty years old, with a whip in hand. He walked up to Vincent and lashed him across his chest. Vincent's shirt tore a bit, but he felt only a sting of pain. The young man chuckled and said, "Let's see how many lashes it will take you to scream."

He kept lashing Vincent, while James looked on in horror. Vincent was bleeding only from his abdomen area, where there were no bones to protect him. Vincent bore it with silence. He refused for emotions to show on his face. The man finally stopped after thirty lashes. He told the old man, "He withstood thirty, so you can have him for sixty."

They spoke as if Vincent was a worthless item that could be replaced anytime. That angered him. He could do nothing unless the chains were cast off him. He watched as they turned their attention to James, who coldly said, "Try it, and you die."

The old man said, "My friend, I have seen fighters like you talk tough, but do nothing in the ring. We will put you there. Let us see how well you do against a beast."

Vincent growled, "Let me go and I will show you who really is a beast."

James watched as the two men exchanged money. The young man opened Vincent's chains, apparently convinced that thirty whip lashes was enough to subdue Vincent. Vincent caught hold of the man and threw him into the crowd, where he collapsed on top of a few old people. They all turned towards Vincent, who broke James' chains. James said, "I can fly us out of here."

"Not without Nilesh."

"How do you intend to defend yourself? Your weapon is gone and all I have is a deafening shriek."

"Use the shriek. Hopefully, Nilesh will hear it and find us."

"Hopefully?"

"Just do it!"

James let out all the pain and anger he had pent up inside him, into one powerful shriek. The nearest people fell to the ground, their ears literally bleeding. The other just fainted. James was about to summon knives and make short work of them, when he felt a hand on his shoulder.

Adriana grabbed Vincent and James. Together, they made it away from the city, running about half a league before stopping. She said, "Well done surviving your first and only trip to Cylinx. We need to get away from here as fast as possible."

Vincent said, "Wait. I need to go back and get Nilesh."

Adriana looked at Vincent and said, "There is no time. We need to leave now."

"You go. I will follow."

"Vincent, you will not find him."

"Why?" James asked.

Adriana looked at James. He understood.

He asked, "Where is it?"

Vincent got confused. Then Adriana opened her bag to take out a Fire Opal gem, and Vincent's world collapsed around him. He stood, shell-shocked. His eyes revealed nothing, but James could sense the emotions building up inside. James gently took the Fire Opal from Adriana and asked, "When and how did this happen?"

"He was the beast you were to fight against. He was wounded from two battles already. He found me amongst the crowd and limped over to me. I had a knife with me. I relieved him of his misery."

Adriana said the last sentence like she had put an end to her own Guardian. Vincent had not moved from his spot. He just stared hard at the ground. James wanted to put his arm around Vincent, to try and comfort him. But how could you comfort somebody when a part of them has died? No one gave James comfort when Riyo died, and he was comfortable with it. Sure, he had cried as he put the Schrol into his arm-guard, but he knew what he was to expect.

Looking at Vincent, James felt scared of him, for the first time since they had met in Talis. Vincent's fists were clenched tightly, turning them almost white. His eyes had water in them, but he refused to cry. He was not blinking. James spoke softly and lovingly to him, "Vincent. It is alright to cry. There is nothing wrong it. Just let your emotions show. Let it come out now."

Vincent shook his head, not wanting to let his emotions get the better of him. James said, "Vincent, cry."

Vincent again shook his head. James slapped him hard across his face and shouted this time, "Cry!"

This time, Vincent's eyes let loose a miniature waterfall. James watched as Vincent let out everything, happy that he could get his friend to express himself. Vincent stopped crying after a few minutes. His face still had tear marks, but his eyes had a murderous look in them. He held his hand out for the Fire Opal. James gave it to him. Vincent studied the gem before announcing, "Cylinx is going to pay for doing this to Nilesh. They will pay for this insult dearly."

James caught Vincent and said, "We only protect those who cannot protect themselves. We do not take advantage of that fact."

"Did they care as to whether Nilesh could protect himself? If it is a fight they are looking for, they have got one."

Adriana did not want her hometown to get decimated by the wrath of Vincent. She pulled the earth under Vincent's feet, till it reached his knees. Vincent took no notice of it. The Fire Opal in his hand went to his arm-guard. His eyes flashed yellow, but his mane did not grow out from his neck. He turned to James and said, "Stand in my way and you will die. Stay neutral and you may just survive."

James produced two knives and said, "Do not do this, Vincent. Please. If you want, take our anger out on every monster we come across. Just do not harm innocent people."

"I am starting to consider innocent people collateral damage."

James played his last card in a desperate attempt, "Including your own parents and friends? Even Patrick?"

Vincent glared at him, but James refused to look away.

James said, "I know what you really can do. I heard everything."

Vincent nearly snarled at James. But he held himself back. Pure anger could be used for some time. But after a while, even anger had to give way to calmness. He spat and said, "Fine! I will spare Cylinx, but only this once. If they try anything with us again, I swear I will do much worse than just kill the people responsible. I will wipe this city off the map of Lasgalan."

James nodded to Adriana, who released the earth around Vincent's legs. They walked away from Cylinx, keeping the sea in view, but staying within the treeline. They were headed towards the Rhodonite Hills. From there, they would climb up, until they reached the Equine Gulf. Crossing that, they would be back on the Dividing Mountains, between Logder and Leonis. As for what lay between them and Yedgal's palace, that they left in the hands of destiny.

# CHAPTER 21

Sabre heaved an unconscious Edward into a cell. He locked the cell and tossed the key to a guard. He watched as Edward slept peacefully. He held out his sword. The blades were hidden as per usual. He smiled and opened up the sword. He swung it hard at the bars of the cell. Edward shot up from his place and tried to use his powers. Sabre chuckled and said, "You cannot use your powers in the cell. After the last unfortunate jail break, we changed the specifics of the cells. If even a small part of your body is inside the cell, your powers will not work."

So saying, Sabre walked away from the cell, leaving Edward alone. He came out to the council room, where Xristos was sitting, along with Byron. Sabre took his seat and said, "I have caught one. He is from Talis. He can manipulate fire and use flames to siphon strength and stamina from his opponents."

Byron casually caused electricity to crackle at his fingertips. He said, "I hope this one will prove more useful than the previous two we have captured."

Xristos smiled at Sabre and said, "Well done. I had sent Raze to Equis to see if he could capture anyone from there. Of course, I do not expect him to turn up for some time. Meanwhile, we must prepare for King Yedgal's return. Byron, have you been reading the books properly?"

Byron nodded and said, "It would not be called the biggest library in Lasgalan for nothing, if I could not find the spells. It is a bit difficult translating the language, but I should be done within a week, if not less."

There was a noise behind Bryan's chair. All three men shot up from their seats. Byron let both his arms catch fire. He said, "Come out slowly."

One Battos came into the light. On realising who it was, all three of them relaxed.

Xristos asked, "Batty, what happened?"

The Battos rumbled lowly, in its own language. Xristos nodded and replied back in the Battos' language. Sabre and Byron exchanged funny looks. They could never understand when and where Xristos had learnt the language. But it had proved useful many times when they could not reach a compromise with the Battois.

Xristos turned to Byron and said, "He says that he has information on the group. It would seem that they have been broken up into six groups of four people each. He wishes to know as to whether he should allow his forces to engage them. He knows that we would prefer them alive, but if it cannot be avoided, he will give permission to his forces across Lasgalan to kill them."

Byron said, "I want them alive. But they are to tell us when they corner someone."

Xristos rumbled back to Batty, who nodded and left.

Byron let his arms return to normal. He said, "The Battois are power-hungry monsters. If they were not so few in number, they would take Lasgalan back to a primordial state."

Xristos said, "But their loyalty is unwavering. That far outweighs them as liabilities."

Sabre was not convinced. He said, "How can the Battois consider themselves so few in number? They are enough to fill at least two cities of Tauris."

"They lack numbers, but can make a charge of a hundred seem like a lot. Their size also plays an important role in making the opponent fear them."

"I still feel that the less monsters we have, the better for us," Sabre voiced his opinion. He felt very scared around monsters, especially Battois. One misdirected breath of theirs would be enough to make sure he would not return from the dead. Despite the charms of quasi-immortality that Byron had placed on them, Sabre kept his distance from potentially life-ending moments. He trusted the Battois the most, which was not saying much. The Jides were unpredictable at best. Sabre stayed as far away from the Constries as he could. He did not have a problem with their poisoned claws. He always carried an antidote for the poison with him, as the poison took five minutes to become fatal. Yoknies had scared him a lot, so he let Shane, their navy commander see to them. Shane always seemed to be at ease on his ships, rather than on solid land.

They had not seen much of Shane since the last meeting they had held. He was heading south towards Covis, for some undisclosed work. Even Xristos did not know what he was planning.

Byron said, "We need to get back to work. I will be in the library if anyone wants me."

The three of them parted company. Xristos sat back in his chair and touched the table. A three-dimensional hologram of Lasgalan popped up. Xristos concentrated on Equis, and zoomed in on the Isle of the Pegasi.

Byron walked back to his room, through the corridor behind his chair, and then to the library. He found Bryan waiting for him, sword in hand. Byron asked, "What happened?"

Bryan gave him a cold stare before saying, "You need help, brother. Bringing father back will not be an easy task. I can help you."

"How? You know nothing of sorcery. You preferred to be the military man, for a good reason."

Bryan's face looked as if a shadow had fallen over it. He remembered the day he had first tried his hand at sorcery. His entire left palm's skin had come off. Had Byron not been there at the time, Bryan would have died.

"That does not matter, Byron. Someone needs to take the strain of the spell, along with you."

"I will be fine. I've trained for over a hundred years for this. I am confident that I will be able to take the strain."

Bryan raised an eyebrow.

"That undertone of your voice would suggest otherwise, little brother."

Byron silently cursed. His brother was notoriously good at listening to peoples' speech and detecting the lies in that. He shook his head and said, "I will manage."

He walked past his brother and up the stairs, to the third level of the library. Chains were stretched across each shelf of the bookcases. Each book was hard bound and red in colour. Byron had insisted on colour-coordinating all the book they had, based on the type of contents they had. The first level, at the ground, had books with blue bindings, signifying that those books' contents were free for anyone to access. The second level, below him, had green coloured books. They were the most numerous in the library. Their contents were slightly dangerous, but all could access those books. However, the books he was looking at, the red coloured ones, were highly dangerous and were not books meant to be read directly before sleep. Those books contained myths, legends, spells, history so dark that they could give someone a waking nightmare. There was a reason there were chains to prevent the wrong people from reading those books.

It was not that Byron wanted a wrong person reading his books and coming up with ways to defeat him. The actual reason was that he wanted the wrong people to at least stay sane. The chains were enchanted to open only when Byron, Xristos, or Bryan wished to access a book.

Byron took out a book, and the chains closed on their own. The book Byron was holding contained spells used to call upon Gods. He knew that he had to call upon Esdah and Sorenth for sure, but he wanted to confirm that no other God was to be part of the spell. He flipped through the pages, not even glancing at the pictures. He found the page he was looking for and skimmed through it. He knew that Bryan was still waiting downstairs for him. He checked the incantations and smiled. His first step to bringing his father back was over. Now he just had to wait for the second step to finish, with five more Chosen Ones to arrive. He put the book back and jumped off the balcony he was on. He landed next to Byran, who said, "Show off."

"Get used to it brother. We have one person in the cells, only five more to go."

Xristos' voice came from the door of the library.

"Make that four to go. Raze has brought back one from Equis, along with potions. She too is from Talis. We are unsure about her powers though."

Byron grinned like a small child and turned to Bryan, "Not bad now, is it, our situation?"

Xristos left the duo and walked to Karan's chambers. He knocked on the door and walked in. He did not expect to see what he did.

Karan was practicing his sword swings, moving with his old pace and agility. He nearly decapitated Xristos as the latter walked into his chambers. Karan realised his mistake and apologised. Xristos just smiled and asked, "How are you feeling now? It must have been quite the shock for you, getting overpowered by a youngster."

"Well, physically I am feeling very good. Mentally, it was a bit jarring. But I will take my revenge out on the man who wounded my pride. Have no fear, General."

Xristos said nothing, but only nodded. He saw that Karan was studying maps, but none of them looked like any region of Lasgalan.

So he asked, “Karan, where do you originally come from?”

“I do not remember, General. I have no memory of my past, except you finding me, about a hundred years ago. After that, my memory has stayed vivid.”

Xristos doubted Karan was giving him truthful answers, but he had been there when Byron had implanted false memories into Karan’s mind.

“Very well, Karan. I hope you can finish the palace restoration in time for the king to rise again.”

“Yes, of course. Though I must ask, why am I building a palace where no one can see it?”

“Do not worry about that. Your work will be appreciated by one and all, soon.”

Xristos walked out of Karan’s chambers, shutting the door behind him.

Once Karan was sure that he was gone, he turned back to the maps on his bed. He smiled and said to himself, “You may think I don’t remember anything, Xristos. But I have a memory sharper than anyone else’s.”

He closed all the maps, except one. It was a map that looked like the mirror image of a map of Lasgalan. It had taken Karan some time to get all his memories back, but he managed to reconstruct an entire map of the land he came from.

It was not exactly a land, though. For Karan came not from Lasgalan or any physical world. He came from a place, where few people had dared to venture into alive, but never come out again. It was the region between Lasgalan and Underworld. No one knew that it really existed, except through legends and myths. He knew exactly what it looked like. After all, it was his family that had been appointed as gatekeepers of the Underworld, by Esdah himself.

Countless generations of Karan’s family had kept the Underworld secure. Their orders were simple: "Kill anything living that tries to enter the Underworld, and stop anything that tries to leave the Underworld, unless by my orders."

Karan and his parents had defended the gates of the Underworld for as long as he was alive. Before them were Karan's grandparents. Karan had an elder sister, who did not want to guard the gates, as it seemed to be very boring for her. She took up the duties of keeping the souls in the Underworld in check. Soon, Esdah took her as his bride, but not before seeking her parents' permission. It had seemed very funny that a God required a mortal's permission, but Esdah was all about following rules.

Karan had later done something to offend Esdah, which even he did not realise at that time was offensive to the God. Esdah had then banished him to the upper world, Lasgalan. At first, Karan thought that he would not be able to survive. But then, he met Byron and Xristos, and his life changed. He had managed to blend in with the people of Lasgalan, until a fight with a Bull had left him fatally wounded. Byron rescued him and implanted false memories of Karan swearing loyalty to his father. But Karan had later shaken off Byron's spell, without the prince realising it. He could now find a way back to the Underworld, and to his family. It had been over fifty years, but thanks to Karan's unique physiology, he managed to retain his youthful body.

Karan knew that there were many ways for mortals to enter the Underworld. The most obvious one was for them to die, after which their souls automatically drifted towards the gates of the Underworld. Another way was for a mortal to somehow find the exact location of the gates of the Underworld, which existed in a different dimension altogether. One had to be very calculative and sure of their mind's limits, if they wished to enter the Underworld alive. However, Karan's family made sure that they died before reaching the gates, in which case they would anyway reach the Underworld, but not return to

Lasgalan to tell their tales of adventure.

The location of the gates was never in the same place for very long. It was sometimes in a remote cave in a forest, sometimes underwater, sometimes high up in the Dividing Mountains. There was a time when there were living people who could go into the Underworld, to talk with Esdah, as he was the most approachable of all the Gods, and then leave. That was the time when the District Lords were not as flimsy as the current ones. Esdah stopped that practice over seven centuries ago. He decided that it was best for Lasgalan, as he felt the Lords were being shown too much of the Underworld well before their time.

Karan understood the wisdom of Esdah. He had seen the Underworld himself, and he knew that one day, his soul too would be one among the countless souls Esdah had under his control.

Karan knew that there was no pattern as to where and when the gates would appear. But he had a feeling that the gates would appear near the palace soon. He had to wait until then, to make his escape. He could not get back to the Underworld, but he could wait out the war, and hope to somehow win back Esdah's favour. All he could do now was bide his time. He walked out of his chambers and headed to an unfinished section of the palace, facing north.

Constries were working tirelessly to build the palace. Karan had been given authority to command them as his own personal army. A few men and women were also there. These people were handpicked by Bryan when he was secretly touring Lasgalan. These were people who he had found discarded by their own families, with nowhere and no one to turn to. They had raised themselves as tough workers and depended only upon themselves for their survival. They were not as efficient as the Constries, but they were good. One woman saluted him as he walked past.

He returned her salute and asked, "How has the progress been?"

"A bit slower than what you had preferred, sir. The Constries have been working as hard as they can, but yesterday a full section of the wall collapsed. We have fixed that, and are back on track. We should finish the work within a week's time."

Karan nodded. He watched as one Constry threw three bricks upwards to another Constry, which caught it with ease. They were both holding onto the wall with only one hand. Karan smiled and turned to the woman.

"Captain. Once this work is over, I would like to personally give each one of you a gift. A token of appreciation for what you are helping Lasgalan reach."

The captain blushed slightly and said, "Please do not trouble yourself. I do not need anything. If you have to, give my workers something."

Karan was impressed by the captain's selflessness. But he was not surprised. He walked on, towards a finished section of the wall, from where he could see the Equine Gulf. This was the one place he could be alone with his thoughts. He glanced outside to check that there was no uninvited person sneaking around the palace walls, not that the person would figure out what actually lay in front of him.

Karan knew that four people were still to be captured. But he did not know what their fate would be, after they had been used to bring back Yedgal. He glanced back the way he had come. The Constries and men were making a hole in the wall, from where soldiers could keep an eye out for threats.

Karan was lost in his own thoughts, when he heard somebody walk towards him. He turned and found himself facing the captain.

"Yes, captain?"

"Sir, I need to talk to you. Privately."

Karan was a bit surprised. The captain rarely did anything without witnesses. Nevertheless, he followed her. She took him to their quarters, where Karan did not see anything wrong. He turned to her, wondering why she had brought him to their room. She had closed the door, desperation written on her face.

"Captain, what happened?" Even Karan was getting nervous. He had never seen her so stressed.

"You asked me if I wanted anything, and I said no. Well, there is something I want."

"What is that, captain?"

"Karan, you know a bit of sorcery, do you not?"

"No. What are you talking about? Byron does sorcery."

"You see, the thing is that..."

"What? Spit it out captain."

The captain put her hand on her stomach, as if trying to find the right words. Karan understood.

"Who is the father?"

"That is the problem, Karan. There is no father. I cannot conceive. Believe me, I have tried."

Karan did not know what to say for a few moments. However, he regained his composure and said calmly, "You should ask Byron for help. He would probably know a few spells that could help you. If you wish, I can speak to him on your behalf."

"No. Please do not do that."

The captain felt relieved that someone could understand her. But she did not know how Byron would react to her request. Meanwhile, Karan put his hands on her shoulders and said, "Look, it is perfectly normal if a woman cannot conceive. There are many more like you in Lasgalan. It is not a disability. Just remember that. Now, let's finish the north wall. You can speak to Byron after that."

"Yes Karan."

## CHAPTER 22

Climbing had never been Jacob's forte, but when Clint ordered him to start climbing Bloodhound Mountain, he had no choice. His legs cried for mercy as he tried finding footholds to rest his feet. However, Clint showed them no mercy and made the three of them climb higher and higher. Clint himself had no problem, using his Raven to fly next to them. He had made Jacob climb first, followed by Hasha and Dan bringing up the rear.

Dan had it easy going up the mountain, using his berserker strength to make handholds in the mountainside. Hasha was using ropes to keep herself lashed to the mountainside. All Jacob could do was hope that he did not slip going up.

Finally, after what seemed like eternity, which was really only half an hour, Clint said, "Cave up ahead. Twenty feet up. Keep climbing."

Jacob got a second wind and almost raced up the mountainside. He crawled out of harm's way, into the cave and collapsed. Hasha came up after him, and helped get Dan up as well. Clint landed in front of them and said, "We rest here for the night. No one moves out unless I say so."

Jacob was too tired to even care. The entire day had gone by uneventful for their group. His Guardian, a Cut Lion called Zoh had virtually slept all day long, while being merged with him. Dan was not bothered, as his Guardian was dead already. Hasha had no Guardian to protect her, so Clint had established himself as her Guardian. Hasha was sceptical at first, but finally relented. It was not cold inside the cave, but there was a chilly wind coming from the back of the cave.

That meant that there was a second entrance to the cave.

Clint told the others to stay put, while he explored the cave. He walked ahead, the light slowly turning to an inky black. He kept his quindent in spear form, keeping it extended in front of himself, as if he was blind, to check for obstacles. He did not want to go too far away from the trio, in case something untoward happened to them. He folded his wings as much as he could, but they were getting hit by protruding rocks where he could not see them.

A howl sounded ahead of him, freezing him in his position. He did not know which animal was up ahead, but the sound made his blood curl. He backed away slowly, not wanting to face away from whatever had made that sound. He made his way back to the group, where Dan and Hasha were joking around, while Jacob was almost ready to sleep. Clint shook him a bit, to get him up.

"What happened, Clint?" Hasha asked.

"We may have to get ready to climb again."

Jacob groaned.

"Why?"

"I am not sure where this cave goes. But this is called Bloodhound Mountain for a reason."

"Understandable. But we are safer in this cave, than we are outside, with nowhere to run. We will stay here for the night. But why did you want us to detour all the way here, taking out about two days, coming, and going from the Dividing Mountains?"

"Sapphire roses." Dan said.

Clint looked at Dan, as if wondering how he came to that conclusion, before saying, "Yes. Our enemy may want to get them, in case we kill their comrades. We should take as many as we can find and leave. We will have back-up potions then."

Dan interrupted him, with the most obvious question.

"Does anyone even have experience making these potions?"

Silence followed. Clint sat down on the ground and unmerged. He sighed as he placed his Guardian on his lap. The Raven was sleeping soundly, as if it had expended its quota of energy for the day, staying merged with Clint. Clint said, "We will be needing food soon. I do not think rabbit is going to help Jacob and I last the night like this."

Hasha laughed and said, "Way ahead of you, Clint. I stole some food from the breakfast table today."

She brought out four large pieces of beef, with strips of bacon.

Clint looked at her in amazement.

"How?"

"You guys are not the only ones with gifts."

Dan smiled and said, "Not bad, Hasha. There's still hope for you to join our club."

"Let's see. Now, let's eat."

Jacob reluctantly got up and helped himself to some bacon. Clint did not eat. He wanted to get away from the Mountain and start looking for Yedgal's palace. He watched as Dan produced different weapons, using his gem's powers. He kept at it, producing weapons faster and faster. Dan looked up at Clint, who signed quickly and subtly, "We will head straight for where you can remember the palace is. If we find it, we fall back for help."

Dan looked away, and gave a small nod. He was about to sign back, when a sharp howl sounded from behind them. Jacob and Hasha, who were facing away from the other two, towards the cave's entrance, froze. Clint was on his feet. As Cyrus was tired, he did not merge. He levelled his quindent and faced the back of the cave, where he could make out two red dots slowly coming closer towards them. Dan turned towards the entrance, wondering if they could make a dash for it. That route was also cut off by two beasts, who stayed where they were. As Clint watched, his opponent came into full view. Clint was sure that his time had come.

The Underworld Hound that had been simulated for them was like a trivial thing, compared to the beast he was facing. Red eyes first came into view, flanking a black snout filled with glistening white teeth. The ears were pointed downwards, red in colour. The shoulders looked huge for the legs that they were connected to, though that was not much of an advantage for the group. One paw alone would have been as big as Clint's palm. Each of the animal's legs could have used as miniature pillars to hold a small tree in place from falling. The body of the Crimson-eyed Bloodhound was about three and a half feet long. Clint saw that it was wide enough for him to put his hands around, but his hands would never meet each other. The tail of the Bloodhound was red, almost like blood. The tail was pointed up, which hopefully meant that it would not kill them right away. It came to a stop seven feet from Clint's quindent.

Dan noticed that the Hounds were not moving at all, as if waiting for a signal to attack the four of them. He quietly said, "Guys, do not take a step back. If you do, they will move in for a kill. I am not sure that we can move as fast as them."

Jacob slipped his knuckledusters onto his fingers. He closed his fists, and the claws on the knuckledusters popped out. He was hoping to give the animals a scare. The Bloodhounds were not impressed. They showed their own claws, which popped out of their paws, giving Jacob a good view of the three inches of serrated pain that they could deliver per claw. Jacob asked Clint, without turning to him, "Should I..."

"Do not even try using your powers. They will attack us."

Clint watched as the animal facing him suddenly dropped its tail. It leapt at him, flooring him straight away. The other two leapt at the trio. Hasha barely had time to summon a defence, when one of them almost knocked her out cold. Jacob leapt into its path and roared. There was a flash of yellow light, and Zoh "leapt" out of Jacob's body, throwing the Bloodhound in the opposite direction. The two animals got up and faced each other, circling each other and sizing the opponent up.

The Bloodhound that leapt at Dan got hit by a red mace in the jaw. It got back to its feet, unsure of what to make of the young man. Dan swung his mace a few times on the ground, showing the Bloodhound who was in charge.

Clint's captor had not moved. It watched as Clint struggled to move. Clint did not try to get its paw off his sternum. It felt as if a stone block had been placed on him.

It looked Clint dead in the eye, and opened its mouth. Clint's quindent was out of reach, Clint having dropped it when he had been floored. Clint's bag was leaking all kinds of colourful liquids. Somehow, each potion seemed to neutralise the other. That explained why they were still alive and the cave had not exploded. Clint was ready to accept his fate, when it turned out that fate had other ideas for him.

Cyrus, who had been near the meat and fast asleep, shot towards the Bloodhound, successfully pecking out one eye. The Bloodhound jumped back in surprise, releasing Clint. Clint rolled to the side, grabbed his quindent and got it back into cylinder form. Cyrus had been caught by the Bloodhound and was in its mouth. Clint locked eyes with his Guardian, understanding what was about to happen. The Bloodhound closed its jaws and Clint could hear the sound of bones getting crushed by the jaws. The Bloodhound suddenly looked surprised and spat out a Schrol. It lunged at Clint, who opened his spear and drove the point into the roof of the mouth of the animal, skewering its brain in the process. He grabbed the Schrol and took his spear out of the mouth of the animal. The other two Bloodhounds looked at their fallen comrade, towards the five opposing creatures and turned around to run. Dan spat out some blood and said, "So much for being vicious killers."

Clint passed the Schrol over his arm-guard and tested it for weapon production. He shrunk his spear down to a small size and slung it onto his back. He did not like the fact that Cyrus was dead. But he accepted it. Dan nodded to him, understandingly. Clint spread his wings, just to see their size. They were considerably much larger than Chris'. He produced another seven-foot long quindent and stabbed it into the ground, where it sank three feet into the ground. Clint took it out and willed it to disappear. Dan told him, "If you produce projectile weapons and let go of them, they can still be used by others. Arrows are the safest, as they cannot be used again. But, since this is your weapon of choice, stick to it."

Clint said, "We wait for morning. I will guard all of you. Zoh is also there to back me up."

Jacob rubbed his Guardian's nose, which the Lion quite enjoyed. Clint could swear that it was smiling contently, with its eyes closed. Jacob asked, "Should we collapse the back end of this cave, in case those animals decide to try an attack at night?"

"That will not be necessary, young man."

A new voice sounded from the back of the cave. A man stepped into their view. Clint snarled and asked, "How many times do we need to run into you? Did our last encounter not teach you anything?"

The man slung a longbow off his back. He did not have a quiver with him, but when he drew his drawstring back, a gold arrow formed, appearing to be nocked. Dan produced a shield to defend to Hasha. Jacob shouted, "Why don't you just run away, you coward?"

The man appeared a bit scared upon hearing and seeing Jacob. He saw the Leonid snarling at him and turned the bow towards the boy. Clint saw his opportunity and threw his quindent at the man. The man instinctively fell back, firing the arrow. It flew past all of them, hitting Clint's bag, which exploded on contact with the arrow. The cave started to shake, and Dan raised his shield to protect Hasha and himself. The man got over his shock.

He ran at Jacob, grabbing Dan and him by the waist. He took out an Argentic Transporter, which hummed for a second, before disappearing in a silver flash.

Clint stared in shock at Hasha, who looked equally distraught. He took her by the hand, ran for the cave entrance and flew out into the evening. Hasha held onto both his hands as he did a large loop around the Mountain. From the height they were at, they could see small bodies of Bloodhounds moving all over the Mountain. Clint turned and started heading west. Just then, Hasha had an idea.

"Get to the ground. I know a place where we will be safe."

"Where?"

"My house. Was that not obvious?"

"We cannot. As much as I would like to get to safety, this will go against my orders."

"Then just get some new orders. Dive."

Hasha figured she had about five seconds before Clint let her go and let her fall to her death. Finally, Clint said, "Which direction to your house?"

"Head south. If we hit the river, we have gone too far south. We will need to backtrack in that case, north to the nearest city."

"Got it."

Clint started to climb, lost in his own thoughts. But he made sure that he was heading in the right directions. Meanwhile, Hasha had managed to climb onto his back, which was wide enough for her. She put her hands around his chest, to prevent herself from falling off. Clint kept turning from side to side, whenever he felt that she was slipping to one side. The evening sun was in his peripheral vision. He heard Hasha snoring softly on his back, and decided to glide for a while. The winds carried him, and he also felt like sleeping. But he knew that he could not. He wanted to wait till nightfall, so that he could see the city lights and then get a good approach.

Clint was flying for about an hour, when he felt Hasha starting to get up. He pitched himself down slowly, allowing Hasha enough time to get alert. She surveyed the landscape around them and said, "Dive a bit more. I cannot see much from being in and out of the clouds."

Clint snickered, "Big mistake."

"Why? What are you going to…?"

Clint furled his wings in and did a steep dive. Hasha held onto his shoulders, screaming. Clint suspected that she was actually enjoying the dive. Nevertheless, he pulled out of his dive with about a thousand feet left before they hit the ground. Hasha shouted, "I am going to get you killed!"

"Why? I told you to hold onto me."

"You most certainly did not!"

"My bad. Now, which way?"

"See those woods about a league ahead? Head for those. I should get my bearings once we are close by."

"Don't you guys live in the city?"

"Nope. Garon's family, our family and some others live outside the city. We wanted some privacy."

"Fair enough. Speaking of Garon, how do you think he's doing with his group?"

"Should be surviving, if he is smart. After all, he'd better come back to…"

Hasha stopped herself, but it was too late.

Clint chuckled and said, "Back to you, you were going to say? I could tell from the way you said the rest of that statement."

Hasha's face turned red. She was thankful that Clint could not see it. She said, "You would not understand, even if I tried to explain it to you."

Clint said, "Trust me, I could be some of the few who would be able to."

"How? How would you know what it is like to have feelings for someone you know you may or may not get in life?"

"I know the feeling, all too well, I am afraid."

Something had changed in Clint's voice. Just a moment back, it was full of humour. Now, it sounded like he was speaking at someone's funeral.

Hash did not want to, but she asked, "Who was it?"

Clint sighed, "There were a few people. My first girlfriend was a good hunter. She and I had it going good for a year. Then one day, she went for a regular hunt. I was slightly ill that day. I waited for her to come back before dusk, which she did not. The gates of the city were closed. I snuck out and went in the direction she had gone. I did not find her then. Towards dawn, as I was coming back, I saw a murder of crows slowly taking apart a humanoid corpse. I shooed them off, only to find her body desecrated beyond recognition. I buried her in the woods itself. Telling my parents about it was harder than telling her parents about her death."

Hasha kept quiet until they reached the ground. She slid off Clint's back and both of them headed into the woods. She had seen Adnanam as they had come in for a landing, so she knew which direction to go in. As they walked on, she kept glancing back at Clint, checking if he was still with her. Night had almost fallen and if not for Clint's constant tapping of her shoulder, she would have been scared to death if she turned around to see someone behind her.

After about fifteen minutes of walking, Hasha stopped. Clint readied a sword, thinking that they had run into danger. Hasha said, "Do you smell smoke?"

Clint sniffed the air and said, "Ever since we landed. I thought that it was normal. It was faint when we landed. As long as we have been walking, the smell has been getting stronger."

Hasha knew that forest fires were common in Tauris, just before and during their monsoon season. Logder rarely had forest fires. She said, "Never mind. Once we are at my place, we can rethink our next steps. But first, we need to get out of the forest. It is giving me the creeps."

"Lead on, madam."

They trudged on. Hasha wanted to make the journey seem shorter, so she asked Clint, "Who were the others?"

"A friend of mine had gone to another city to live his life. This was in one of our ports. Later on, I had heard that there was a pirate who creating hell in that area. I was already in the army by then, so I went there. I found out that he was the pirate. Putting him jail would have been enough, but then I found out that he was also running a slave trade, using his piracy as a cover for that. The worst part was that he did not care who he was selling. Men, women, children, brainwashed teenagers. It did not matter to him. He was trying to explain what he was doing, but I gave him no time and I lost my cool."

Clint did not look at Hasha, but she understood.

"That is why I am also called "sentinel" in Covis. I belong to a part of the army that deals with protecting people's rights, as well as the people themselves."

Hasha did not say anything for a few moments. Clint walked on behind her and said, "Listen, if you do not like my company, now that you know who I really am, I am sorry. I cannot change the way I am."

"Surprisingly, I feel safer in your company now." Hasha laughed.

Clint managed a small smile. He looked ahead, behind Hasha, and his smile dissolved.

He pointed to a large orange glow ahead and said, "We found the source of the smoke."

Hasha could just about make out what he was pointing at. They ran towards the glow. Once they reached the edge of the woods, Clint stopped Hasha. He went first, his black wings camouflaging with the environment. Hasha saw a large fire engulfing a house. With a chill, she realised that this was Garon's house. She ran out in front of Clint, and used her Ring to produce water to douse the fire. Clint waited till the fire had died out. He went to Hasha's side and asked, "Whose house is this?"

"Garon's."

Clint saw something glinting in the ashes of the house. He turned and saw that it was a silver ring. He saw it was stuck on a stick. He tried to remove the stick, only to realise that it was attached to a skeleton. He jumped back, quickly uttering a prayer that they learnt in the army, to pay their respects to the dead. It was a man's skeleton, and he had a bow in hand. It looked as if the man had gone down fighting. Clint thought that the fallen man was Garon's father. He heard a sob next to him, only to see Hasha struggling to keep herself together. He quickly gave her a hug, so as to shield her eyes from the carnage that she had just witnessed. He said, "Let's go to your house. You will feel better."

Hasha weakly pointed in one direction. Clint picked her up and flew over the woods in that direction. He was not prepared for what he saw next.

It looked as if someone had used a large amount of impure flat bomb. A crater, hundred metres across, about fifty metres deep was in the next clearing. Hasha almost choked. Clint understood. He landed next to the edge of the crater, which was tinged in green, due to the vapour coming out of the crater. Clint looked down towards the centre of the crater, hoping to see someone alive, but he knew that it was crazy to even think that. Hasha had sat down hard on the ground, in a ball and was crying her eyes out. Clint looked around to see if anyone was around, but it was past sunset. Everyone would have been in the city itself. Clint's first priority was to help Hasha get over her loss. That was easier said than done. But he had recently lost his mother. He too knew what it felt like. He sat down next to Hasha, covering her with one wing, so as to make her feel a bit more comfortable. He stared at the crater, waiting for Hasha to finish crying, when he saw someone approach the crater, across from where they were sitting. The person did not appear to have seen them. He got off from his Horse and walked to the edge of the crater. Clint did not want to, but he pointed the man out to Hasha, signalling for her to not do anything rash while he confronted the man.

Clint knew that he would not be seen very easily, so he spread his wings and shot up, out of the man's view. He circled the man and body-slammed him into the crater. The man's Horse stayed put, not willing to move, which was fine by Clint. He shot into the crater, grabbing the man by his neck, and throwing him on the ground next to Hasha. Hasha restrained him by producing a large block of ice on top of his chest.

Clint put a sword under the man's chin and said, "So you have come to see your handiwork. A bit shoddy, I must say."

The man looked at Clint's sword, before turning his attention to Hasha's Ring. His eyes widened with some sort of realisation and he said, "You people will help save us from Yedgal."

That line threw Clint off a bit.

"Who are you, and why are you not very shocked to see us?"

"I am afraid I cannot tell you my name. Names have a lot of power, you know. Just know that I am a member of the Pegasi tribe. I was recently captured by Yedgal's forces, and then released. I came to Logder to visit a friend of mine. But now I see that he and his family are no more."

"Not all of them are dead." Hasha spoke for the first time since seeing the damage done to her home.

"How can you say that?"

"I am your friend's daughter."

The man said softly, "Your father was a very noble man, young lady. He was a good soul, who never hurt anyone. He helped us in the rebellion against Yedgal the last time the tyrant was alive, almost fifteen years ago. He will rest in peace, knowing that you are fighting for the same cause as he once did."

Clint understood that they could trust the man. He flipped the block of ice off the man and helped him to his feet. Clint noted the man's weapons, a pair of knuckledusters. But unlike Jacob's, this man's knuckledusters had hoof designs on them. They would have been effective for knocking someone out cold, rather than kill a person.

The man sized up the two of them. He said, "It looks like I have no further business here. I will leave you now."

The man walked across to his Horse, which had not moved from its spot. It was grazing, unmindful of where its owner was. The man rode off into the trees. Clint turned to Hasha.

Her eyes were still red from crying. Tear marks were present on her cheeks, but she made no attempt to wipe them. She looked at her Emerald, as if contemplating what to do with it. She finally sat down and asked Clint, "You do know that we have a problem, right?"

"We have three actually, but what are you focussing on?"

"Dan and Jacob have been captured. We do not have their bags, and yours was blown up. We just have mine. We have to make sure that the potions are rationed properly. What were your problems?"

"Dan and Jacob have been captured. That leaves four more people to be captured by Yedgal's forces, optimistically speaking. The second problem is that Jacob was taken, but whether his Guardian was taken with him, or died in the cave collapse, is a question that is to be answered. The last problem is that tomorrow is a new day. And we have nowhere to go for the night. The cave was comfortable and secure enough for one night, and I sure am not going to like sleeping in the forest."

"We will manage. But tomorrow, your freshening up will be a question mark."

Clint scratched his head and said, "True enough. We will cross that bridge when we come to it."

Hasha took a small pebble and threw it, half-heartedly, into the crater. She sighed and said, "Ake will be sad when he hears about this. Not as much as me, though. He always knew that he was adopted. I guess that served its purpose. He will be solely focussed on the mission at hand."

"You know, Hasha, maybe you should learn to open up a bit. Keeping everything bottled up inside is not going to help your mental stability."

Hasha stared at him as if he had said something crazy.

She said, "I just cried my eyes out in front of you, watched two homes that I knew burn up. I could not even give my parents a proper funeral, and you want me to open up."

The last two words were spoken with an angry edge to them. Clint knew that he could not push Hasha more towards the edge, otherwise he was risking his life. He said nothing else.

He wanted to head back to the Mountains, but that would take another half-day out of their way, if he flew Hasha all the way. He could smell the smoke coming off the crater, which made their sleeping spot a bit uncomfortable. But soon, Hasha was asleep. Clint decided that he would not sleep, in case they were taken by surprise. He would wait till dawn and wake up Hasha. They would freshen up at the river, which was south of their location. They would then go up the river and head north into the Mountains. Ideally, Clint wanted to reach the Mountains before dusk the next day.

He sat down next to Hasha's sleeping form, spear at the ready. He nearly fell off to sleep twice, but he had trained his mind to keep his biological clock independent of the sun. Around midnight, he checked on Hasha, who was still sleeping. He could see that the green smoke coming off the crater was not so thick, as when they had first arrived. He rose from his place and went towards it, determined to give the dead their due respect.

He slid down the side to the bottom, where the ruins of the house could be seen. He did not see any bodies, but felt that they were within the house. He opened his quindent, pushed it into the ground, upside down, and started praying for the souls of those who had perished within the house. He wanted to get back to Hasha fast, so he ran through the prayers. To mark the ending of the prayers, he lifted his quindent and, with the side that was earlier in the ground, he drew the figure of a Raven in the dirt. It was not visible, but Clint knew that he had drawn it correctly. This was the first time that he had ever said those prayers, as his seniors in the army believed that the youngsters were not to be burdened with the impact of the prayers after saying them. Now, he understood their wisdom.

As Clint finished drawing his Raven, he felt as if a few weights had been added to his shoulders. His knees threatened to give out beneath him and he felt a bit sluggish. His quindent felt heavier in his arms. Clint wanted to believe that the work of the previous day was finally telling on his body, but he knew that it was really the impact of the prayers. He flew out of the crater, back next to Hasha, who did not even stir after getting a rush of wind from his wings while he was landing. Clint decided that he also should at least lie down, if not sleep. His mind would be a bit at ease the next morning. He did that, waiting for dawn to arrive.

Once Clint saw the sky change slightly from obsidian to charcoal grey, he got up and stretched himself. He did not want to, but he woke up Hasha, who took a moment to remember where they were. Once she was ready, he flew her south to the Logd River. He did not have much to do to freshen up. He made Hasha wait at the bank, while he dived into the river, and came out, water dripping all over himself. He made no attempt to dry himself. As the sun was not yet out, he decided to wait while Hasha changed and freshened up. There was a tree that covered the upstream part of the river a bit, through which nothing could be seen. Clint suggested that Hasha change behind that.

At his suggestion, Hasha arched an eyebrow at him and asked, "Being a straight-laced person, are you?"

Clint went a bit red in the face. He just said, "Change quickly. Then we can get a move on."

Once she was done, Clint decided to walk with her till she could walk no more. But they needed food as well. Hasha took out the last of her meat from her bag, which both of them ate while walking upstream. They kept by the riverbank, in case they needed to change shores quickly. Clint spotted a herd of deer ahead of them, about two hours after sunrise. He asked Hasha, "Do you think you can snare some of them, while I kill them?"

"Probably. But be quick."

Ten minutes later, they had a fire going, with deer meat on the skewers. Clint was turning the skewer, while Hasha was stoking the fire. When the meat was cooked nice and tender, Clint took it off the skewer and sliced it cleanly off the bone. He threw the bones into the fire, which seemed to act as a fuel for the fire. Hasha first made a face when she ate the deer, claiming that it was too salty for her liking. Clint told her to eat it quietly, as they would not be eating again for a while, and that she needed all the energy that she could get.

Clint was finishing his piece of venison, when he heard a menacing snarl. He dropped his piece into the fire, forming a quiver of arrows and a bow. He spun in his place, nocking one arrow and fired without waiting to stop to position himself. The black arrow struck the ground fifty feet from the fire. No animal was seen though. Clint stood up and looked around. Whatever had made that sound was keeping quiet.

Hasha stayed in her place. Clint sniffed the air and did not smell anything out of the ordinary. His instincts told him to move away from where he was. He was about to sit down again, when he saw a movement in the branches of the trees above him. Without hesitation, Clint fired a second arrow to that location. It was a tricky shot, but Clint found his target. A Jide dropped to the ground, shot through the stomach. Clint was about to heave a sigh of relief, when he saw a dozen Jides descend from those very trees, headed right for the duo near the fire.

Hasha shot icicles towards them, forcing Clint to duck and roll towards the nearest rock. He saw three Jides come at him, their mouths open to get his neck within them. Clint shot one of them with an arrow. Before he could get another arrow ready, one of the Jides clamped its jaws onto his right shoulder, forcing him to scream loudly. Almost instantly, the noise around him died out. He punched the Jide with his left hand, only to have it remove a bit of his flesh and leave some teeth in his arm. Clint kicked it away from himself, realising at the same time that all the twelve Jides were dead.

He managed to stem the bleeding on his shoulder by tying a part of his pants on the wound. But he knew that the wound was very deep, and that he might need surgery. The Jide had managed to go all over his shoulder, and his pectoral muscles had taken some of the bite, if not all of it. Sweenet and blocker would not be able to heal his muscles. He got up, using his real quindent as a support and made his way to Hasha, who was flat on the ground, eyes wide open, looking as if she had been stunned, or worse…

Clint wanted to confirm his fears, so he quickly checked for her pulse. She had one, though it felt higher than what Clint had ever encountered. Clint checked her breathing, which seemed alright. He waved his hand over her eyes, but she did not respond to his gestures. She did not seem to have any external injuries, and none of the Jides were even close to her to have touched her. In fact, it looked like some unseen force had intervened and caused the scene around them.

Clint could not risk any potion with her, as she could not digest carmine. He grabbed her left arm and vigorously rubbed his palms across it, hoping to warm her blood as it raced back to her heart. She still did not respond. Clint was getting desperate now. He could not allow another girl to head towards death while he was around her. Clint ran to the river and filled his bottle with water. He sprinkled some water on her face, hoping to get her out of her stunned phase. Her skin was still warm, so she was not dying soon.

Clint decided that there was only one other way to get Hasha back. He propped her up against the rock he had rolled to. He poured a small amount of water into her mouth and waited for a response.

To his relief, Hasha started to cough and retched to her side. Clint waited for her stop. When he could see that she was alright, he told her about what had happened over the previous minutes.

Hasha said, “The last thing I remember was a high-pitched scream. I thought that it was some kind of weapon used to disorient people. What was the source of it?”

“Your guess is as good as mine. Honestly, I did not hear anything. But whatever it was, it looks like it was able to kill the Jides.”

Clint decided that they could not go by ground anymore. He stowed his quindent and told Hasha to climb onto his back. He spread his wings and took off. He climbed higher, until they were hidden in the clouds. He had a vague idea as to which direction they had to go. Soon, the air started becoming cooler, which meant that they were heading towards the Dividing Mountains.

The snowy patches soon revealed themselves and Clint headed for a flat part on the slope. He landed cautiously, not wanting to alert any nearby monsters of their location.

Hasha and he started heading north and further towards the centre of the mountain range. It was a bit of a climb, but they managed.

After about an hour, Clint heard a crashing sound ahead of them. He stopped dead in his tracks and produced a sword in each hand. He made Hasha hide behind a bush, while he hid behind a tree and waited for the source of the sound to come his way. He heard a lot of footsteps coming his way. When he was confident of being within striking range, he jumped out from his hiding place, only to find an axe and sword at his throat.

He assessed his would-be victims before saying, “You.”

The young man wielding the axe said, “Yes, us. Now, can we put our weapons away peacefully before we turn this place into a massacre?”

Clint laughed and called out, “Hasha, you can come out. Our friends from Talis are here. More importantly, your brother is here.”

Hasha came out from her spot, and got a huge hug from Ake. Gonth and Robert looked like they had done all the fighting in their group.

Just then, Clint fell to the ground. His wound being kept covered for so long, had revealed itself again. The last thing Clint heard was Robert saying, “Not good.”

# CHAPTER 23

Xristos could have never imagined being able to capture four youths in the span of less than two days, especially considering their powers. He stood in the throne room, watching as ghostly figures repaired the walls and ceiling. The throne itself was being repaired as well.

Originally black, it was slowly turning to white, with the six gems of the Districts of Lasgalan placed in a semicircle near the top of the throne. The steps to the throne too gleamed white. There was a hole on one wall, which was in such a place, that it looked like a natural spotlight on the throne. Byron wanted to fix that, but Xristos felt that it added to the regal look of the throne. One throne was at the right side of the king's throne, meant for Bryan, as he was the next in line for the throne. There was a wide walkway in front of the throne, where any subject of Lasgalan could walk in to speak to Yedgal. On either side of the walkway, four more thrones marched off, at a distance of five metres from each other. The right-hand side thrones were meant for Byron, Giriod, Shane and Sabre in that order from the king's throne. The left-hand side thrones were meant for Xristos, Karan, Listro and Raze in that order from the king's throne.

Each throne was made differently, depending on the person's personality. The colour on all thrones was white, though. Xristos smiled to himself and went down to visit the prisoners. Now that four had been captured, he was not really worried about time. Byron, however, seemed very anxious to get on with bringing his father back from the dead. He said that he could use the spells on the prisoners as they arrived, as then they would have one person less to worry about, because the spells might kill the person in the process. Xristos was a little orthodox and wanted to wait for all six prisoners.

He headed to the cells, where two new boys had been kept just the day before, in the evening. That was the hard work of Listro. Xristos recognised one of them, who was an Equine.

He stopped before Dan's cell and asked, "Third time captured, am I right?"

Dan lunged at him, determined to catch Xristos' neck. Xristos just backed up a foot, out of Dan's reach. He continued, "Do not have any fear, young man. You will help bring in a new age to Lasgalan."

"I doubt that Xristos."

Xristos moved to the cell which housed a girl. She was from Talis. Xristos did not know her power, but that did not worry him. She was sleeping, so he went to the last person, a boy from Leonis. From what Listro had told him, it seemed that this boy had the power of being intimidating. That would be useful power for Yedgal to have. The boy sat in a corner of the cell, cracking his knuckles.

None of the four had any weapons on them, which was good. The only problem was that no Guardians were found with them. Listro had said that he had seen none with the two boys that he captured. Sabre said that he had knocked the Guardian out of the body of the boy that he had brought. Raze had brought the girl from Equis, and it had taken the combined strength of Xristos, Sabre and Raze to kill the Dragon that emerged from her body. Nothing happened at that time, though a Citrine gem that was supposed to emerge then, did not emerge.

Xristos watched as the guards completed their shift and walked out. A new set of guards were to come soon. Xristos decided to change things a bit. He ordered the new set of guards coming in to position themselves outside the jail block. It would be better for them, as then there would be no chance of a jailbreak. He kept the keys of the cells with himself.

Once Jacob saw that no one was in the jail block, he ran to the door of his cell and tried to get Edward's attention. He managed to do so and asked, "How long have you been here?"

Then, Dan and Victoria came to their cell doors as well. Dan caught the bars of his door and shook them as if he was trying to pry them apart.

Edward said, "Don't bother. Even if a part of your body is inside the cell, your powers will not work. The man who brought me here said so."

As if to prove his point, Edward stuck his hand out and tried to summon flames. He had no luck.

Dan said, "This is the third time that I have been locked up here. Even my Rhodonite will not work. Trust me, I tried."

Edward said, "The back of our cells are soft. We could try and scrape through them to get out."

Victoria said, "We do not know what is on the other side. We could well land up in a monster's cell, or plummet through the air and die on impact with the ground below. We need to sit here and hope that someone comes for us."

Edward weighed his options carefully and said, "No one is coming."

Dan asked, "Why not? Given that they do not know the exact location of the palace, they would at least be on the move."

"You do not understand, Dan. When we segregated you into groups, we later decided that, if you were captured, we would fall back to the nearest cities, coordinate with the other groups, and then wait for the palace to reveal itself, before launching an assault on the palace."

Victoria spoke in an icy voice, "Why?"

"If we, by which I mean the six of us stronger youngsters, tried to come to your rescue and got captured, our powers would be taken as well. That is something we did not want happening. It would have been better if Yedgal got weaker powers and then we took him out, as our powers are on a much higher level than yours."

Jacob asked, "Are you calling us weak, or are you calling us cannon fodder?"

"Both. See, we have a higher chance of surviving whatever ceremony they plan to use us in. You guys would perhaps die. Once the bait is no longer there, we could attack the palace without any problems. It was a risk we were ready to take."

Jacob laughed and said, "Clint has gone back on his word, by the way."

It was Edward's turn to be surprised.

"Why?"

"He told us everything the moment we came to Logder. We did not believe him at first, but you just confirmed it. As for your question, Clint said that he would come to rescue us if we were captured. He was not going back to any city. We only had to make sure that neither Hasha nor he were captured. So we took the fall when we were captured."

Edward was stunned. He knew that Clint was a guy that obeyed his orders. Hearing that he was defying his orders from Talis, and was on his way to get them, did not sit well with Edward. He said, "Four of us are here. Considering our powers, especially mine, Yedgal will have no problem subduing or killing our friends. Now, we just have to see who are the other two coming here."

Victoria said, "We may have another problem. My bag of potions was taken when I was brought here. If they manage to create more potions from that, they will be almost unstoppable. We may not be able to get out of here, but we better come up with an escape plan fast."

Edward was about to say that no plan would be efficient, unless they were broken out of their cells. Just then, they heard the main door to their block being opened. The four of them crept back to the back of their cells. Three men walked in. Victoria recognised the man who brought her to her cell, while Dan and Jacob recognised their captor. There was also the man who Dan had slammed into a wall. How he was able to walk was a mystery to Dan.

The three men opened the first cell, which was Dan's. Dan did not resist as they tied up his hands. He waited till he was outside the cell, before trying to use his berserker strength. He failed to even summon strength from his legs. His captor made him walk through a room that he had never seen. They reached their destination.

It was a room about fifty metres long, twenty metres wide and had a ceiling so high that it was not visible. Daylight shone in through the many windows that lined the room, providing a great view of the greenery outside. But the real attraction was in front of Dan.

A pit was located in the centre of the room. It was pitch black, in contrast to the white marble floor that Dan was standing on. It was over five metres across, and looked as if it was cut through the mountain, heading all the way down to the Underworld. Across the circumference of the circle were six black tables, each eight feet long and five feet wide. They were mounted on pedestals that were three feet high. A young man, who they had never seen before, stood watching them as the four of them came in. Dan was made to lie on one table, of his choice, while his hands and feet were secure with ropes. He could turn his neck to see that the other were bound in a similar manner, each table a different colour, except for Edward and Victoria, as they were on orange tables, the colour of Talis. His table was blue, and Jacob's turned yellow as he lay down on it.

Once all of them were secured, the three men stood near the door, as if awaiting further instructions. The young man walked up to Dan, with a small knife in his hand. He inspected Dan's arms for a moment, before slicing a vein and letting the blood trickle slowly down the table, towards the pit. He did the same with the other three.

He stepped out of view and spoke to someone that they could not see. The cut was starting to burn Dan and he smelt burning skin. He did not know what was on that knife, but it was clearly not good for him and, by extension, any of the others. He tried to focus on other things, like the fact that Victoria was just one table away from him.

A booming voice was heard echoing across the room, in a language that none of them understand. Instantly, Dan felt the cut become longer, as if it was expanding across his arm. He screamed in agony, feeling his blood boiling. He turned to look at Victoria who was screaming as well. Blood was coming out of her mouth and her body was writhing, as if she wanted to break free of her bonds. Her eyes were turning red from the pain that she was experiencing.

The voice continued, and Dan understood that it was some sort of chant that the young man was doing. Dan felt his entire lower body spasm and suddenly felt his feet cool down. He understood that the blood from his legs was being brought up, towards the cut. It was only a matter of time before he would feel nothing at all.

He closed his eyes, wanting to go as calmly as possible. Sure, this was not the end that he had envisioned for himself, but if was going to die and his friends later managed to kill Yedgal, he would be remembered as one of the people who was part of that same group. He felt Frea trying to break free and control his body, but it seemed that even his Horse was no good against enchantments. Dan's heart was working against him now, trying to pump blood into his body at a frantic pace, to make up for the amount of blood he was losing. Any faster, and Dan was sure that his heart would burst out of his chest. He remembered what Edward had said about them not surviving this ceremony. He hoped that Edward would survive to wreak havoc on Yedgal's forces.

# CHAPTER 24

Ake watched over Clint's sleeping form as the six of them set up a temporary camp in a cave. He was really tired of hiding in caves. He even had a distaste for them, after he had seen the conditions of the people who worked in mines. Robert and Hasha had gone to look for some food that would be close by. That left Ake with Vesper and Clint. Gonth was near the entrance of the cave, standing guard. He looked a bit gloomy, which Ake knew was alright, given their circumstances.

Both Robert and Gonth had lost their Guardians while the group was fighting Battois on the foothills of the Dividing Mountains on the Talis side. But Robert took it in stride. He said that he now had nothing to lose, and was ready to fight to the death, if it meant bringing down Yedgal. Ake did not mind that attitude, though it sounded a bit too harsh, coming from a young man who was not even twenty.

They had tried to heal Clint as best they could, applying blocker all over his shoulder. Extracting the teeth of Jides was not easy, as they had to restrain him, not knowing what each tooth pull would make him do, as he was unconscious. All the teeth had been extracted and thrown into a stream.

Hasha had told him about their house's destruction, along with the encounter with the man who claimed to be from the Pegasi Tribe. Ake had quietly mourned his family's death, not speaking to anyone for an hour. He had cried a little, but he managed to calm himself. Now, he was going to keep his head straight and focus only on their mission. He knew that they had limited resources, in terms of potions. Hasha had her bag, as well the four of them from Ake's group.

Clint's face was one of eerie calm. Looking at him, one would have thought that he was one who had no worries in the world. Ake wanted to wake Clint up, as he was the reason that they were waiting. Ake was wondering where his sister and Robert had wandered off, when he heard a gallop of a Horse, nearing their hideout. Gonth and Ake both readied their weapons in a flash of purple and green. Vesper moved towards Clint's still frame. Ake heard the galloping come near the cave and suddenly stop. Then, he caught the scent of Robert, Hasha and fresh blood. He dropped his weapons, telling Gonth to do the same. He glanced outside the cave to see how Robert had gotten hold of a Horse, that too so far from Equis.

To his surprise, Robert was an armoured Centaur, which he said was his original merged form. Hasha was riding him, with a Dragon carcass in tow. Hasha jumped down from Robert's back and started to drag the carcass towards the cave, as Robert was taller in his merged form. Robert folded his legs under himself and closed his eyes in concentration. His armour melted back into clothes. They saw his hindquarters shrink, as if going into his back. A few seconds later, Robert was back to normal. He helped Hasha get the carcass into the cave, where it took up almost half the space inside. Ake, Robert and Gonth started to chop and slice away at the meat, but it was gruelling work. The scales on the Dragon did not help them. It was a small Dragon, though. It was about fifteen feet long, snout to tail. It would have been about six feet to the shoulder.

Vesper got a fire going, where the meat was being cooked, but without the fat. Ake decided to put a cooked piece of meat near Clint's nose, hoping that the smell would get him up again.

Clint's eyes opened after a few seconds. Ake eased him up gently with Gonth's help. Clint helped himself to a part of its hind leg, though he said that it tasted sweet. This time it was Hasha who told him to eat it quietly, as they would not be eating again for a while, and that he needed all the energy that he could get.

Clint heard the stories that Ake and his group had, which sounded less terrifying than facing three Crimson-eyed Bloodhounds. He did not tell Ake about the prayers he had said for his family. Once they finished their lunch, they covered the fire with a lot of dirt, careful not to let any smoke out. They left the cave, with Robert taking Vesper on his Equine back. Clint spread his wings and flew above them, but within the canopy of trees. Ake and Hasha led the group, talking among themselves. Gonth brought up the rear of the group, with his purple sword and shield in hand. They were heading north and a bit west, towards Leonis. Clint knew that their journey was going to be a few days, at the very least, since Vesper and Hasha would tire out the fastest. Also, he was not fond of travelling at night.

Ake was lost in his own world. He casually jumped over fallen trees and rocks, forcing the others to follow him. The air was getting a bit cooler, but it was not windy. Then, Clint saw it.

A lake lay in front of them. It was a small one, about fifty feet across. The water was almost clear, allowing Clint to see to the bottom of the lake. It looked about thirty feet deep, which was alright by Clint's standards. But he could not remember ever seeing this lake on any map of Lasgalan or a detailed map of Talis. He did two whole circles around the lake, checking for traps, but could see none. Ake could not smell any monsters as well. He went to a clump of trees and scratched at the trunk, hard. Clint knew that he was marking his territory, in a way. There were other ways, more primitive as Clint saw them, but he was not going to question Ake.

Clint screeched loudly, his voice echoing off the surface of the lake. As if it was a response, a deep roar sounded back. Clint and Ake exchanged worried looks. Clint climbed higher into the sky, wanting to get a heads up of what was coming towards them. Ake ran back to the group, who were ready with weapons.

Clint could not see anything in the distance. He looked at the water, wondering if there was some invisible monster around. He formed a spear and threw it into the water. It flew fast and true. It seemed to sink to the bottom. Clint was about to think that the roar was nothing of significance, when many things happened at once.

He heard another screech behind him. As he turned towards the source of the sound, he saw a flash of blue near the group. Before he could register what that meant, he got slammed in the chest by a long flat weapon. He just had time to think, "We were not taught to tackle flying swords."

He realised that two Jides were coming at him. He was falling towards the lake, and he heard the water under him explode. He knew that this was bad news. He turned and narrowly avoided a death bite from a Yoknie. He shot towards his friends, who were fighting many Battois. Ake and Gonth were driving one towards the water, while it spewed flames at them. Clint got his regular quindent out and stabbed the monster with a single point, before opening the five points within the Battos. Just for good measure, he threw the body into the water, near the Yoknie. He had to let go off his quindent as well, but he did not mind that. The Yoknie forgot about him and proceeded to chew the body up, taking it underwater.

Robert had evidently had enough of the Battois. He let loose his beastly side. Blue energy lines surrounded him, transforming into armour. His Equine half formed as well. He charged the monsters alone, right through the flames. He produced shields to prevent his face from getting destroyed, as his form did not give him a helmet.

Ake watched as Gonth's blue energy solidified into a Horse above him. He grabbed one Battos and threw it like a ball at some of the Battois. He produced two swords and started slashing away at the monsters.

Clint turned towards the Jides, who were not making any attempt to attack him. Clint turned to Ake and said, "Get ready to help Robert and me."

Ake nodded.

Clint flew up to meet the Jides in the air. His body started to turn red, which Ake was not happy to see. The red aura solidified into a Raven. Clint produced two swords and shot towards the Jides. He was so fast that Ake had trouble tracking him. His swords went through the Jides like a hot knife through butter. Neatly dissected, the monsters fell towards the water. Clint turned and headed for the group. He could smell the Battois heading their way, so he headed right for them. To his surprise, Robert ran alongside him. There was a stretch of open land, where they could see the Battois charging towards them. Clint waited till the last moment before pulling up into the air, using Robert as a distraction for the monsters.

Robert was fearless, Clint gave him credit for that. He headed for a tall rock and leapt off that, right into the middle of the group of fifty Battois. He started to attack them, occasionally shielding himself from the flames. Meanwhile, Clint was attacking the periphery of the small group. Together, the two of them hacked away at the group, until there was one monster left. It backed away slowly, not wanting to get close to them. Then, it turned and ran the way it had come. Clint calmly formed a bow and quiver. He nocked a black arrow, which had a serrated tip, and let it fly. The arrow found its mark. The Battos hit the ground and did not get up again.

Clint and Robert were still in their beast mode, but Clint had a strong willpower. He forced Cyrus back and took control of his own mind. Then, before Robert could do anything, Clint produced a large shield and smacked Robert in the face with it. Robert fell to the ground, taking on his human form again. He was still conscious, and accepted Clint's hand to get back to their friends, who were about five hundred metres away. Regrouping, they decided to move faster through the Mountains.

Clint could tell that they were getting to a very high altitude, where the air was quite thin. He came to that conclusion when Vesper and Hasha both complained of light-headedness and were forced to sit on

Robert while they tackled challenging slopes and jumped from cliff to cliff.

It was almost sunset, when they came to a small fortress. Calling it a fortress was too much, as it was obviously a temporary camp, made out of wood and not stone. It was big enough for about a hundred soldiers.

Ake tried to listen for any conversation happening inside the camp, but he was a bit far to catch any words. Clint was not willing to send him even further ahead. Clint asked Vesper, "Could you please cause a small fire to erupt around the camp, to get the soldiers outside?"

Vesper said, "I can. But I also have to worry about controlling it."

Hasha said, "Do not worry. I have got your back."

Vesper closed her eyes and extended her left-hand outwards. A small fire started behind the camp, growing larger by the second, until it was as large as the camp walls. Then, they heard screams from within the camp.

Clint waited for the first people to come out of the camp. Ten people emerged, looking as if they had been woken up from sleep. Ake got into action and dispatched them with some well-placed arrows. Clint and Robert ran to the entrance of the camp, killing whoever they could. But then, when it seemed that they had won and got the camp to themselves, a new surprise announced itself.

A screech made Ake glance to the back of the camp. A Constry was facing them. But it looked like a hybrid Constry. Instead of four arms, it had six. It had four eyes, not two, each one silver in colour. It stood fifteen feet tall, which Ake thought was unfair to them, as they would not be able to reach the head of the monster. It screeched again, in warning to the group, as if it would have preferred that they leave it in peace.

Clint unfurled his wings and said, "You guys distract it. I will get it from the top."

Robert said, “Do not be a fool. It has six arms, not four. We are only six. Besides, I am pretty sure that the poisoned claws will make short work of us.”

“Poisoned claws?” Gonth asked, sounding surprised.

“Yes. How did you not know that?”

“Never mind. We need to kill this monster. Any ideas?”

Ake said, “We cut off the arms.”

Hasha said, “Brother, you do know that they can regenerate any body part, right?”

“Yes. We will have to keep it distracted, while Clint does his work.”

Clint smiled and said, “Very well. Attack it.”

# CHAPTER 25

Patrick was not feeling good at all. He had almost led his team to death half a dozen times, being easily distracted after being told that he was going back to his own District. Karen had saved him all those times, being able to hold off the monsters they intercepted, with her fiery breath. Her breath, as it turned out, was not hot, but worked on a level comparable to a Battos'.

As they sat in a cave, waiting for the small rainstorm overhead to clear, Patrick put his head in his hands and said, "I'm sorry guys. I thought that I could help you once we arrived. But I guess that you are more up to the task than me."

Chris' voice was sharp like a knife.

"Then why did you say that you could help us? We would be dead by now, and no one would even know. It was only thanks to Karen that we are here. Maybe you think you have nothing to lose if you die here, which is pretty much true, but the three of us do. If we die, we would be one less fighter strong to take down Yedgal."

Chris would have probably continued, but Isabella put her hand on his chest. The second time they nearly died, Isabella's Horse, Esquire had unmerged and saved Chris. There was a geographically important gorge which Patrick had forgotten about. Chris would have had no time to escape his death. Esquire had unmerged and while falling down, kicked Chris back up to the group. He had died, and Chris retrieved Isabella's Rhodonite for her. Now, she could become a Centaur whenever she wanted.

Karen's Bull, Qezre, had died taking a Constry with him. Karen's Amethyst allowed her to transform into a Minotaur. But it added a permanent effect to her body. Her arms and legs became ripped, her body became sturdier. Her sense of smell was heightened, though her hearing was not enhanced a lot.

Patrick knew that he was the weakest out of all of them. He had tried to prove himself capable after the second close encounter, but it had not worked. Chris was not making things easy for him, and Patrick knew that Chris would have preferred him out of the group. Karen was the only one who did not give him any grief, but even she must have been nearing the end of her string.

Patrick watched as Chris walked towards the entrance of the cave and glanced out, to see the setting sun through the dark clouds. Just then, Isabella tensed.

Before they could register what was happening, five Battois walked out from the back off the cave, which should not have been possible, as Chris had collapsed that part of the cave. The trio backed up quickly, almost sending Chris off the side of the hill they were on. The Battois stopped ten feet from them. Karen said, "I will hold them off. Chris, fly these two away."

"No, Karen. They want you. I can take them."

Before Karen could protest, Chris pulled her back and threw her down the side of the hill. The fall would not kill her, being only thirty feet onto solid ground. Chris caught hold of Patrick and said, "Take care of yourselves."

As Patrick and Karen watched from thirty feet below, the mouth of the cave spewed blue flames. The last thing they heard was Chris' signature screech, used to cause havoc to the enemy's hearing.

Karen reacted fast. She grabbed Patrick's wrist and dragged him under a cluster of boulders. Patrick managed to squeeze into a small gap between the boulders, being very thin. Karen stuck as close to the boulders as possible, trying not to reveal too much of herself. Patrick could not see much, but Karen could.

The Battois walked out of the cave, all five of them. One of them glanced in the direction of the boulder, which made Karen very worried. If the monsters charged towards them, they were dead. One monster carried the limp bodies of Chris and Isabella, which he set down on the ground. Karen was ready to grieve for them, when she saw Isabella's leg twitch. She would have sighed in relief, if she had not seen Chris' situation.

Chris looked like he had taken the full power of the flame upon himself. His wings did not show much damage, but one of them was bent at a funny angle. He did not furl them in, which made Karen a bit worried as to whether he was alive or dead. His face was red all over, and parts of his skull were showing. His eyes were shut, and one shoulder was evidently dislocated. It was shoulder on which his wing was bent. Karen suspected that, if his wing took sufficient damage, his arm bones too would give way. His shirt was completely ripped, where most of the Battois' flames would have made contact. Karen looked for any sign of him breathing, but could not see anything.

The Battos who was carrying Isabella and Clint stood guard over their bodies. It rumbled to its companions, in what Isabella assumed was their language. Then it did something that Karen would have never imagined a monster of any type would have done to a victim.

It took some of its own saliva in its hand, and rubbed it over Chris' face and torso. All the cuts and bruises on Chris' body slowly disappeared. His wing did not mend though. His dislocated shoulder stayed as it was.

The Battois fanned out, evidently searching for the two of them. Karen and Patrick waited, not moving unless needed. Karen had not changed into a Minotaur, which was good, as her flames would have attracted the attention of the Battois. How they had not smelled the duo yet was a mystery. After about ten minutes, the Battois gave up on their search and headed back into the cave. Karen was about to follow them, but Patrick stopped her.

Karen asked, "Why not? If we can kill them and get our friends back, all the better."

"How do you know that it is not a trap? Chris brought down the back of the cave. We saw that. Then how did those monsters get through the rubble? Even if it is not a trap, we have no idea how many more Battois are waiting inside. We need to get away from this area as fast as possible."

Karen wondered what had happened to Patrick suddenly. He was not like this when they first entered Leonis. Maybe the loss of Isabella and Chris had shocked him and his mind was now working out every possible scenario. Nevertheless, she nodded and said, "Which city now?"

Patrick said, "There is one south of the minor Fang River. It is very secure. Hopefully, we can get a message out to Talis. This city is loosely guarded as it is mostly a farmer's city. So do not destroy anything there. It is the lifeline of some of the eastern cities of Leonis. We call the city Larente."

"Fine. How fast can we get there?"

"If we call it a night now, move out at dawn and do not stop even while we are eating, and call it a night again at sunset, about one and a half days, if we run like mad. We can reach it by tomorrow night, if we get lucky and do not run into monsters. But we first need to get down from the Mountains, and cross two tributaries of the Fang River. There will be no cities on the most direct route there."

Karen walked to the side of the cliff that they were on. She could not see all the way to the bottom of the mountainside, but she could see a winding path leading down. She pointed it out to Patrick, who said, "It is a risk. We will be open to attack from all directions. If we go now, we may not be attacked. It is your call. You are the leader here."

"No. This is your District. I will follow you. You are the leader here, not me. It is your call."

Patrick's mind was busy running fighting scenarios in his head. He said, "We take the direct route down."

Karen said, "My body might be able to take the fall, but I am not grabbing hold of you. My poisoned nails can kill people like Garon within minutes. You might not even last that long."

"Are your nails still poisoned after taking up your Amethyst?"

"Actually, I am not sure. But I do not want to risk testing it out on you now."

"Then we take the road."

Patrick and Karen got to the winding road, which was a trail cut into the mountainside. Karen led the way, relying on her sense of hearing and smell as the sun went down. From time to time, they heard roars of Lions, causing them to run for a bit down the trail. Finally, they reached the bottom of the trail.

The sun had set some time back and they were running almost blind into the wilderness. Patrick started to use his Ring for light, showing the next few metres ahead, before shutting the flames off. He was afraid that the light would attract all kinds of creatures to their location, which was not something that he wanted happening.

They had walked about four leagues, when Patrick stopped. He said, "We rest here for tonight. Tomorrow we take off running. Feed yourself before we leave this place. No fire here. If you need, I can light up this area for a few moments. But do whatever you need to within that time."

"You got it."

# CHAPTER 26

Vincent worked himself to the death bringing down the Jides hovering in the air, fifty metres above his group. Adriana produced spear after spear for him, and he threw them at the monsters.

James was taking shots from the air, attracting some of the monsters towards himself, but they were more focussed on Vincent. James had a better vantage from his position, and he could see more of them pouring in from over the mountain tops. They were not even at the peak of the mountain they were on. He threw knives after knives at the monsters heads, getting the blades into the heads of the monsters without a second knife needed to finish the job.

Adriana was hurling rocks from underneath the ground at the monsters that got too close to Vincent or her. They were on a plateau where they were planning on resting for the night. The sun was setting, which allowed them to see their opponents. Vincent used his sense of smell to hit his targets. James was getting tired of being in the air, so he dropped down next to Vincent and the duo took out targets even faster, with a monster getting two hits from different angles at times. But they just kept coming. James used the ace up his sleeve and let out a screech. His screeches were becoming worse every time he used them. Vincent barely had time to shut his ears, as dead Jides fell all over them.

Vincent pulled his fingers out from his ears and asked James, "How do you manage to pull off worse screeches with each passing moment?"

James shrugged his shoulders and said, "No idea. Maybe as the situations get worse, I get to go higher. Or perhaps, the longer I have my Schrol, the better I get."

Adriana said, "I do not know about better, but you just killed creatures, who do not have external ears, with sound. You are a force to be reckoned with. Not as much as Vincent though." She added quickly.

Vincent said, "We will stay here for the night. Perhaps the stench of these dead bodies will mask our scent from any other monsters who might be seeking us out. Put them in a circle around us and take off their heads, just to be sure that they are dead."

James got to work and placed the heads around them. Adriana watched him work and told Vincent, "We have a problem. Yours and James' potions are with Victoria, but she is not here. Worst case scenario is that she has been captured. Best case scenario, she is doing what we are. Surviving."

Vincent glanced up at the stars and replied, "It does not matter. You are there. We have not used up a lot of potions anyway, in these last two days. We are supposed to fall back to the nearest city in Equis, but after Cylinx, I just want to finish this job fast and go back home."

James dropped down next to them and said, "You make it sound like it is a burden on you. Think of it as your righteous path."

"Exactly my point James. I did not ask to be born like this. The powers are good, but this divine duty and righteous path thing is not something I am comfortable with. What happens if we lose, and I am the only survivor? I will be reliving these days in my head, until my death, wondering how I could have changed the outcome of what had happened."

Adriana watched as the two boys talked. She understood what was running through their minds. James did not mind the additional responsibility that came with his life. Vincent, on the other hand, wanted the responsibility taken off his back. She could not claim to understand what they were going through. Vincent, in the meanwhile, was getting ready to go to sleep. He curled into a foetal position and was snoring within minutes. Adriana and James stayed up and talked softly. Somehow, James managed to get Adriana to open up about her past, as she had grown up in one of the roughest places in Equis. Soon, Adriana was pouring her heart out to him. James was a good listener. Every time Adriana would stop, he would nod and say, "Continue."

Adriana spoke of the boys who she had known in Cylinx, before they either left for other cities for better futures or died while working for Cylinx. As it turned out, Adriana had quite a dull history in her sixteen years of living in Equis. When James asked how Isabella was comfortable with Adriana's lifestyle, all he got was a conspiratorial wink.

James laughed and said, "In Covis, you would have put into jail for that negligence. You would have been released at eighteen."

"I take your word for it. But unfortunately, I live in Equis. Quite literally on the other side of the country."

James allowed himself a smile. He did not want to laugh as he might wake up Vincent.

"James, you are only fourteen. Have you ever thought about your future?"

James looked at her with menacing eyes. Adriana supposed that was to deter her, but she had grown up looking at those kinds of eyes. So she did not retract the question.

James formed a knife in his hand and glanced at Adriana's stomach. Adriana figured that he would make quick work of her, before she could ask Vincent for help. James, however, just turned the knife in his hand, let it disappear, and then said, "A spy or an assassin."

Adriana's heart sped up a little bit. The way James said those words, with such finality and confidence, made her feel a bit more secure. If he was planning on taking one of those jobs, he would have been planning and training from a young age. She was now sure that he could take her out quickly and painlessly. She lay down on the ground and said, "You might as well get some sleep. Tomorrow we get to the Equine Gulf's strait. The swim will not be easy. It will be a long one, and we may probably face Yoknies as well."

James said, "I am not sleeping. With our big hitter having a good snooze, it is only right that I stay awake and guard you guys. Besides, I have always been more of a night person. As for the swim, I can take you on my back and carry Vincent in my arms. Picture that."

Adriana did and nearly burst out laughing.

"Very funny, James. Now let me sleep."

She crashed out on the ground and James got up to walk around. He took off as gently as possible from the ground and made wide circles around the sleeping duo. He climbed higher and higher, till Adriana and Vincent were small figures on the ground. James' vision during the night was significantly better than his vision during the day. He could make out different colours, see accurately for about fifty metres. But his sight powers were nowhere at par with Garon's. Ake had once said that Garon could see the heat given out by objects, see through objects, see in pure darkness, and move properly even if blindfolded. James scanned the sky for threats. Being an almost foggy area, he could see properly up to about thirty metres. He could not smell any monsters, and he could not see any moving through the trees.

After about three hours of hovering in the air, James dropped down next to his companions. He lay down on his stomach, spread his wings over his friends to camouflage them against the ground and dark surroundings, and waited for dawn to arrive. He did not sleep the entire night.

James was the first one up before dawn. As he had not slept the night, his eyes were bloodshot. He felt weak in the legs, and his wings were very stiff. He forced them to furl inwards, walking away from the duo, who were still sleeping. He had no change of clothes, but still had to freshen up. He walked up to some bushes, looking for a certain herb that would mask his body odour for the rest of the day. He and Vincent had been using those herbs ever since they escaped Cylinx, some time back. Adriana had shown them the herbs.

He found the herbs and plucked them from the bush. He crushed the stem, leaves and flowers before rubbing the flowing juice onto his arms. He took some more and rubbed it across his face, neck, legs and back. As usual, the herb had a cooling effect on his back and he felt like he had got a good night's sleep. He gathered up whatever was left of the bush and took it back to the duo. The sky was turning grey, dawn not far away. James shook Vincent awake and gave him half the quantity of herbs he had. Vincent nodded and the odour from his body too was gone, replaced by a lovely fragrance.

As Adriana was still sleeping, James and Vincent talked about getting across the Equine Gulf's strait. Vincent did not mind James' idea of carrying the two off them, though it would be a strain on his body for the two leagues of flying that had to be done. James was confident that he could handle it. He told Vincent about his conversation with Adriana the night before. Vincent did not seem surprised at all.

When James asked him why, Vincent replied, "Sometimes staying on the ground can help you understand your friends better, rather than hovering fifteen feet above them."

James looked over to Adriana and said, "She is kind of interesting, I must say."

Vincent promptly said, "James, do not even think about it."

"Oh, trust me, after hearing about what she has done, I am thinking about it."

Vincent grabbed James' arm and said, "That was not a warning. You try anything with her, and I put a projectile through your heart."

James replied nonchalantly, “So then, are you warning me to stay out of your way, so that you can get to her?”

“Well played James. But the answer is no. I am going to kill Yedgal, take her back to Cylinx, you to Covis, and settle myself in Leonis.”

James raised an eyebrow and asked, “When do you want to wake her up? She sleeps very heavily, as we know. Might take some time for us to find and get her to a proper place.”

“True. If we can find a spring or something, nothing like it. Preferably a hot spring.”

“Vincent, we both just had a bath, in a manner of speaking. Do not wash it off. We have a full day to smell like this, no matter what happens. Besides, our body odour is not as bad as theirs.”

James pointed to the dead Jide bodies around them, which were reeking of sulphur. Some bodies were starting to decay, while others remained intact. From the corner of his eye, James saw something move, just beyond the trees.

Without turning his head, James said, “Something is here.” He flicked his eye to the left. Vincent smelt the air and said, “Yes. Food. Wait here.”

Vincent’s claws sprang out from his fingers. He shot towards his prey silently, giving James enough time to mentally prepare an obituary for the unfortunate animal. Vincent came back, holding three dead deer. They had been killed cleanly, with three large claw marks across their neck. Vincent started to clean the meat off the bone, using a short yellow sword.

James asked, “Can we eat these raw? I would not like to have a fire going. That would give away our location.”

“We could, if we wanted to die from food poisoning. Come on, man. We have been in the wilderness for some time now. Have you ever eaten uncooked venison?”

“Just messing with you, Vincent. You carry on. I am getting the wood."

Vincent dug a hole two feet deep and they had the fire going soon. The fire was small, but hot enough to start cooking the meat. The sun had almost cleared the horizon by the time Adriana woke up. She saw the meat being cooked and half crawled, half walked to the fire. The wind was picking up, which explained why their fire was two feet below the ground. As per usual, they kept the fat in a separate, airtight bag and inside Adriana's bag. They had made it a point to eat the fat of any animal they caught as their last meal of the day. Adriana gestured for the herbs, which James would have given to her, but Vincent said, "You wash up first. Then you can think about using the herbs."

Adriana said, "There is no water source here."

"Follow me."

They followed Vincent to the trees. After about two minutes, they heard a gurgling sound. They came to a spring that looked as if it had not been touched in centuries. The trees were fifty feet tall, with a canopy that was not very thick. A ray of sunlight fell on the centre of the spring. The water was clear to the bottom, three feet down. Vincent filled his canteen with the water and James did the same. Adriana asked Vincent, "How did you find this place?"

"Where do you think the three deer came from?"

Adriana put her hand in the water. It was warm and seemed like the ideal temperature for her to take a bath in. She turned to see both the boys had their backs to her, weapons at the ready. She got the message. She slipped out of her day-old clothes, took out her spare clothes and went into the spring. The water, which was seemed warm, was cooler towards the bottom. No fish were to be seen. Adriana trusted the boys enough to guard her. She went down on her knees and let the water come up to her chin. She closed her eyes and went under. She emerged a few seconds later, feeling rejuvenated.

She decided to have a little swim and relax in the spring. She could see the back of James' neck beaded with sweat, despite the breeze blowing and the cool weather around them. He and Vincent seemed to be having a conversation. Adriana did not bother asking them what they were talking about. She finished with her swim and stepped out of the spring. She said, "You boys can look back now."

Vincent turned first, and he was shocked by what he saw. He seemed to be at a loss for words. James too was in shock. But he managed to say, "Adriana, what happened to you?"

If their eyes could have popped out of their sockets, Adriana thought they would have. But she did not know what they were having trouble comprehending. Then Vincent pointed it out to her.

Adriana's dark, maple skin had given way to a light, bronze coloured one. Her dark and rough hair had become glossy and very straight. Her nails looked like they had been dipped in milk and the milk had bonded with the very cells of her nails. Her cracked lips had become smooth. The water might as well have done a complete makeover on her, given the way the boys described her. Adriana was used to boys giving her undivided attention, but the way Vincent and James gave her their undivided attention was different. Almost good different. They cared about her.

James drank some water from his canteen, spat it out almost instantly and emptied the remaining water to the spring. Vincent asked, "Why did you do that? You need water to drink from time to time."

"Taste it. You will understand."

Vincent tasted the water from his canteen. He realised that it was pure salt water. His taste buds, being partly that of a Lion's, fired the message to his brain. He nearly released his breakfast from his stomach, but managed to spit out the water. Vincent came to a conclusion.

"We must be near the Equine Gulf. Perhaps that is why the water is very salty."

James contradicted him and said, "We are near the sea anyway. That is why the water is salty."

Vincent scratched his head and said, "Silly me."

Adriana was busy admiring her new look. She figured she looked a year younger, though neither boy said anything. James was trying to compose himself, while Vincent tested the water. He put his entire arm, up to his elbow, in the water and took it out moments later. Sure enough, even his stone-coloured skin, which was greyish, turned to a shade of marble. It gave his arm a funny look, dark white from his finger to elbow, and grey from the elbow upwards.

Adriana laughed and said, "You would make a good statue."

Vincent scowled and gestured for James to give Adriana the herbs. Adriana did not feel any different after applying the juice on herself.

They walked on, keeping the sea in view, though they had to move inland from time to time, but they headed south most of the time. They moved from piedmont plateau to piedmont plateau. The sunlight was obscured from them, only coming down to the forest floor at regular shafts.

By noon, Vincent was getting restless. No monsters had attacked them. He could not smell them, which meant that they were either far from the group, or they were dead. A large flock of geese flew above them. James, absentmindedly, formed a bow and quiver of arrows. He sent one arrow flying at the geese. It hit the leader, who fell ahead of them. The flock carried on without stopping. They came upon the fallen bird, who was calling out in misery. James' arrow had missed its heart. As a result, the bird was going through torture by living. A slow trickle of blood was pouring out from its chest.

Adriana told James, "Finish the job."

She closed her eyes as James decapitated the goose, relieving it of the pain. Vincent was on a tree, trying to get above the canopy to see what lay ahead of them. He was hidden by the branches and leaves for a few moments, until he came down and said, "You guys better come with me."

Considering that they were not very high up in the Rhodonite Hills, the Equine section of the Dividing Mountains, James did not expect to get much of a scenery in front of him. They moved on for fifteen minutes, picking their way through the dense undergrowth. Sometimes, James had to fly Adriana across areas where her form would not allow her to cross normally. Vincent was moving like a Lion, jumping from tree to rock to ground without making a noise.

Finally, they saw the tree growth come to a halt ahead of them. They emerged from the trees, to get a magnificent view of the Equine Gulf's strait. They were about a thousand feet above the surface of the water, with a narrow cliff ahead of them. They could see the famous Isle of the Pegasi faintly in the distance, to their left. But their target was ahead of them.

Two and a half leagues of water separated them from the other side of Equis. They saw the Dividing Mountains rising right from the coast, which gave the Mountains a weird appearance. A small piece of land was visible about a league from them, in the strait itself. Vincent pointed to it and said, "We can stop there for a break, before heading onwards."

James unfurled his wings and said, "I'm sold. Let's do this."

He walked to the end of the cliff and was about to take off, when he heard a loud growl from behind them. He was going to turn, but Vincent pushed him off the cliff. James levelled out and came back up to them. He could make out a small shape heading towards them. It was coming fast. Vincent got Adriana onto James' back and yelled, "Get out of here! I will handle this monster."

James said, "No. You cannot handle this one. It is an Underworld Hound."

"Exactly why I am telling you to go. Now, go!"

James stayed away from the cliff as he saw Vincent charge into the trees, his aura bright. They could hear defiant yells and howls from within the forest, but James did not go closer. Adriana waited for James to do something. But all James did was fly her away from cliff, towards the piece of land in the strait. He placed her on it and said, "Wait here for us."

He zipped back to the cliff, wondering whether Vincent was already dead or on his way to death. He heard the Hound snapping at something, but no sound of Vincent. He shot through the canopy and found himself three feet from the Hound, its teeth stained red with blood. Under the foot of the animal, Vincent lay. His eyes were closed, but his breath was uneven. His bloodied chest was about three ribs away from being completely opened, to reveal his heart. His abdominal cavity was completely exposed, though his liver and one kidney were still intact. James and the Hound eyed each other for a moment. Then, the Hound slowly moved towards James, who moved backwards. He hoped that Vincent would try and move away from the monster, but that was wishful thinking. Vincent would not be able to even crawl two feet, without losing a lot of blood or his organs. James moved as far back as he could dare, to the edge of the cliff. The Hound snapped in warning at James, but James did not flinch. He could see Vincent slowly move his hands around on the ground, but Vincent wisely did not make an attempt to get up.

James produced a long sword in his dominant left hand to keep the Hound at bay, but he had to get around the monster to get to Vincent. The Hound was getting tired of their little standoff, and tested James. It jumped a little high at the young boy, who instinctively formed a shield with his right hand and smashed the monster in the face, sending back a few feet, almost near Vincent. Then, disaster struck.

As the Hound was hit backwards towards Vincent, the latter suddenly shot up from his place and caught the Hound by its neck. He forced it down to the ground and locked eyes with James, who was shell-shocked at how Vincent had managed that move. Vincent roared in triumph and his aura surrounded both him and the monster. James barely had time to move, when everything in reach of the aura burst into flames and the force of the blast blew him away from the cliff, down towards the sea.

James managed to stop his fall and came up again. Everything that was flammable was on fire. James could make out the still form of the monster, so he threw the monster to the side and found Vincent's body. The body was not hot, and the aura was not coming off it. James held the body gently and flew off to Adriana, who was waiting for them. She nearly screamed when James lay the still body of Vincent on the ground. She looked up at James for an explanation, but James was struggling to keep himself together. He dug through Adriana's bag and took out a vial of sapphire potion. The blue liquid was placid at first, but vapours started to come off the surface of the liquid as soon as sunlight hit the vial. James shielded the vial with his body and was about to open it, when Adriana asked, "Are you sure that he is dead?"

James looked into her eyes and said, "He cannot be alive, not in his current state. Apply blocker all around his stomach. Hopefully, we can bring him back. Also, be ready with sweenet in case he has got broken bones."

Adriana carefully applied small amounts of blocker over Vincent's stomach. The hole sealed itself up. James waited for a minute and poured a few drops of sapphire potion into Vincent's mouth. Adriana had a worried look on her face. James put his hand on her shoulder and, "Vincent will pull through. Now we just have to wait for him to wake up."

"What happened up there? You guys could not have killed the Hound. You need Acid Hounds for that."

James told her what had happened. She sat down hard on the ground and watched Vincent. She final said, "If he does not pull through, what are we supposed do with the body?"

"Hey, I said he will pull through. We gave him sapphire potion. Sweenet will repair his bones if needed."

A sound from Vincent brought them both to his side. His limbs were twitching, and his head was moving from side to side. James got behind his head and held it hard to prevent damage to his neck. Vincent's face became one of rage, the moment he felt James' hands on his head. Before he opened his eyes, he lashed out his right hand, grabbing James' throat and throwing him to the edge of the water. It was a good thing that the island was about twenty metres across, or else James would have been in the water. Vincent was on his feet, his eyes wide open, blazing yellow in colour. He popped out his claws and walked fast towards James.

James formed a bow and quiver, firing arrow after arrow at Vincent. He yelled, "Adriana, hold his feet in the ground."

Vincent stopped three feet from James, Adriana having brought the ground up to his waist to stop him. James got a bit closer and yelled, "Vincent, snap out of it! It is me, James!"

In response, Vincent attempted to slash open James' jugular. He roared in challenge at James. James said, "Adriana, shut your ears tight. This is going to be bad."

Adriana ran as far away from James as she could, on the small island. James locked eyes with Vincent and softy said, "Sorry about this, buddy."

Vincent bared his teeth, but James was not intimidated. He closed his eyes, took in a long, deep breath, and unleashed a sound of hell. Adriana could hear it clearly through her plugged ears. The shockwaves that she felt from that sound were very bad themselves. She could only think about what Vincent was hearing. She remembered that James had got people's ears to bleed in Cylinx, from a distance. There was no way Vincent was not going deaf hearing a louder sound at a much closer range.

When James finally stopped his screech, Adriana unplugged her ears. She had concentrated on keeping Vincent's legs in place, and had not failed in her task. Vincent was still in his place, holding his head and howling in pain. His ears were not bleeding, though. Adriana asked James, "What did you do to him?"

James studied Vincent before replying, "I focussed my sound to give his body a good shock. I did not concentrate the sound to his ears, which would have overloaded his senses and caused him to go deaf. He should snap out of whatever he is in."

"You said the same for getting him back alive."

"That worked, didn't it?"

Vincent had stopped howling, but he still had a murderous look in his yellow eyes. That meant that he had not entirely snapped out of his anger. Adriana said, "Does he have a girlfriend?"

James shrugged his shoulders and said, "Not that I know of."

"Fine. Then stay out of this."

"Stay out of what?"

Adriana tossed her hair back and approached Vincent. He did not lash out at her. He was breathing heavily as Adriana kissed his cheeks. It was not something that James would have risked doing to Vincent, but he was not going to argue with Adriana. He watched as the yellow colour faded from Vincent's eyes. His previously pale face became flushed as blood rushed back to the surface of his skin. He blinked a few times, as if getting up from a deep sleep. He took a second to realise that Adriana's lips were on his cheeks. He instinctively leaned away from her and said, "Stop, stop! I have a girlfriend!"

Adriana stopped and drew her head back. She made a sad face and said, "But I was feeling nice."

"You may have been feeling nice, but I sure was not feeling nice. I made a vow with her not to even kiss another girl or get anywhere along those lines with another girl, unless we decide to part company."

James said, "Damn. Did you also take an oath to practise celibacy? I am just curious here."

Vincent glared at him and said, "No."

Adriana said, "Look, it was the only gamble I could take. If there is one thing I excel in, it is making people come back to normal, thought the means I employ are a bit questionable."

Vincent asked sarcastically, "A bit. You forget, both of us know your dull history."

"I know. And as men of honour, which I do not doubt you are, I expect you to keep that to yourselves."

"Well played, Adriana. Now, do you mind letting me go?"

James mischievously asked, "Do you promise not to try and kill me if we do so?"

"Shut up James."

Adriana pulled the earth down from his legs as he looked out to the southern horizon. Through the layer of mist, Vincent could make out the beginning of the Dividing Mountains. He pointed towards the nearest peak and said, "James, take us there."

# CHAPTER 27

Byron always prided himself on performing sorcery with perfection. However, it seemed that he would have to swallow his pride for once, forced down his throat by his own brother.

Bryan was not one bit pleased to find that his brother had defied their father's commandments and killed three out of the four prisoners that they had. According to Byron, it was better to be safe than to be sorry. His reasoning was the escape of their last two prisoners, one of whom had breathed his last a few moments before Bryan had entered the room where Byron had performed the revival ceremony to bring back their father. Bryan slapped Byron hard across the latter's face, with a Lion's paw. The claws drew some blood from Byron's face, but he put his palm to his cheek and healed himself.

Bryan said, "I should oust you from the palace. You are unfit to be called a prince. If you have any sense of remorse, stop this ceremony."

Byron said, "It is too late to stop this. I can wait until the next people are brought in. Then we use them as well."

Bryan could not stand it anymore. He turned to Raze, Listro and Karan, who were standing at the door and said, "Bury these three with the rituals of their respective Districts."

He turned to Edward, who was the only one who had survived the ceremony. Bryan sliced the restraints off him and carried him back to his cell. He gently placed Edward on the floor and walked out, closing the door of the cell behind him. He walked to the throne room, where he saw five Battois present two more people to Byron. Bryan immediately commanded, without them seeing him, "Put them in the cells. I will see to them. Only when I say, will they be used."

Byron cursed his luck. Bryan had played his ace to counter him. As the elder son, Bryan's word carried more weight than Byron's. The only person who could overturn Bryan's command was their father. So, Bryan's command was followed. The duo, who were one girl from Equis and a boy from Covis, were barely aware of what was happening around them, as they were partially drugged. The Battois left Bryan and went their own way.

The boy was evidently in a lot of pain, as his facial expressions gave it away. Bryan realised that he was the same one who had escaped last time, but he did not say anything. Physically, nothing seemed wrong with the boy, but he was in pain. One of shoulders seemed a bit large for someone of his size. Then, Bryan realised what had happened.

The boy's shoulder had been dislocated. It would be impossible to tell when and where he had sustained that injury, but it was no doubt the source of his pain. Bryan hurried back to his chambers, where he found a small vial of sweenet. He could not consume any of the potions that they had found with the girl from Talis, though everyone else in the council could. He ran back to the boy's cell and opened it. He knelt at the boy's side and prised his jaws open. He poured two drops into the boy's mouth, which was enough for the shoulder to pop back into its socket. The boy, though drugged, must have felt the relief coursing through his arm, as his facial expressions became relaxed. Byron came to the cell and found Bryan leaving it.

He asked Bryan. "Why did you do that? He was incapacitated, no threat to us. You just helped him get over a month's worth of injury."

Bryan replied, "It is because I have honour, more than you. Also, if I have to fight him, it would be a better death for either of us if the other was at full strength, with nothing holding us back. You would not know much about that. You always relied on sneak attacks and never fought hand to hand. In a proper fight, you would be injured beyond fighting, if not dead. Remember, there is nothing wrong in fighting with honour."

# RECAP OF NAMES AND LOCATIONS

**NAMES of the chosen ones:**

**Ake:** A fourteen-year-old boy, from Logder. Favoured weapon is double-bladed axe. Standing in at 6'3" and 82 kgs, the Grey Wolf, Hadver watches over him. Power is super hearing.

**Anne:** A fourteen-year-old girl, from Leonis. Favoured weapon is her mind, which is sharper than the others'. Standing in at 6'2" and 75 kgs, the Claw Lion, David watches over her. Power is brute strength.

**Chris:** A sixteen-year-old boy, from Covis. Favoured weapon is solid metal mace. Standing in at 6'0" and 70 kgs, the Mountain Raven, Cronder watches over him. Power is changing body structures.

**Clint:** A seventeen-year-old boy, from Covis. Favoured weapon is trident-cum-spear. Standing in at 6'5" and 80 kgs, the Black Raven, Cyrus watches over him. Power is that he can assess any threat and find a solution to fight it.

**Dan:** A fifteen-year-old boy, from Equis. Favoured weapon is bow and arrow. Standing in at 6'0" and 76 kgs, the Blue Roan, Frea watches over him. Power is that he can sense the emotions of animals and humans.

**Edward:** A seventeen-year-old boy, from Talis. Favoured weapon is flames that he can produce and use to fly, among other things. Standing in at 6'4" and 76 kgs, the Fire Dragon, Ontemp watches over him. Power is that he doesn't crack under pressure.

**Elesa:** A fourteen-year-old girl, from Logder. Favoured weapon is sword. Standing in at 6'2" and 85 kgs, the Grey Wolf, Ketta watches over her. Power is uncontrolled rage that supplies great amounts of strength.

**Emmanuel:** A seventeen-year-old boy, from Tauris. Favoured weapon is club of mountain birch. Standing in at 6'6" and 78 kgs, the Hump Bull, Aral watches over him. Power is that he doesn't back down from a fight, even if he knows that he will die.

**Garon**: A fifteen-year-old boy, from Logder. Favoured weapon is dagger. Standing in at 6'5" and 84 kgs, the Ag Wolf, Edmund watches over him. Power is super sight, for any environment.

**Gonth:** A fifteen-year-old boy, from Tauris. Favoured weapon is sword and shield. Standing in at 6'2" and 81 kgs, the Poison Bull, George watches over him. Power is that he can see the result of any battle beforehand, with whatever information he is given.

**Isabella:** A fifteen-year-old girl, from Equis. Favoured weapon is traps made by her. Standing in at 6"0" and 86 kgs, the Blue Roan, Esquire watches over her. Power is her ability to sense traps or ambushes from a distance.

**Jacob:** A sixteen-year-old boy, from Leonis. Favoured weapon is knuckledusters. Standing in at 6'1" and 83 kgs, the Cut Lion, Zoh watches over him. His power resides in his ability to intimidate others.

**James:** A fourteen-year-old boy, from Covis. Favoured weapon is knives. Standing in at 6'3" and 82 kgs, the Mountain Raven, Riyo watches over him. Power is turning invisible.

**Karen:** A fourteen-year-old girl, from Tauris. Favoured weapon is scythe. Standing in at 6'4" and 70 kgs, the Poison Bull, Qezre watches over her. Power is being an expert at torture.

**Robert:** A fifteen-year-old boy, from Equis. Favoured weapon is hands, being a specialist in hand-to-hand combat. Standing in at 6'2" and 85 kgs, the Strawberry Roan, Darius watches over him. Power is being able to hide his emotions from others.

**Trest:** A fifteen-year-old girl, from Talis. Favoured weapon is a customised scalpel. Standing in at 6'0" and 70 kgs, the Fire Dragon, Dersyu watches over her. Power is quick healing, and can heal others quickly as well.

**Victoria:** A sixteen-year-old girl, from Talis. Standing in at 6'1" and 80 kgs, the Sharp-Winged Dragon, Phiroze watches over her. Power is pheromonal manipulation.

**Vincent:** A sixteen-year-old boy, from Leonis. Favoured weapon is javelin. Standing in at 6'0" and 85 kgs, the Claw Lion, Nilesh watches over him. Power is accurate missile projection up to half a league.

**NAMES of the District Ring Bearers:**

**Adrian:** A fifteen-year-old boy, from Tauris.

**Adriana:** A sixteen-year-old girl, from Equis.

**Hasha:** A fourteen-year-old girl, from Logder.

**Thomas:** A fourteen-year-old boy, from Leonis.

**Vesper:** A fifteen-year-old girl, from Talis.

**NAMES of the Gods:**

**Esdah:** God of the Underworld.

**Sorenth:** God of War.

**Ara:** Goddess of Ice.

**NAMES of the Antagonists:**

**Yedgal:** The Dead Tyrant, killed by Rendaf's father.

**Xristos:** General of Yedgal's army.

**Raze:** Captain of Yedgal's private guard.

**Bryan:** Crown Prince, animalistic shape-shifter.

**Byron:** Bryan's younger twin, delves in sorcery.

**Giriod:** Yedgal's resurrected uncle.

**Sabre:** Yedgal's cousin and right-hand man.

**Shane:** Yedgal's brother and naval expert.

**Listro:** Leader of Yedgal's spy units.

**Karan:** Right-hand man of Xristos.

## NAMES of the Districts with Some History:

**Covis:** The Raven District, founded by Lord Covin. Sacred gem is the Schrol. Ruled by Lord Nora, overseen by King Rendaf.

**Equis:** The Horse District, founded by Lord Equin. Sacred gem is the Rhodonite. Ruled by Lord Baki, overseen by King Rendaf.

**Leonis:** The Lion District, founded by Lord Leonin. Sacred gem is the Fire Opal. Ruled by Lord Xast, overseen by King Rendaf.

**Logder:** The Wolf District, founded by Lord Logder. Sacred gem is the Emerald. Ruled by Lord Huy, overseen by King Rendaf.

**Talis:** The Dragon District, founded by Lord Talin. Sacred gem is the Citrine. Ruled by Lord Veryu, overseen by King Rendaf.

**Tauris:** The Bull District, founded by Lord Taurin. Sacred gem is the Amethyst. Ruled by Lord Amlay, overseen by King Rendaf.

## ABOUT THE AUTHOR

The author, Darius C. Modi, is (at the time of writing) a Xavier Business School, St. Xavier's University student from Kolkata, India, who loves fiction and is an avid reader. The main inspiration for the series was The Lord of the Rings and The Hobbit Trilogies. He grew up fascinated by European mythologies, particularly Greek, Roman, Norse and also liked Egyptian mythology.

He likes movies and is not afraid to push his writing to extreme measures, to see what it can develop into. He thinks of how the book has to start, where in the plot he wants it to end, and then fills in the middle. Plot twists and unexpected turns are what he enjoys and leaves things open to his readers to think about for themselves, rather than be too specific on descriptions.

Darius writes while listening to a mixed bag of music, from Mozart and Beethoven, to Queen and Led Zeppelin, letting the ideas flow with ease. His imagination is all over the place, and he prefers to be at his books for a long time. His ideas are sometimes bounced around among friends, just to get a different perspective, and see how much of that can be incorporated into the story.

www.ingramcontent.com/pod-product-compliance
Lightning Source LLC
LaVergne TN
LVHW090131160826
845673LV00017B/1481

* 9 7 8 8 1 1 9 4 8 3 8 3 9 *